the au pairs

Melissa De La Cruz

SIMON AND SCHUSTER

SIMON AND SCHUSTER
First published in Great Britain in 2004 by Simon & Schuster UK Ltd
Africa House, 64–78 Kingsway, London WC2B 6AH
A Viacom Company

Originally published in 2004 by
Simon & Schuster Books for Young Readers,
an imprint of Simon & Schuster Children's Division, New York

 Produced by 17th Street Productions,
An Alloy company.
151 West 26th Street, New York, NY 10011

A CIP catalogue record for this book is
available from the British Library

ISBN 0689872526

1 3 5 7 9 10 8 6 4 2

Printed by
Cox & Wyman Ltd, Reading, Berkshire

For Papa and Mommy. For Chito. For Aina, Steve and Nico.
Because being with my family is the best vacation there is.

For Kim DeMarco and David Carthas,
the coolest people in the Hamptons.

For my husband, Mike,
with whom every day is a day at the beach

There are only the pursued, the pursuing, the busy, and the tired.
— F. Scott Fitzgerald, *The Great Gatsby*

"It's all about the Benjamins, baby."
— P. Diddy, *No Way Out*

SUMMER AU PAIRS NEEDED IMMEDIATELY

For four energetic children
between 3 and 10 years old.

Join a NYC family for the
best summer of your life in

East Hampton, July 4–Labor Day

Pay: $10,000.00

Driver's licence a must.
Familiarity with the Hamptons a plus.

Send resumes and head shots to
HamptonsAuPairs@yahoo.com

Port authority, take one: Eliza experiences public transportation

ELIZA THOMPSON HAD NEVER BEEN SO UNCOMFORTABLE in her entire life. She was sitting in the back of a Greyhound bus, sandwiched between the particularly fragrant bathroom and an overfriendly seatmate who was using Eliza's shoulder as a head-rest. The old bag in the Stars and Stripes T-shirt had little bubbles of spit forming on her lips. Eliza took a moment to pity herself. Seriously, how hard could it have been for her parents to spring for a ticket on Jet Blue?

The nightmare had begun a year ago, when some people started looking into her dad's 'accounting practices' at the bank and dug up some 'misdirected funds'. Several details had been leaked – the papers had a field day with the thousand-dollar umbrella stand on his expense reports. The lawyer's bills added up quickly, and soon even the maintenance on their five-bedroom, five-bath co-op was just too much.

The Thompsons sold their 'cottage' in Amagansett – which was actually the size of an airplane hangar – to pay their mounting legal expenses. Next they sold their beachfront condo in Palm Beach. And then one afternoon Eliza came home from Spence, her elite all-girls private school (which counted none other than Gwynnie Paltrow as an alum), to find her maid packing her bedroom into boxes. The next thing she knew, she was living in a crappy two-bedroom in Buffalo and enrolled at Herbert Hoover High, while her parents shared a ten-year-old Honda Civic. Forget AP classes. Forget early admission to Princeton. Forget that year abroad in Paris.

Her parents had told everyone they were simply going to go recover from it all 'upstate in the country', though no one had any idea how far upstate they had really gone. To Manhattanites, there's as big a difference between the Catskills and Buffalo as there is between Chanel Couture and Old Navy.

But thank God for rich brats. The call from Kevin Perry had come just yesterday – he was looking for a summer au pair and could Eliza make it to the Hamptons by sunset? Kevin Perry's law firm had been instrumental in keeping her dad out of the Big House, so he was one of the only people who really knew about their situation. The au pair job was her one-way ticket out of godforsaken Buffalo; so what if she had to work for old friends of her family? At least she wouldn't have to show up for work at the Buffalo Galleria on Monday. The girl who used to have personal shoppers at Bergdorf's had come this close to waiting on pimply classmates determined to squeeze themselves into two-sizes-too-small, cheap-ass polyester spandex. She shuddered at the thought.

The woman next to her grunted and exhaled. Eliza discreetly

spritzed the air with her signature tuberose perfume to camouflage the offensive stink. She fiddled with her right earring, a diamond that was part of the pair Charlie Borshok had given her for her sixteenth birthday. Eliza wasn't sentimental, but she still wore them despite breaking up with him more than six months ago. She'd done it in self-defense, really: how do you explain Buffalo and bankruptcy to the sole heir of a multi-million-dollar pharmaceutical fortune? She'd loved Charlie as much as she knew how, but she couldn't bring herself to tell him or anyone else about exactly how much they'd lost. It was almost like if she said it out loud, it would make it true. So Eliza was determined to make sure no one ever found out. She didn't know how she was going to cover it up exactly, but she was sure she'd come up with something. She always did, after all.

Take today, for example. So, fine, she was on the Manhattan-bound Greyhound, but she'd already found a way to get out of taking the Jitney to the Hamptons. She was relying on Kit to take her, just like he'd always done before. Sure, she could spend four hours in a glorified bus (and hello, the Jitney was a bus even with its exclusive name) – but why should she, when Kit drove his sweet little Mercedes CLK convertible out of the city every summer Friday just like clockwork? All she needed to do was hitch a ride. She and Kit had grown up across the hall from each other – they were practically siblings. Good old Kit. She was looking forward to seeing him again – she was looking forward to seeing everyone who was anyone again.

*   *   *

The bus pulled into the yawning chasm of the Port Authority and discharged its passengers under a grimy concrete slab. Eliza shouldered her Vuitton carryall (the only one her mom let her keep from her formerly extensive collection) and walked as fast as she could to get away from the awful place.

She looked around at the sprawling bus station, wrinkling her nose at the blinding fluorescent lights, the holiday rush of the crowd on their way to the 34th Street piers for the fireworks, the pockets of pasty-faced tourists holding American flags and scanning LIRR timetables. Was this how the other half lived? Pushing and pulling and running and catching trains? Ugh. She'd never had to take public transportation in her life. She'd almost missed the bus that morning before she realised it might actually have the temerity to leave without her.

Life had always waited for and waited on Eliza. She never even wore a wristwatch. Why bother? The party never started till she arrived. Eliza was dimpled, gorgeous, and blonde, blessed with the kind of cover girl looks that paradise resort brochures were made of. All she needed to complete the picture was a dark tan and a gold lavaliere necklace. The tan would happen – she'd hit Flying Point and slather on the Ombrelle, and, well, the lavaliere was tacky anyway.

She wandered for a while in a bit of a daze, looking for exit signs, annoyed at all the plebian commotion. A harried soccer mom with a fully loaded stroller elbowed her aside, throwing her onto a brunette girl who was standing in the middle of the station, holding a map.

'Oh, gee, I'm so sorry,' the girl said, helping Eliza back to her feet.

Eliza scowled but mumbled a reluctant, 'It's okay,' even though it hadn't been the girl's fault that she had fallen.

'Excuse me – do you know where the . . . ?' the girl asked, but Eliza had already dashed off to the nearest exit.

On 42nd Street, horns honked in futile protest at the usual gridlock. A long, serpentine line for the few yellow cabs snaked down the block, but Eliza felt exultant. She was back in New York! Her city! She savoured the smog-filled air. She hoped idly that she would make it in time. She didn't really have a back-up plan in mind. But one of the things she loved about Kit was how predictable he was.

She walked a block away from the taxi line and put two fingers in her mouth to blow an earsplitting whistle.

A cab materialised in front of her turquoise Jack Rogers flip-flops. Eliza smiled and stowed her bags in the trunk.

'Park Avenue and Sixty-third, please,' she told the driver. God, it was good to be home.

Port authority, take two: Mara has small town girl written all over her

MARA WATERS CONSULTED THE GRUBBY PIECE OF PAPER in her hand. Mr Perry had said something about the Hampton Jitney, but as she looked around the Port Authority complex, she couldn't find signs for it anywhere. She was getting anxious. She didn't want to be late for her first day.

She still couldn't believe she was in New York! It was so exciting to see all the flickering neon lights, the mobs of people, and to experience the brisk, rubberneck pace – and that was just the bus station! In Sturbridge the bus station was a lone bench on a forlorn corner. You'd think they'd spruce up the place a bit to herald the occasion of someone actually leaving that dead-end town, but no.

When the phone call came the day before, she just couldn't believe her luck. There she was, dressed up as the Old School Marm at Ye Old School House at Old Sturbridge Village, sweating underneath an itchy powdered wig and shepherding complacent midwestern tourists through the nineteenth century, when the news came. She'd got the job as an au pair! In the Hamptons! For ten thousand dollars for two months! More money than she could even imagine. At the very least, enough to pay for her college contribution and maybe have enough left over for the sweet little Toyota Camry she had her eye on from Jim's uncle's used-car dealership.

Of course, Jim hadn't been too pleased she was leaving him for the summer. Actually that was the understatement of the year. Jim had been *p-i-s-s-e-d*. It had all happened so quickly that Mara hadn't even had a chance to tell him she'd applied for the job, and Jim wasn't the kind of guy who liked Mara making plans without him, or plans that didn't include him, or, really, any plans at all that he hadn't approved of beforehand. This whole Hamptons thing had blindsided him. It, like, totally ruined his plans for the Fourth of July! He was going to show off his souped-up El Dorado at the local auto show. Who was going to help him polish the hood now that Mara was abandoning him?

She and Jim had been inseparable since freshman year. More than a few people had told her she was too good for him, but they were mostly related to her, so what were they supposed to say? Mara felt a twinge of guilt for leaving but brushed it away. She had other things to take care of at the moment. She walked up tentatively to a uniformed officer in a ticket booth and rapped on the glass window.

'Yeah?' he asked curtly, annoyed at being interrupted.

'Hi there, sir. Could you please tell me where the Hampton Jitney is?'

'You wan' da Longuylandrail?'

'No, um, it's called the Jitney?'

'Jipney?'

'It's a bus? To the Hamptons?'

'New Joisey transit ovah theh.' He shook his head. 'You wan' da Hampton, take LIRR on Eight Ave.'

A passenger waiting on line overheard and chirped, 'You won't find the Jitney here; it's on Third Avenue.'

'But really, you're better off taking the train. Less traffic,' piped a lady holding several shopping bags behind him.

'Forget the train. Jitney's worth it.'

'I don't know why anyone bothers to go to the Hamptons anyway.' The lady sniffed in exasperation. 'It's just inundated with all those horrid summer people. Woodstock is so much nicer.'

'I don't know about that. You can't get decent sushi anywhere in the Catskills,' the first guy disagreed.

The two began a colourful argument about the relative merits of the Hamptons versus the Hudson Valley, completely ignoring Mara.

'Third – Third Avenue, did you say?' Mara asked.

'Huh? Oh yeah, just take the one-nine over to Times Square, then take the shuttle over to Lex and walk one block up towards Forty-third; it's on the south side.'

It was all Greek to her. She nodded dumbly, feeling more like a hick than ever.

'But I'm telling you, dear, the train's much better!' yelled the lady with the bags.

Mara left the line and opened the crumpled e-mail again to make sure she had read the directions correctly when she was caught off balance by a girl who tumbled into her, narrowly missing falling flat on her face.

'Oh, I'm sorry,' she said, helping the pretty, long-haired blonde to her feet. Mara noticed a tennis racket slung over the girl's shoulder and was about to ask her about the Jitney, but when she looked up, the girl was gone.

Squaring her shoulders, she decided a taxi was probably her best bet and joined the packed line in front of the station to wait for a cab. Mara looked around her happily. She was so thrilled to be away, it didn't matter how long it took to get where she was going.

JFK baggage claim: Jacqui picks up more than her luggage

KEEP LOOKING, A LITTLE BIT TO YOUR LEFT, UH-HUH,
these are real, all the way down, yeah, baybee, you like what you see?
I know you do, pervert, three, two, one . . .

BINGO.

The thirty-something guy with the slicked-back hair, faded jeans and sockless mocassins touched Jacarei Velasco on her arm. It was a soft tap – a mere flutter, really; he didn't pat her arm so much as hint at the start of a caress.

'Manuela?'

That, she didn't expect.

'Que?' she asked, raising her wraparound shades to assess him further. Bronze tan. Oversized Rolex. Aviator sunglasses. The shoes were obviously handmade. He'd do.

'Sorry, I thought we'd met somewhere before, Miami Beach maybe?' he said, smiling so that the faint wrinkles around his bright blue eyes crinkled charmingly. He shrugged and turned away. Well, if that wasn't the oldest line in the book. But she wasn't about to let him get away that easily. 'Maybe we have,' she called.

The guy turned. 'The Delano bar? Last year?'

Jacqui shook her head, smiling.

'Ah, well. Rupert Thorne,' he said, shaking her hand firmly. 'Those yours?' he asked, spying a matching pair of shiny black patent luggage on the ramp.

Jacqui nodded. 'I'm Jacqui Velasco.'

He motioned deftly to a uniformed driver to pick them up.

'Where to?' he asked.

'The, ah, 'Amptons?'

'Exactly where I'm headed.' He nodded approvingly. 'City's no good in the summer. Fry an egg on that concrete. Not to mention the smell.' He grimaced.

'Are you from New York?' Jacqui asked, amused by his complaints.

'Originally. We've got a place over in Sag. But I've got the cross-country commute. I'm still on Malibu time.'

She smiled, letting him yap while her mind was elsewhere. She wondered where this was headed. In São Paulo she was so accustomed to being hit on by older men that figuring out how much she could get away with was a favourite pastime. As a sales-girl at Daslu, the most fashionable store in Brazil, she had zipped the country's richest women into handmade Parisian ball gowns. She was no mere wage slave, either, more like a glorified stylist, as

11

the store only employed girls from roughly the same social class as its customers. Jacqui's family wasn't rich, but her grandmother sent her to a prestigious convent school in the city, where Jacqui was a middling student. At Daslu she was adept at conducting ongoing flirtations with many of her patrons' husbands. Keep him entertained while the missus spent most of his paycheck on Versace leather trousers and she picked up that sweet commission. It was all part of doing business.

And it came naturally to Jacqui: ever since she'd started filling out her C-cup bikini top, men had noticed her. Their eyes lingered on her chest, her hips, her long black hair, and Jacqui came to believe that being beautiful was the only thing she was really good at. It was certainly the only thing anyone ever paid attention to.

But her life changed when she met Luca. Sweet, earnest Luca. The American boy she met in Rio during Carnaval. Luca, with his goofy grin and his omnipresent backpack. He was the first guy she ever met who didn't hit on her immediately. Like many revellers, she was masked at the time, but unlike most of her friends, who were staggering on the cobblestone streets trying to hold their liquor, Jacqui had been content to stand on the sidelines. After all, every year was the same wild frenzy. She didn't know it then, but she was dying for a change. She found it when Luca, an American high-school senior, asked her for directions and then walked away, even when Jacqui gave him her warmest smile. They'd only exchanged a few words, but when he turned to leave, something in Jacqui wanted to follow him. And she'd certainly never felt like that before.

Unlike the overly obnoxious wolf-whistling boys from her hometown, or the salacious older men from the city, Luca didn't even seem attracted to her at first – which certainly piqued her interest. Jacqui had no false modesty about her looks. Her black hair fell in long, inky waves down her sun-kissed shoulders, and as for her body, let's just say Gisele would have wept.

Luca was spending his spring break backpacking through South America – hiking Machu Picchu and the Aztec trail – and seemed totally unimpressed by Jacqui's glamour. He listened to Jacqui like he really cared what she thought, and she was quickly charmed by his lazy smile and enormous backpack. They spent a wonderful two weeks together – hitting the samba clubs, downing liters of *cachaça*, climbing the peak of the Corcovado, sunbathing in Ipanema. He had even convinced her to go camping with him in Tijuca one weekend. They had snuggled in his sleeping bag, kissing under the night sky.

Luca had told her the sexiest thing about her was her brain. It was like he was the first guy to even notice she had one. Their first night together, Jacqui couldn't go to sleep. She kept smiling to herself, not believing her luck. She tossed and turned, clutching at her stomach, feeling happy and frightened at the same time. So this was what love was like.

Then, after an amazing week, he just disappeared. He left without so much as a goodbye or a note with his e-mail address. She didn't even know his last name. Jacqui was crushed. For the first time in her life, Jacqui was in love. The only key to his

13

whereabouts was that he had once mentioned his family normally spent the summer in someplace called 'the Hamptons'.

It had been only two days ago that Jacqui logged on to the store computer and googled 'the Hamptons' yet again. But this time she found something new: Kevin Perry's classified ad for 'the summer of her life' in East Hampton. She heard back from him almost instantly. (Jacqui's head shot had that effect on people.) It was urgent; could she hop on a plane tomorrow to arrive in town by July 4? *Claro que sim!* She was convinced she'd find her Luca in the Hamptons somewhere. And if not, she could always fly back home. It wasn't as if she *really* needed the job.

Rupert consulted his watch, breaking her reverie. 'If we leave now, we'll still have time to hit the beach before sunset. My car is waiting outside,' he said, pointing to the curb, where a stretch Hummer was waiting.

'Sure.' Jacqui shrugged. She hadn't had any concrete plans on how to get to the Hamptons. She just figured something would turn up like it always did.

Jacqui gave him her flashiest megawatt smile. The one that always led men to promise chinchilla furs and hand over platinum AmEx cards. 'Lead the way.'

Eliza tells a couple of not-so-white lies

THE CAB DROPPED ELIZA OFF IN FRONT OF HER FORMER building, an imposing prewar high-rise that was one of the city's most sought-after addresses. Its bronze gilt doors shone in the bright sun. How she missed it. In Buffalo her family occupied the first floor of a row house. The bathroom had never been renovated, and Eliza swore there was mould behind the tub. Every time she showered, she felt dirtier than when she'd started.

Her old bathroom boasted a panoramic view of Central Park and a gleaming eggshell-white tub that Eliza had personally picked out from the Bofi showroom with her mother's decorator. Original paintings by Jackson Pollock and Willem de Kooning hung in the hallways, heirlooms from Eliza's maternal grandmother, a former debutante who kept company with the abstract expressionists in the fifties. Woody Allen had once scouted their living room as a possible location for one of his movies. The only movie Eliza could ever imagine being filmed in her new home was something out of *The Texas Chainsaw Massacre*. Okay, so she was exaggerating. Slightly.

Cracking linoleum tile in the kitchen. Rusted aluminum siding. Wall-to-wall putrid avocado shag carpeting. A cramped six hundred square feet! Even their former servants had lived better. Her parents kept reminding her it could have been worse. Much, much worse. Dad could have ended up in – but Eliza couldn't go there. Bad enough that it had even been a possibility.

The weekend doorman opened the cab door and recognised her immediately.

'Miss Eliza!'

'Hi, Duke.'

He tipped his cap. 'Been a long time.'

'You're telling me.'

'You guys back in the building?'

'Not exactly,' she said, trying to appear casual. She looked down the street. There was no sign of Kit's convertible.

'Kit around?'

'Mr Christopher?' Duke scratched his forehead with a black leather glove, which was part of the uniform – even in ninety-eight-degree heat. 'I think he just left.'

She cursed under her breath. She couldn't believe she'd missed her ride.

'Mr and Mrs Ashleigh are upstairs, though. I can ring up.'

'No thanks,' Eliza said, suppressing a temptation to gnaw her nails. What on earth was she going to do now?

Just then a familiar red convertible pulled up in front of the red canopy. An agreeable-looking guy with a blond crew cut hopped out of the front seat without waiting for Duke to open the door. He gasped when he saw Eliza.

'Liza!'

'Kit!'

'What the hell are you doing here?' he asked, before enveloping her in a bone-crunching bear hug.

Eliza ignored the question. 'It's great to see you!' she said, rubbing her fingers on his spiky hair and giving him a noogie.

'I forgot something – I just gotta run up and grab it. You goin' to Amagansett?' Kit started jogging backwards into the marble lobby. 'Hey, you want a ride?'

'Sure!' she said, relieved. Good old Kit. Eliza let Duke put her bags in the trunk and settled in the front seat to wait for Kit.

'Damn, girl! I missed you!' Kit said when he returned. He fired up the engine and they cruised top-down on Park Avenue. 'You, like, went AWOL.'

'Yeah, well, after everything that happened,' Eliza said offhandedly, 'my parents wanted to get out of the city to just relax, you know? So they decided to ship me off to boarding school. *Quel* drag.' Eliza found Kit's Marlboros on the dashboard and helped herself to one. Her hands shook slightly as she rooted in the glove compartment for a lighter. 'Lights out at eleven and the hall monitor is a tool,' she said, firing up a Zippo and inhaling.

Kit grunted in sympathy. 'Dad threatened that once. But I don't have the grades for Andover. So, uh, how are the 'rents, anyway?' Kit asked tentatively.

'They, um, spend all their time in Florida these days,' she improvised. Eliza knew what everyone had read in the papers, but no one knew just how bad it had got. The gossip pages and business section had lost interest after her dad got off without an indictment, and before long the Thompsons had feigned exhaustion and disinterest over all the hubbub and left Manhattan for good.

'I didn't know you guys were down in PB!' He smacked the steering wheel, looking relieved. 'We gotta hook up during winter break!'

'Of course!' She felt sick to her stomach having to lie to one of her best friends. Especially since he automatically assumed the Thompsons had retired to Palm Beach. God, she missed their place by Mar-a-Lago.

It was all her dad's fault. She felt an all-too-familiar bitter resentment welling up inside her. It just wasn't fair. Her parents could hide out in Buffalo and avoid all their old friends. But Eliza was sixteen – not sixty – with her whole life ahead of her. She wasn't about to waste her chance. She wanted back *in*, no matter what it took.

'So it's just you this summer?' Kit asked.

'Yeah, thank God I bumped into you! I thought I'd have to take the Jitney. Ugh. You know I got kicked off last time because I wouldn't turn off my phone.'

Kit grinned. 'I remember. It made the *Post*.'

'Anyway, I'm staying at my uncle's place on Georgica,' she said. It wasn't such a stretch, really – Kevin Perry was one of her father's lawyers and after the last year, well, they were practically family. Eliza decided she was really just 'helping out', and if she got paid doing it, what was the harm? Come to think of it, she was really more like an honoured guest. After all, she had grown up with his twin daughters, Sugar and Poppy.

'Cool. That's not too far from our new place. Got any plans for tonight?'

'No, what's up?'

'A couple of the gang are hitting Resort – there's a party in the VIP room around midnight – then afterwards there's P. Diddy's Red, White, and Blue soiree at the PlayStation2 House.'

'Sounds cool.' Eliza nodded. She knew the guys who ran the PlayStation2 House. A couple of New York club promoters had convinced Sony it was a good idea to fund a weekend party house to 'market' their new games. In the Hamptons it was unofficially known as a model landing pad. Kind of like the Playboy Mansion but with nubile flat-chested eighteen-year-olds who were more likely to be found marching down a runway than spread-eagle in a centrefold.

'I'll put you on the list.'

'Hey, have you seen Charlie around, by the way?'

Kit gave her a furtive glance. 'Last I heard, he was dating some hoochie he met in summer school.'

'Huh.'

'I'm sure it's not serious.'

'Kit, you're too sweet.'

She remembered Charlie's face, crumpled in disbelief, when she told him over Christmas that it was probably not a good idea for them to see each other anymore. For weeks afterwards he had left her voice mails wondering where she had gone. She wasn't at school. She wasn't at Jackson Hole after school. She wasn't at Barneys on Saturday mornings or at Bungalow 8 on Thursday nights. Then she changed her mobile number to a local Buffalo area code (some luxuries are just necessities), and she stopped getting the messages. Eliza had thought it would be easier if she just disappeared – she knew that she might break down and tell him everything if she saw him, and that was a risk she simply could not afford to take.

The convertible inched its way out of the city, and Kit paid the toll at the Triborough Bridge. Eliza savoured the freeway signs as they sped east, Long Island towns with funny-sounding names like Hicksville, Ronkonkoma, and Yaphank bidding her on her way, taking her back to where she belonged.

She relaxed for the first time that day. So far, so good. Kit had bought her story about boarding school and her 'uncle', she was already invited to some pretty fabu soirees in the Hamptons, and even if her ex-boyfriend was currently unavailable, Eliza loved him and was coming back to retrieve what was rightfully hers.

Mara discovers the rules
for Hamptons travel

'AH, DE HAMPTONS, BERRY, BERRY RICH PEOPLE
there,' the bearded cabdriver told Mara when she told him where
she was headed.

'So I've heard,' she agreed. Her sister Megan, the *US Weekly*
addict, had given her the full run-down before she left. 'I hear
Resort is hot this summer but stay away from the Star Room –
it's so over. And try to get a table at Bamboo if you can.' As if
Mara had any idea what she was talking about. For Mara the
Hamptons was the episode on *Sex and the City* where Carrie goes
to stay with a friend and accidentally sees her friend's husband
naked. Mara knew it was some sort of rich summer place, but she
went to the Cape every summer – it couldn't be much different
from that, could it?

'Very, very rich people, yes. You lika Jerry Seinfeld? Billy Joel?
They inda Hamptons all dee time. The guy who dated Jennifer
Lopez before this Affleck. He has big party this weekend. Piff
Daddy.'

'P. Diddy?' Mara laughed.

'Yeah, him. I useta drive limo for him. Big party. Big, big fireworks. So many beautiful people. So thin. All the girls, thin, thin, thin.' He angled back to appraise Mara. 'You thin. You rich?'

'No, I'm not rich,' Mara said. 'I'm going to be working for some rich people, though.'

'Ah, not rich. Working girl, eh?'

'That's right.'

'Here Forty-third and Third. Jitney over there,' he said, waving towards a large silver-and-green bus with The Hampton Jitney in cheerful lettering on the back.

'Great!' Mara said, giving him the exact amount on the meter. 'Here you go, thank you very, very much!' She scurried out of the cab and slammed the door.

'No tip?' the confused cabdriver asked to the empty air.

Mara ran to find another long line waiting for her in front of the Jitney. She shuffled patiently to the front, where a tough-looking middle-aged woman wearing a cash belt stood with a clipboard.

'Name?'

'Mara Waters.'

'Waters, Waters, Waters . . . Huh. I don't see you. Did you make a reservation?'

'Was I supposed to?' Mara asked, a little nervous.

'Sorry. This bus is fully booked. You'll have to go standby on the next. But I doubt you'll get on. It's July Fourth weekend!'

'Omigod. Are you serious? I'm not going to be able to get on?'

'Not without a reservation, you're not.'

'But – but – I didn't know . . .'

'Step aside, miss,' the bus madam said rudely.

'You don't understand! I'll be late for my job, and it's really, really important I get to East Hampton by five. Please?'

'Can't help you. Try tomorrow.'

Mara moved numbly to the side, shell-shocked. She had been on the road since six o'clock in the morning and now this! It was just like Kevin Perry to forget to mention the reservation policy on the Jitney. He just assumed that like everyone in New York, Mara would know the drill.

'Please – is there any way?' she asked, inching back to the front.

'I told you, miss, you'll have to STAND ASIDE!'

'Excuse me! What's the holdup?' asked an elegant woman in an oversized straw hat, holding a tiny lapdog in her handbag.

'No reservation,' the grouchy clipboard-nazi said, pointing to Mara.

'I didn't know. I really need to get on this bus or I'll be late for my job,' Mara explained, her eyes welling up.

'Fine, fine, fine.' The woman sighed loudly behind her sunglasses. 'You can take Muffy's seat as long as you hold him,' she said in a martyr's tone.

'Oh, thank you! Thank you so much!' Mara said as the lady deposited her dog and its carrier in her arms.

Harried and still a little upset, Mara was finally allowed to climb aboard the bus and take a seat. She squeezed in next to her benefactor, who promptly put on a frilly eye mask and fell asleep as the bus pulled away.

Mara looked out the window at the receding New York skyline. In Queens they passed Shea Stadium, festooned with American flags and patriotic bunting. An hour went by. Traffic on the freeway was brutal. Mara pressed her nose against the glass, counting the aboveground pools that sprouted in every backyard once they hit Long Island proper.

It reminded her of Sturbridge. She should really call Jim to try and work things out. She didn't like leaving things the way they had, and she hated to think of anyone being mad at her. Just as she was wondering whether she could try him again, her phone began to ring.

The slumbering silence was suddenly broken by a wheezy DA-DA-DA-DA-DA-DUM, DA-DA-DA-DA-DA-DUM. The digitised opening bars of 'Sweet Child of Mine'.

'Mobile phone!' hissed her seatmate, lifting her eye mask. 'Who's got the mobile phone?'

'Turn it off! Turn it off!' demanded a pinched-looking girl a few years older than Mara, looking up from her knitting.

'The noise! The noise!' quavered a bald middle-aged man holding up the latest Harry Potter novel.

Mara frantically began searching for her tiny phone inside her overstuffed backpack. A cantankerous voice thundered from the front seat. 'No mobile phones allowed! Will you please turn that off!' Everyone craned their necks to see who had broken the most august law on the Hampton Jitney. Fifty pairs of irritated, sleep-rumpled eyes glared in Mara's direction. The clipboard-wielding bus madam who'd already given Mara grief for getting on the bus without a reservation gestured angrily. 'You there!'

'Sorry! Sorry! I didn't know!' Mara said, fumbling with her phone. 'Hello???' She brushed her long brown bangs off her face with a hurried sweep.

'Mar! It's me! Hey, I – '

'Jim! I can't talk now!' she said, snapping the phone shut and cutting him off in mid-protest.

The long-haired Chihuahua in her arms stared her down with an indignant look on its pointy face.

'What's wrong, pup?' she cooed nervously, holding up the dog close to her. As if in answer, the dog peed in her lap.

'Hey!' Mara yelped.

'Oh. He does that to some people.' Muffy's owner yawned. 'You should really have turned off your phone. Didn't you see the sign?' she added, motioning to the image of a mobile phone inside a circle with an angry red slash drawn across it.

Mara sank lower in her seat. It was going to be a very long ride.

Somewhere on the Montauk Highway: Jacqui can really hold her liquor

THE SMARMY MOVIE PRODUCER WAS STARTING TO look very, very attractive, but that was probably Johnny Walker talking, Jacqui thought.

For the most part Rupert had acted the perfect gentleman; in fact, he had barely paid her any attention except to refill her whiskey glass. He had been glued to his mobile phone's wireless earpiece, yelling into the little receiver about some botched film deal. By the time they reached Noyak, Jacqui had already watched three episodes of *That 70s Show* on the Tivo, played numerous games of *Halo* on the Xbox, and watched as the landscape out the window changed from crowded metropolis to suburban wasteland to picturesque vineyards.

'I'm sorry, sweetheart,' he said, taking a moment to squeeze her left knee.

Hmmm. She didn't know how she felt about that.

Maybe she'd feel better after just one more drink, she thought, reaching over for the crystal decanter. Rupert had said to 'help herself', and she wasn't one to pass up on the limousine's amenities. Who knew when she'd ever be in a stretch Hummer again?

Rupert finally put away his phone and turned to her. 'Sorry about that. The floozy signed the contract, but now she's trying to get out of it to do a movie with Tom Cruise. Didn't mean to be rude.'

Jacqui waved it away, still holding her cocktail glass.

He smirked and poured himself another shot of bourbon.

'Cheers,' he said.

'Saúde.' To your health.

They clinked glasses. Rupert took a hearty sip and smacked his lips. 'Much better,' he said, unbuttoning the topmost button on his oxford shirt. 'So, what are you doing in the Hamptons this summer?' he inquired.

'Au pair,' she said.

'No way. You're serious? I was sure you were a model or something. And that's not a line. I see pretty girls in my business every day.'

'Não sou modelo.'

'Actress wannabe?'

Jacqui shook her head. She had absolutely no desire to generate even more attention for herself.

'Just a nanny, huh?'

'Au pair,' she corrected.

'Right. Right.' He smiled. 'Who's the lucky family?'

She told him about the Perrys and gave him their address on Lily Pond Lane. He looked impressed.

'Perry? Not Kevin Perry?'

She nodded.

'The lucky bastard,' Rupert said, now grinning broadly. 'Maxine and I know them,' he said as he put a hand on her knee. 'My wife, you know. We just got married last year. It wasn't my idea,' he added as he ran a hand up her toned thigh, stopping just short of her denim miniskirt. He let his hand rest there – just below – to see what she would do.

It must have been the alcohol because even if she had expected this, Jacqui wasn't as repulsed as she normally would be.

'We won't get into East Hampton for another hour with this traffic,' he murmured, leaning in to smell her hair. 'What do you say?'

Jacqui giggled into her glass. Really, men were way too predictable. 'I don't know, what do you say?' she asked, finally pushing his hand away.

'Well, I think we should get to know each other a little . . .' he began to suggest when they were both jostled by the limo swerving to miss a Mercedes convertible.

Jacqui looked out the window and saw a cute guy giving the limo the finger while a blonde girl laughed beside him.

'Luca?' she called. It looked like him – from the back – was it? She couldn't be sure. Thinking of Luca sobered her up. What the hell was she doing in the back of a limo with a guy twice her age?

It was time to take control of the situation.

'Rupert,' she said, turning around to let him know she needed to be dropped off in East Hampton pronto and she wasn't about to play any more games. But Rupert was already on the other side of the car, answering his mobile phone.

Thank God for Hollywood diva crises.

East Hampton, New York: God, Eliza missed this

THREE HOURS AFTER THEY SET OFF FROM PARK AVENUE, Kit and Eliza arrived on East Hampton's main drag. Eliza felt a wave of nostalgia and affection at the sight of the familiar tree-lined shopping street with the shiny new Citarella anchored at the end of the block. The store here stocked even better salmon pâté and stuffed grape leaves than the one on the Upper West Side. A few blocks away stood the Creed outpost, a pink jewel box of a store, where she had spent hours trying on perfumes last summer, finally selecting one especially made for the duchess of Windsor.

That's what Eliza loved about the Hamptons – Manhattan's most elegant boutiques and gourmet food stores transplanted to a gentler setting. The Hamptons were just like the city, except with only one-tenth of its inhabitants – the top one-tenth. It was the social equivalent of Harvard, Eliza decided. Of course, there were too many of the hoi polloi these days – wannabes who piled into illegal fifty-person 'share houses', where the beds were stacked up right next to each other like the school gyms that doubled as disaster-recovery zones whenever there was a flood or a fire or a tornado or one of those other terrible things that happened far, far from here.

Regrettably, the Hamptons were getting more media attention every year. There had been a number of cable specials, documentaries, and 'exposés' on everything from the singles dating scene to the environmental problem. It was a favourite target of lazy lifestyle reporters who were forever sounding the death knell and declaring the scene 'over' and the beach 'spoiled by civilisation'. Still, it didn't keep the hordes of up-and-coming Hollywood stars, Grammy Award winners, sitcom royalty, rap impresarios, literary lions, and assorted social-climbing aspirants from calling the place home-away-from-home three months out of the year. After all, a forty-mile stretch of beach only four hours' drive from Manhattan (make that two if you sped on Route 27 after dinner and *The Sopranos* on Sundays) was a total godsend.

'You can drop me off right here,' she told Kit. 'I'm meeting my uncle by the windmill.'

'Okay.' Kit nodded, finding a spot by the curb. He popped the trunk and helped her with her bags. 'So we'll see you tonight?' he asked.

'Duh. Of course.'

'Rockin'. Don't forget — if they ask, you're on my list. Any problem at the door, buzz me,' he said, miming a phone call. He kissed her on the cheek. 'Later.'

'Later.' She waved. She walked over to the bench where a Jitney was unloading its passengers. A disgruntled girl wiping away a stain on the bottom of her shirt walked off the bus and sat down next to her.

Eliza barely noticed. She was oblivious to the outside world and already plotting how she would ditch work to go to the party. She wasn't totally clear on the rules per se, but if the party started at midnight, there was no reason she wouldn't be able to go, right? Kevin was just doing this as a favour to her dad. It wasn't as if the Perrys *actually* expected her to watch their children.

Ryan Perry is Adonis in
board shorts

'YECCH. IT'S NO USE!' MARA COMPLAINED, MAKING
one last effort to clean up the mess. She threw the tissue away in
disgust, making a perfect arc into the trash can. It was her best
going-out shirt, too. A nice rayon-poly blend she'd got at
Marshall's for, like, thirty bucks! It wasn't so pretty now that the
little beast Muffy had peed all over it.

Mara looked around, blinking at the quaint small-town store-
fronts that announced exclusive brand names. A white summer
cottage read Tiffany & Co. in the window; another rustic shack
read Cashmere Hampton. A glittering assortment of Mercedes-
Benzes, Jaguars, BMWs, and Porsches made a slow, rumbling
parade down the centre of town, where a giant windmill towered
at the intersection. Mara had never before seen a Bentley in real
life – and in two minutes in East Hampton, she had already
counted two.

Everyone moved at a leisurely, languid pace. Elegant women
with psychedelic silk scarves wrapped around their heads carried

fluffy white dogs in their Hermés handbags. Balding men with women less than half their age walked arm in arm down to the nearby park. Giggling teenagers wearing nothing but the tightest tube tops and the highest platform wedges darted in and out of traffic.

'Do you have the time?' asked the girl beside her. Mara did a quick double take. The long blonde hair, the annoyed expression, the tennis racket . . . She'd seen this girl before, but where?

'It's ten after five,' Mara replied, discreetly checking out the girl's outfit. Mara wished she had thought to wear a little skirt and flip-flops. She was wearing her leather cowboy boots in a misguided attempt to impress. It was ninety degrees and she was boiling.

The girl nodded and started paging through her PalmPilot.

'Excuse me,' Mara said.

Blondie raised an eyebrow without looking up from her task.

'Weren't you in Port Authority this morning?'

'No.'

'Oh. Sorry. I thought I might have bumped into you this morning . . .'

'No. Wrong person,' she said curtly, sliding down to the opposite end of the bench to make her point.

'Oh, okay. Sorry,' Mara said. They lapsed into an awkward silence.

The two girls sat on the bench and studiously ignored each other.

A silver Aston Martin Vanquish convertible pulled up in front of the bench, and the two girls immediately sat up a little straighter. A tall, tanned guy wearing a holey Martha's Vineyard T-shirt and cutoff board shorts eased out and walked barefoot on the sidewalk. Cue: dreamboat music.

Guys like that are so out of my league, Mara thought. Not that she was in the market for one – she did have a guy at home. *What was his name again? Jim. Right.*

Of course, the hottie went straight up to that prissy blonde who'd been so rude to her earlier. It just made sense.

'Ryan Perry! It's been too long,' she cooed.

'Hey!' Ryan said, bending over for a quick hug. 'How was the Jitney?'

'What Jitney? I rode in with Kit.'

'Very cool. How's he doing?'

'Not bad. There's a party tonight. At Resort,' she said, self-importantly flipping her hair.

'Yeah, yeah. I heard.' He grinned. 'I got the e-vite.'

'Maybe I'll let you be my date,' she teased, basking in the glow of his attention.

Ryan Perry was the type of guy girls swooned over and guys considered their best buds. That he was superlatively good-looking was intrinsic yet somehow irrelevant to the totality of his charm. He had that sunny, good-natured disposition that came from being incredibly lucky both in looks and in life. He wore the mantle of privilege carelessly and would have been just as

35

appealing driving a Pinto as a Porsche. He was the kind of guy who was loyal to his girlfriends and could always be counted on to bring the biggest litre of tequila to any party. Of course, he could also be counted on to empty it.

Mara watched them flirt without the slightest bit of envy. They might as well have been from another planet as far as she was concerned. Mara had always felt she was just a 'sorta'. You know, 'sorta cute', 'sorta smart', 'sorta popular' but nothing special. So when Ryan suddenly called her name, he had to repeat it three times since she was so shocked to even be noticed, let alone recognised. She wasn't the only one. The other girl was now looking at her with renewed, if slightly hostile interest.

'Mara? Mara Waters?' Ryan asked, giving her the full benefit of his dazzling dimples. One on each cheek. Mara could hardly bear it.

'Uh. Me?' Mara squeaked.

'I'm Ryan Perry,' Ryan said, offering his hand. 'My dad was supposed to come get you guys, but he had to do something for Anna. This your suitcase?' he asked, picking up her oversized roller bag.

'Uh-huh.' Mara nodded, dying as her bag went clackety-clackety-clack all over the cobblestone tiles. She almost wanted to disappear when the bag careened wildly and the magazines she'd stuffed in the back pocket went flying. She swore the first thing she would do when she got paid was find out where to get her hands on one of those cute canvas monogrammed tote bags everyone seemed to carry around here.

Ryan held his door open so Mara could climb inside.

'So . . . have you guys met?' Ryan asked.

'Yes,' Mara replied.

'No,' the other girl said.

'Oh-kay.' Ryan laughed. 'Eliza, Mara, Mara, Eliza. We're all really glad you're both working here this summer. God knows Anna has been totally freaked out the past couple of days.' He drove off the highway onto a road with a Private Property: No Trespassing sign. Seeing the concerned look on Mara's face in the rearview mirror, he said, 'Oh, don't worry. The Mortons let us use it all the time. The traffic's so bad here, everyone has to use the back roads to get anywhere.'

'Don't I know it,' Eliza agreed.

Mara nodded. But her mind was still on what Ryan had said earlier. We're so happy you're *both* working here? Huh. Looked like there was more (or a lot less) to this Eliza girl than she had first thought.

Mara is the odd girl out
on Lily Pond Lane

THEY DROVE PAST A PRACTICALLY UNENDING LINE OF
ten-foot-tall hedges – Mara could barely see the roofs of the
houses. Ryan steered the car steadily down the one-lane back
road, occasionally calling out hellos and waving. Several groups
walked on the side of the road, carrying surfing or water sport
gear. Others pedalled English Raleigh bicycles, shopping bags
from Dreesen's tucked in their baskets. Practically every other car
was a convertible. Eliza spent the entire time glued to her mobile
phone, making calls to various friends and updating them on her
plans for the evening.

'Hey, was that . . . ?' Mara asked, turning around so quickly
she almost gave herself whiplash.

'Yeah, that's Steven Spielberg. They have a house near us on
the pond. We always see him at Nick and Toni's,' Ryan mentioned offhandedly. His dad had a standing table at the restaurant, one of the most popular gathering spots for bold-faced
names.

'Oh.' Wow. Mara tried not to look too impressed. 'I saw Tom Hanks once,' she offered.

'Really? Where?' Ryan asked, sounding genuinely intrigued.

'The airport,' she said sheepishly. 'He gave my sister an auto-graph. She chased him all the way to the men's room.'

Ryan laughed.

'Tom and Rita used to come to your mom's fund-raisers all the time, didn't they, Ryan?' Eliza lifted her chin from her phone and asked in an extremely bored voice.

Mara felt slapped in the face.

They drove up to another row of hedges into a private driveway that snaked up to a white mansion with huge Grecian columns. In the driveway were a Mercedes SUV, a Range Rover, a vintage Corvette convertible, a Porsche Cayenne SUV, and two motor scooters. Talk about an auto show.

'Here we are,' said Ryan, bringing the car to a stop on the gravel drive.

A stretch Hummer limousine with rims that spun in reverse even though the car was stopped was parked out front.

'Oh my God! Look at that!' Mara hooted. 'What a dumb car.'

'It's an H2 stretch. Top of the line,' Eliza said in an irritated tone.

A chauffeur emerged from the front seat and walked the four car lengths to the back to hold the door open. A pair of mile-long tanned legs that ended in white furry sheepskin boots swung out. Jacqui Velasco certainly knew how to make an exit, or an entrance, if you will. She let the newcomers take in her presence, then turned around and hitched her hip to the side, kneeling on the car door to say goodbye to her patron.

'*Obrigada,*' she said, a little unsteadily from the numerous cocktails on the ride.

'No, thank you, *bellísima.*' Rupert Thorne winked, pulling her in for a kiss.

'Naughty boy,' Jacqui said, wagging her finger when Rupert licked rather than pecked her cheek.

'I'll see you around,' he promised.

Not if I can help it, Jacqui thought grimly. She straightened up, slammed the door, and found Ryan, Eliza, and Mara watching her, all with different expressions on their faces. Ryan looked amused, Mara intimidated, and Eliza impressed.

'Kick-ass boots!' Eliza said to Jacqui.

Apparently boots in summer were okay after all, thought Mara.

'Thank you,' Jacqui said with a slight accent. 'We just got them in from Australia the other day.' She smiled at Eliza. 'Jacqui Velasco.'

'Eliza Thompson. That's Ryan Perry, our boss.' She snickered. 'And, uh . . . I forgot your name. Mary, right?'

'Mara,' Mara said with steel in her voice. She wasn't going to let Blondie here push her around. 'Mara Waters, nice to meet you.'

'So did you have to go on a waiting list or something to get those? I've been dying for them!' Eliza said, falling in step with

Jacqui.

The two headed inside the house, chatting about footwear, their nearly identical wraparound sunglasses pushed up on their heads. Mara stood somewhat at a loss, wondering if she should follow them, already feeling completely out of place.

Ryan pulled her battered nylon suitcase from the trunk and handed it to a white-jacketed butler. 'Don't let Eliza bother you too much,' he said. 'She can be a pain, but she's actually really nice. She's just going through a lot right now.'

Mara couldn't fathom how 'really nice' could ever apply to the Attitude Queen, but she wanted to be agreeable. If only she wouldn't blush every time he looked at her.

A chubby ten-year-old girl with unruly curls ran out of the side door, wearing a bright pink bathing suit, goggles, and flippers. 'You're IT!' she said, barrelling into Ryan.

'Madison Avenue!' he said, lifting her up and spinning her around.

'Stop! Stop!' She giggled. 'Put me down!!'

Ryan let her go and said, 'Hey, say hi to Mara. Mara, my little sister Madison.'

Madison scooted inside the front door, Ryan and Mara following.

'By the way,' Ryan said, holding the door open. 'I thought that limo was a dumb car, too.'

Mara couldn't stop smiling even after he had left.

This is what 'let's burn the money to keep warm' looks like

'HI! WELCOME TO CREEK HEAD MANOR!' A FROWSY, overweight woman in a pink sweatshirt with a Nokia hanging on a chain around her neck beamed at them as they entered the house. 'I'm Laurie, Anna's personal assistant. Anna's not back from her Reiki session yet, so she asked me to welcome you and give you a tour of the house.' She clucked at the sight of their footwear. 'Sorry, but I'm going to have to ask everyone to take off their shoes before entering. The zebrawood hasn't been oiled yet.' Laurie proudly explained that Anna had flown in an artisan from South America to work with I. J. Peiser's Sons on the floor design. According to Laurie, they did everyone's floors, though it occurred to Mara that 'everyone' must not be anything like anyone Mara knew.

Eliza grumbled at the inconvenience, Jacqui laughed, and Mara felt embarrassed to take off her cowboy boots – one of her grey socks had a huge hole in the toe. Laurie kept up the chatter as they tiptoed around the edges of the vast living room, which was dominated by an enormous floor-to-ceiling picture window that stretched from one end of the house to the other. 'I love this feature!' she gushed as she pressed a button on the wall and automated curtains revealed an uninterrupted view of the Atlantic coast. The waves lapped gracefully at the shore, and seagulls waddled across the sand.

'We've been putting out poisoned bread to keep them off, but it's not working.' Laurie sighed. 'Shoo! Shoo!'

Mara's eyes widened at the view – it was amazing. Eliza picked at her cuticles – she'd been a guest at the house before, and besides, the Thompsons' old place had almost the same view (maybe even better since their next-door neighbours, a prominent Hollywood actor and his starlet wife, had liked to sunbathe nude on their terrace). Jacqui yawned – the sight didn't hold a candle to the golden beaches of Angra dos Reis in Costa Verde. No one braved a comment on the seagullicide programme.

The house smelled sweet but slightly suffocating. Immense bouquets of freshly cut flowers were placed everywhere in carefully considered arrangements. The sculpted glass coffee table was decorated with a spray of fat, blooming, Georgia-peach-coloured roses in a crystal decanter. Matching sideboards spilled over with hollyhocks, irises, and calla lilies, and an enormous Ming vase in the foyer held a magnificent cluster of six-foot-tall acid-yellow sunflowers.

Laurie's mobile phone rang with a piercing shrill. 'Laurie here!

Anna, hi! Yes, they've made it! No, I didn't see an invitation from Calvin Klein yet. Oh, okay. I'll try.' She shut the phone off and told the au pairs, 'Anna says hi!'

She led them to the kitchen, an airy, light-filled rustic wood room with shiny marble countertops and no visible appliances. Laurie breathlessly explained that the cabinets were cut from original floorboards salvaged from an eighteenth-century French chateau. To keep the serenity of the line, the refrigerator, freezer, and dishwasher had been recessed and built into the antique cabinets. Oh. My. God. Mara kept having to remind herself to close her gaping mouth.

The kitchen led to a formal dining room that could easily seat thirty. An immense baroque chandelier hung from the double-height space. Next to it was a second dining room for everyday meals and a breakfast room with a 'cosy' nook. The first floor also had an indoor lap pool, a yoga studio, and a fully equipped Nautilus gym. The billiards room was a by-the-book re-creation of King George's library, complete with a first edition Shakespeare folio underneath a locked glass case. Laurie caressed the glass as if it were her own treasure.

On their way to the back exit they bumped into Ryan, who was holding a book and climbing up the stairs. 'How'd you like the renovation?' he asked. 'The house certainly didn't look like this last year,' he added a little wistfully.

'It's very nice,' Mara said politely.

Ryan winked. 'Laurie, don't forget to tell them about the

mirror in the bathroom. It's an exact reproduction of Marie Antoinette's!' he said with mock enthusiasm.

The girls' expectations shot up when Laurie told them the house contained several guest bedrooms. Now, that was more like it. Eliza hoped she would get the same room she'd had when she visited last summer while the Thompson's house was being fumigated. But the preternaturally perky assistant led them outside, all the way to the servants' quarters – a small, tidy cottage a good five-minute walk away, where they were deposited in a small room on the topmost landing.

It couldn't have been more different from the main house. The attic bedroom consisted of a bunk bed, one single bed, two bureaus, a ratty armchair, one bathroom, and a lone lightbulb hanging from the ceiling.

A spider made its way across the grimy carpet, the lone occupant to welcome them to their new home.

Don't worry, girls, this is a partnership

'TWENTY THOUSAND SQUARE FEET AND ALL THREE OF US have to share *one* godforsaken room?' Eliza griped, smoking out of the tiny attic window.

Mara kept silent, unpacking her suitcase. Since Eliza had taken the single bed and Jacqui the top bunk, she had been left with the claustro-inducing bottom bunk, but she wasn't going to complain. She was still flabbergasted by the size of the estate. (Twelve acres, Laurie had told them in a hushed tone.) Mara didn't realise real people actually lived this way – that marble bathrooms the size of her whole house weren't just something you could find in an episode of *The Fabulous Life Of* . . . on VH-1 or something out of an *It's Good to Be* . . . special on E! As far as she could tell, the Perrys weren't famous, but they were sure loaded.

'Eh.' Jacqui shrugged. 'What can we do? Is not like we have choice,' she said, borrowing Eliza's cigarette to light her own.

'Could you guys not smoke in here?' Mara asked, waving her hands in dismay.

Eliza blew a smoke ring in response.

A rap on the door caused the two girls to stub out their cigarettes on the soles of their shoes. Eliza kicked the butts under the
bed. 'Come in!' she said brightly.

A maid in a black-and-white uniform peeked into the room.
'Mrs Perry calling. Follow me, pliss.'

The three of them were led to the backyard, a stunning
expanse of greenery surrounding an Olympic-sized pool that
flowed into a small waterfall, emptying into a bubbling Jacuzzi
tub. Mara spied tennis courts in the distance, a putting green,
and a basketball court. Back home in Sturbridge, their backyard
was a sliver of brown, fenced in on each side by chicken wire.
There were several chairs rotting from too many winters left outdoors and an ancient hibachi by a dying maple tree.

Several kids were chasing each other with Super Soakers on
the patio, and a little boy with water wings was running
between everyone's legs, screaming. In the middle of the chaos
stood a slim, frosted blonde in a metallic gold bikini and
stiletto mules.

'Cody! Stop making that noise! Stop it! Let go of my leg . . .
let go of my leg!' She wrenched his tiny baby hands from a
bronzed calf the size of a chicken wing. 'Ugh.' The woman grimaced in distaste. She straightened up, only to be met by a nine-
year-old boy wielding a loaded water gun.

'GOTCHA!' The kid squealed.

'William! Don't even *think* about it!' she threatened.

It was no use. He pulled the trigger, sending a powerful blast of water at her head.

'JESUS! Did you take your meds today! DID YOU? LOOK AT WHAT YOU'VE DONE!' she said, taking him by his thin shoulders and shaking the bejesus out of him. He started to bawl.

'Okay. Okay. Fine. I didn't mean it. Scoot,' she said, shooing him away.

She turned to the three teenagers, wiping dripping wet bangs away from her face. 'I'm Anna Perry, sorry about all this,' she said grandly. She shook Mara's and Jacqui's hand with a limp shake, but when she turned to Eliza, her countenance mellowed. 'Oh! Eliza, darling! You made it. Wonderful!' she said, giving Eliza her cheek to kiss. 'How's your mother? Do tell her I said hi. Did she get the books I sent?'

Eliza gritted her teeth and smiled. 'Yes, she did, Anna.' Thinking she had been 'helpful', Anna had sent Eliza's mother several books in *The Idiots Guide to . . .* series (*Wine, Housekeeping, Getting a Job after Fifty,* etc.). The attached card had read: *Now that you don't have a staff, here's something I hope can help you out as you transition into your new life.*

'I'm so glad you all made it. I was a little worried about the traffic. Anyway, as you know, my husband, Kevin, hired you. Oh, thank God, here he is now.'

The girls turned to see a hefty, bald man, in an immaculately pressed Hawaiian shirt and Bermuda shorts, making his way towards them.

'Kevin, did you manage to remember to send over the bottle of Petrus as a hostess present? Yes? Okay, good. How much was it?'

He told her. She winced. Making her way into the good graces of the grand hostesses of the Hamptons was costing them an arm and a leg, but Anna was determined to chair the big ovarian cancer benefit next month.

'Kevin Perry,' he said. He shook each of their hands warmly, lingering just a hair too long with Jacqui's handshake. *Typical*, thought Jacqui. *But maybe this could come in handy.*

'How's your dad?' he asked Eliza.

'Same.' Eliza shrugged.

'Why don't we sit over here?' Kevin said, motioning to the round patio table. Anna followed him, teetering on her heels and almost slipping on the wet tile. The girls took their seats. Mara noticed that every screw in the teak veranda had been hand-turned to a ninety-degree angle, orthogonal to the direction of the boards. Did the Perrys expect this level of stringent perfectionism from everything, and everyone, around them?

'We want to formally welcome you girls to the Hamptons,' Anna began crisply. 'As you can imagine, we have a very busy night ahead of us. I thought we'd just have a little barbecue for the kids since it's the Fourth of July. We usually do something more elaborate, but we've been invited to a party at the Perelmans' later.' She paused so they could let that name sink in – they were hanging out with Ron Perelman! The Revlon mogul married to Ellen Barkin – the tippy top of the Hampton A-list! Unfortunately, Mara and Jacqui had never heard of him, and Eliza couldn't care less about Ron Perelman – he didn't have any kids her age.

'So tonight we'll do just a simple affair – nothing too fancy.' Anna laughed. 'Just a few burgers, maybe some hot dogs. Don't you think?'

'Oh, definitely.' Kevin nodded.

'There's a grill out back, and we could even do some seared tuna, maybe? There's an avocado salad in the fridge that might go nicely with that. Or is tuna not patriotic?' she asked with a little laugh.

'Tuna sounds good,' Eliza ventured.

'It's Pacific ahi, just came off the plane from Hawaii,' Anna told her. 'Delicious. Maybe with a little mirin sauce? Like we did last year?' Last Fourth of July the Perrys had hosted a catered, white-glove party on their private beach to celebrate the holiday. Eliza remembered the succulent tuna steak served on silver platters.

'Sure.' Eliza shrugged. 'Maybe with some white wine?'

'A perfect menu. Except, of course, the kids can't have alcohol. And this will be a lot more intimate.' Anna smiled without showing any teeth. 'Anyway, enough about the barbecue. It's at seven since the kids aren't allowed food after sunset.'

'Honey? Can we get back to business, please?' Kevin asked.

'Of course, of course,' Anna said.

'We just want to stress that this is a partnership. You're part of the family now. Call us Anna and Kevin, please,' he said. 'We see this as an opportunity for the kids to have a good time this summer. I think we're all going to have a little fun, aren't we?' he said, winking at Jacqui.

'But of course, we have some goals in mind,' Anna continued. 'First off, there's William. He's been diagnosed with ADHD. He can't keep still for a moment and keeps forgetting to take his meds. He *must* calm down this summer. He's got to learn how to sit still or they're not taking him back at St. Bernard's in the fall.' She passed them a list of daily prescriptions.

Mara stared at the list, mystified. *A nine-year-old on drugs?*

Eliza was unfazed. William's regime was longer and more complicated than the heart medicine her father took every day, sure, but that was modern parenting for you. And with that thought, her eyes glazed over. *What should I wear to the party later?*

Jacqui was getting impatient. When could she begin the search for Luca? *This blonde insect should stop yapping already.*

'Next, Madison *must* lose weight. As I see it, she's carrying about fifteen more pounds than she should. Kids can be so cruel, and I don't want any daughter of mine to be "the fat one".' She didn't make the quotation mark sign with her hands, but they could hear it clearly in her tone. 'I've put her on an eight-hundred-calorie diet.' She handed out a detailed folder with nutritional charts and calorie serving information. 'I'd really prefer if she only ate raw foods. It truly helped my digestion, and it's a very

51

healthy way to live.' She suddenly craned her neck, like a dog on the trail of a bad scent, and hollered towards the pool. 'MADISON! Put that cookie down! Put it down! Do you want to be a piggy your whole life?'

Raw food? Mara wondered. *What the hell?*

The Christian Dior halter? Eliza mused. *Or the Gucci tank top?*

Water, I need water, Jacqui wheezed. All that whiskey in the car was giving her a premature hangover.

'Zoë is six and is starting first grade in the fall. I want her to learn to read this summer. We sent her to the best kindergarten and pre-K and she still can't do her ABCs. It's so embarrassing.' Anna shook her head.

Six years old. Reading. Got it, Mara thought.

Or maybe the Dolce mini? Eliza wondered.

Jacqui was starting to feel faint from dehydration. She gripped the edge of her seat to keep herself upright.

'And as for Cody . . .' Anna's visage softened slightly. 'The baby has got to conquer his fear of water. I mean, we're in the Hamptons . . . and he won't even go in the pool!'

'What else? Oh. House rules. Curfew is midnight. It's the same for the twins. Ryan you've met. You can drive any car that's not being used, and you'll need to, to get into town and take Zoë and Madison to ballet and yoga and William to his three therapists. Every Sunday we'll all sit down for a weekly progress meeting. You'll be paid in three installments, the first is in a few weeks. Other than that, we don't really have a lot of rules here.'

Well, that was good to know, thought Mara.

Thank God, thought Eliza.

Water, thought Jacqui.

'Lastly, I absolutely *insist* that you girls have a great summer with us. Like we said in the ad – this is going to be the summer of your life! Please make yourselves at home, and we'll see you later at the barbecue?'

'Sounds like fun,' Mara said.

'We'll be there,' Eliza assured Anna. Seared tuna, avocado salad? She was famished!

Jacqui nodded.

'Ciao,' Anna said with a wave of her hand. They were dismissed.

'Uh – honey . . . ,' Kevin Perry said.

'Yes?'

'Don't you think they should *meet* the kids?'

Where there's smoke, there's usually fire

'SO WHAT DID YOU THINK OF MOMZILLA?' ELIZA asked when they were back in their rooms.

'*Problema.* Women like that at my store. *Meu deus.* Never satisfied,' Jacqui prophesied.

'How do you know them?' Mara asked.

'Long story.' Eliza shrugged. What business was it of theirs? 'My dad went to college with Kevin. He called asking if I was available for the summer. I'm only doing this as a favour. I know these kids. Absolute terrors. My advice? Stay as far away from them as possible.'

Well, that isn't really practical, Mara thought, *since we were hired to take care of them.*

'Anna's a total witch, too. She's his second wife. Cody – the three-year-old – is the only one that's hers. The others are Brigitte's. She was crazy. Anna was Kevin's personal assistant. She was having an affair with him for years,' Eliza said as she checked herself out in the mirror. White halter top, sequin-embellished

miniskirt, white sandals with satin ties that laced up the calf –
yes, that would work for tonight. Jacqui pulled on a pair of low-
waisted jeans and a tube top. Mara changed out of her stinky
poly-blend blouse for a T-shirt, shorts, and sneakers.

Second wife. Stepkids. Personal assistants. Affairs. It was too
much for Mara. Had she walked into some whacked-out soap
opera? She was still wondering how she was going to heat
Madison's food to only '100 degrees Fahrenheit so as not to spoil
its natural essence'.

At sunset the three walked towards the pool, where the smell
of gasoline hung heavy in the air. Packs of hamburger meat, hot
dogs, and sesame buns were stacked next to an open, smoking
grill. Finding no one around, the three girls sat around the table,
which had been set for dinner with a white linen tablecloth, ster-
ling silver cutlery, and porcelain plates.

'She said seven, right?' Eliza asked.

'Yeah,' Mara said, feeling a little apprehensive. Something was
wrong here.

Jacqui got up. 'Where do you think the wine is?' she asked,
poking in the Igloo cooler she found near the pots of citronella
candles.

Suddenly all four kids burst through the screen door, clam-
ouring for food.

'Something smells,' William said, wrinkling his nose at the
smoking fire pit.

'Is something burning?' Madison asked.

'I'm hungry,' Zoë said.

'Me too,' Eliza replied. What was going on? Where were the eats?

'Camille always made me a double cheeseburger,' Madison said. 'With lots of onions and pickles,' she added hopefully.

'Who's Camille?' Mara asked.

'She was here three days ago,' Madison said, playing with her napkin. 'But she did a bad thing and had to go away.'

Just then Anna wafted by, humming to herself. She was wearing a grass skirt over her bikini and had put an orchid in her hair (which was still showing the slight aftereffects of William's water attack). 'The invitation said Hula Couture,' she said with a laugh, walking out to the patio. 'Isn't this fun? I got Michael Kors to sew it up for me.'

Kevin followed, wearing a formal tuxedo jacket over his Hawaiian shirt.

'Is everyone having a lovely time?' Anna asked.

'No!' William roared. 'There's nothing to eat!'

'We're hungry!' Madison whined.

'What?' Anna said, walking over to investigate. She found the three au pairs sitting at the table in front of empty plates. 'Why isn't anything ready? I distinctly remembered informing you we were having a barbecue tonight.'

'Oh!' Mara said.

They had assumed they were *invited* to the barbecue. None of them had realised they were supposed to be *cooking* it.

'You said to be here by seven,' Eliza said weakly.

There was a frosty silence as the misunderstanding sank in.

Anna frowned. 'Huh. Well, Kevin and I have to get to the party in a few minutes, so I guess it doesn't matter. You can take them to Main Beach afterward to see the fireworks.'

'No problem, we'll get on it right away,' Mara said, standing by the grill and handing Jacqui a flipper.

'And remember the tuna for Madison,' Anna reminded them as she hoofed it out of the patio without saying goodbye to the kids.

'Mama! Mama! Cody wanna Mama!' the baby cried after her.

'Sh . . . shh . . . ,' Mara said soothingly. 'Mara's here.'

But Cody continued to howl.

'This is bullsh – ,' Eliza said, catching herself, as grease splattered on her skirt and Jacqui burned another patty.

Mara pried the tuna off the grill. She wondered if it was safe to feed it to Madison; didn't fish need to be cooked? Mara decided to keep it where it was. Hopefully Anna wouldn't find out she had broken the raw food rule on the first night. She'd have to remember to ask Madison who this Camille was and why she was sent away.

'Don't they have a chef?' Mara asked. She had observed enough servants around the property.

'Uh-huh. Cordon Bleu. But he doesn't do kiddie meals apparently. It's probably below him.' Eliza shrugged. She was used to handling difficult help. Laurent, their former French chef, refused

to cook anything other than five-star meals. He would throw a
tantrum when her dad demanded a well-done steak. Her mother
eventually had to replace him with someone more flexible.

'Hey, did anyone see the rest of the ahi?' Eliza asked.

'There's just this itty piece,' Mara said.

Jacqui shrugged. She'd found a six-pack of beer underneath
the soda cans and had helped herself to one. 'Miller Lite?' she
offered.

Eliza shook her head. She unwrapped all the waxed paper
packages in a panic, but they all contained ground meat.
Apparently Anna had decided not to waste the precious tuna on
the likes of them.

The reality of her status finally sank in: she had been installed
in an attic room instead of the corner bedroom. Fed burgers
instead of tuna steak. She wasn't a guest on the Perry estate. Eliza
Thompson, former 'it girl', was now the help.

Main Beach: you can only keep Eliza down for so long

THE BEACH WAS AS CROWDED AS CENTRAL PARK DURING a free concert. The fireworks show had begun, and as rockets whizzed up to the heavens, Beethoven's Fifth Symphony thundered from temporary overhead speakers. Stylish picnickers popping champagne corks and feasting on three-pound lobsters sat on checkered tablecloths and sent fuzzy photos via their mobile phones to provide latecomers with location coordinates. Almost no one looked up. They had better things to do, like blanket-hop to exchange effusive double-cheek air kisses and discreetly check out each other's flowered Murakami handbags.

The three au pairs secured a place on top of the hill, primo real estate, thanks to Eliza's pushiness. She found them a postage-stamp-sized area bordered by two identical silk jacquard blankets and managed to expand their territory by letting Cody cry his lungs out as the rockets boomed. Nothing like an irritable toddler to motivate self-involved single Hamptonites to get out of the way.

Mara couldn't help but overhear some of the chatter around them.

'How's the black truffle ravioli?' a woman asked her guests as she handed out monogrammed china filled with plump, glistening pasta and smothered with a white cream sauce.

'Superb. And the *cervelle de canut* is divine with this Riesling.'

'Did someone bring the opera glasses?' another asked, motioning for a pair of binoculars.

She had never seen anyone picnic like this before. Back home, picnics meant a couple of sandwiches, a bag of chips, and a litre of soda. Not a four-course menu with a different wine accompaniment for each entrée. Wresting her eyes away from the neighbouring sheets, Mara turned back to her own group.

'Madison, where did you find that candy bar?' she asked.

Madison looked up guiltily and stuffed the entire Snickers bar in her mouth. Mara shook her head. She would have to find out where the kid hid her stash or they were all dead. She did a quick head count. One, two, three . . . That couldn't be right. 'William! Eliza, Jacqui, have you seen William?!' she asked.

The two shrugged indifferently.

'You guys stay here; I'll try to find him,' Mara said, beginning to panic. She walked carefully around the perimeter, calling his name as softly as she could. 'William?' she whispered. 'William? Where are you?'

'Sorry, sorry,' she said, tiptoeing by an uproarious group of clean-cut guys in matching khaki trousers and Teva sandals, puffing on cigars as they cheered the spectacle in the sky.

'No worries. Why don't you join us?' one asked, offering her a plastic cup filled with bubbly.

'No thanks. I'm just looking for a little boy.' Mara shook her head.

'We're all big boys here.' He winked. 'C'mon, stay awhile.' He looked about twenty-two, red-cheeked, and well meaning, but she wasn't interested in older guys (even older guys with the maturity of teenagers).

'Really, I can't. I'm working.'

'What do you do?'

'I'm an au pair.'

And with those four little words, his posture changed. He raked his eyes over her body. 'Then you've got absolutely no excuse *not* to stay. It's not like you've got a real job, right?'

Mara turned away without answering him, completely offended.

'WILLIAM!!' Mara began to yell in desperation, not caring if she caused a scene. The hyperactive nine-year-old finally reappeared, making aeroplane noises and screaming every time the rockets boomed.

'Don't ever do that again!' Mara scolded. 'You can't just disappear like that! It's not safe!'

'DON'T TELL ME WHAT TO DO!' William screamed. 'YOU'RE NOT MY MOMMY!'

'I know I'm not your mommy, but I work for your mommy.'

'No, you don't – you work for ANNA,' William spat.

Back at the blanket, Mara recounted what the Dartmouth-undergrad-look-alike had said to her. 'It was like I said "au pair" but he heard "hooker"!'

Eliza rolled her eyes. She could have warned her about using the '*a*' word to describe herself. 'Most of the young investment banker types around here think au pairs are easy summer lays with little or no responsibility. Stay away from them; they rent tract homes in Westhampton and are totally not worth your while,' Eliza advised.

Madison removed a Ziploc full of gummi bears from her pocket. She nudged her brother. 'The other au pairs were a lot nicer.'

'Wait. What other au pairs?' Mara demanded.

'Camille, Tara, and Astrid. They were taking care of us because Nanny went back to England this summer,' Zoë piped up.

'What happened to them?' Eliza wanted to know.

'They were fired,' William said gleefully. 'It was funny.' He hugged his knees, remembering how the Porsche Cayenne careened through the streets of East Hampton and screeched to a halt at the Jitney stop and how his stepmother used bad, bad words as she threw their suitcases out of the window.

'Fired?' Mara asked, a chill in her heart. The possibility had never occurred to her. That would totally ruin her plans to earn enough money for her college tuition.

Fired? Eliza thought. Now, that would definitely complicate matters. She was supposed to spend the whole summer here – God help them if they tried to ship her back to Buffalo.

Jacqui didn't much care about being fired. As long as they did it after she found Luca.

'I miss them,' Zoë said. 'Tara was supposed to braid my hair today.'

'What did they d—' but before Mara could finish her question, a particularly loud firecracker exploded and Cody started to bawl again.

'Oh my God, can you hold him? What should we do?' Eliza said, thrusting the toddler into Mara's arms.

'Shh . . . shh . . . ,' Mara said, rocking him on her lap and trying to hum a lullaby.

'Thees one says she's a little hungry,' Jacqui said, pointing to Madison. 'Maybe we give her something?' she asked when Mara had her back turned.

'What's in the basket?' Eliza asked.

'Pringles.'

'Yeah, fine.' Eliza shrugged.

'Here. You,' Jacqui said, pushing the Pringles towards Madison, 'What is your name?'

'Madison, like Madison Avenue in New York City,' the little girl said proudly.

'Ah,' said Jacqui, 'My name is Jacerei. It is a place in my home, too.' Jacqui smiled at her.

But their bonding was interrupted when Mara looked up. 'Hey, where'd William go? William! Stay here! On the blanket! Don't move!' Mara said in her best sophomore class secretary voice. 'Zoë, come on, honey, look at all the colours, aren't they nice?'

'Cody, it's okay, baby, it's only fireworks. I know, they're loud, but it's okay,' she soothed.

A few minutes later the kids were crowded around Mara, who put an arm around all of them. 'Look at that! The Stars and Stripes! Have you ever seen anything so beautiful?' Mara asked the little girls, who were sitting raptly looking at the night sky. The boys were passed out on the blanket, William utterly spent from chasing dragonflies and Cody sleeping in his stroller with his thumb in his mouth.

Eliza looked at her mobile phone. Uh-oh. Time to motor.

'Hey, you know what, I've got to run. I'm meeting some friends . . . ,' Eliza said, brushing grass stains off her knees and starting to walk away.

'Excuse me?' Mara asked.

'Where are you going?' Jacqui asked.

'Party. Wanna come?' Eliza said.

'*Sim.*' Jacqui nodded, standing up.

'Yeah, after all, you've got things under control here, right, Mary?' Eliza asked. But before Mara could answer, Eliza and Jacqui were running down the hill as fast as their stilettos would take them.

Resort is the hottest party in the Hamptons. At least until next week.

ELIZA TOOK A DEEP BREATH AS SHE SCANNED THE MOB scene outside Resort. Five hundred people were elbowing each other to get closer to the velvet-roped entrance, and there was a backup of twenty stretch limos parked on the driveway, waiting to discharge their famous (or merely showy) passengers. Toothpick-sized women with significant cleavage, lathered in layers of foundation, blush, and hair spray, wearing brightly coloured tank tops and formfitting knee-length skirts, picked their way across the gravel in spindly sandals. Their dates, slick older men with artificial tans, jangled enormous gold bracelets on their hairy wrists.

Two spotlights directed up in the air lit the entire scene like a movie set. Several overwhelmed publicists tried to control the crowd while burly, three-hundred-pound bouncers glared at the overeager revellers.

Eliza fought her way to the front armed with the magic words: *I'm on the list!*

'Eliza Thompson!' she screamed at a beleaguered girl in a headset.

After rifling through her pages the door girl snapped, 'You're not on the list. You'll have to wait in line.'

'Under Kit Ashleigh?!'

'You should have said that you were on Kit's list in the first place,' she said sullenly. 'What did you say your name was again?'

'ELIZA THOMPSON!'

'Oh, there you are.' The girl nodded at the gorilla in the three-piece suit. He lifted the rope reluctantly. Eliza tugged at Jacqui's arm, and the two were swept inside the nightclub.

They found themselves in the middle of a chaotic scene, and Jacqui felt the familiar rush she felt whenever she was somewhere new, uncharted, and maybe even slightly dangerous. She licked her lips in anticipation. She was certain Luca was here some-where. She could feel it.

'Hold up!' Eliza said, grabbing Jacqui's arm. 'I see my friends over there.'

Kit was sitting in the middle of the biggest banquette in the middle of the packed VIP room. His face lit up when he spotted Eliza. 'Liza!'

'Kitty cat!' she shrieked, giving him a two-cheek air kiss as if they hadn't just seen each other a few hours before.

'Who's your friend?' Kit asked, wagging his eyebrows at Jacqui.

'Jacqui Velasco. She's, uh, an exchange student . . . living with my uncle's family,' Eliza said before Jacqui could open her mouth. She gave Jacqui a mute plea to play along.

'Sim.' Jacqui nodded. *What was that all about?*

'Cool,' Kit said. 'What are you studying?'

'Design,' Jacqui said.

'English,' Eliza replied.

They looked at each other. Eliza laughed nervously. 'English design, right, Jac?'

'Whatever,' Jacqui conceded. She was too busy scanning the room for a sign of her beloved to deal with Eliza right now. But she was polite enough to smile at Kit, who beamed at her.

'About time you got here!' Kit's girlfriend, Taylor, said to Eliza as she squeezed herself between her man and the hot South American girl.

'You're back!' Lindsay, another friend, crowed, coming to join them.

'My girls!' Eliza said, triumphant.

So many people were coming up to hug and kiss her she felt like homecoming queen. Except that she'd never be caught dead at something as lame as a high school dance. This was homecoming Eliza style: frozen margaritas, flowing bottles of Cliquot, hot guys, good shoes, even better cars parked outside.

'Sweetie, you look fantastic!' Taylor said in an admiring and slightly jealous tone.

'You must be starving yourself!' said Lindsay, the master of the back-handed compliment.

'Is Charlie here?' Eliza asked, a little too eagerly.

'Not yet. Why?' Lindsay asked, narrowing her eyes.

'Nothing. I just thought it would be nice to see him, for old times' sake.' Eliza shrugged.

Lindsay and Taylor exchanged a knowing look.

'Well, look who's here,' purred a voice from behind the champagne bucket. A sloe-eyed blonde with a vixenish pout appraised them coolly. She was wearing a pink beret, aviator sunglasses, and a tight baby T-shirt that showed off a completely flat midriff.

'Sugar!' Eliza said, bending down to say hello.

'Careful – I just had it blow-dried,' Sugar Perry said, turning away before Eliza could get any closer.

'How are *you?*' Eliza asked, sliding into the seat next to her.

Sugar was the most popular girl at Eliza's old prep school. At least, she was now that Eliza had left.

'I'm all right,' Sugar drawled, taking a cigarette from Eliza's pack and tapping it on her hand. 'I'm so over this scene.'

'I know, it's *so* boring. The same every year.' Eliza knew this was the right thing to say in the Hamptons, even though the truth was, she was thrilled to be back.

'You're so lucky your parents sent you to boarding school.' Sugar sighed. 'If only I could get away from mine.'

'It's never going to happen,' added a similarly hoarse voice. Eliza looked up to see Sugar's identical twin, Poppy, looming over them.

'Eliza, you're back,' Poppy said flatly. She had the same long platinum Donatella-Versace-like locks as her sister, the same seductive languor, but where Sugar had the makings of a porn star in a debutante body, Poppy, who was taller and two minutes younger, projected a more innocent air. Sugar was sexy; Poppy was just cute.

Finding the banquette fully crowded, Poppy parked herself on Eliza's lap without a second thought. Eliza didn't have the nerve to complain. She was too excited not to have to answer any difficult questions. Taylor and Lindsay receded to the background, pretending not to be bothered that Eliza had replaced them for the twins without a second thought.

Meanwhile, after downing two quick flutes of champagne and making chitchat with some of Eliza's friends, Jacqui scanned the room again. These people were nice enough, and yes, she could tell they were rich, but after meeting Luca, Jacqui had started caring less about those things. Before him she probably would have made her way straight over to the handsome Almost Forty who was staring at her from across the room — Jacqui knew the benefits of seeing an older man (hello, expense account) — but Luca had changed everything. For once she had found a guy who really liked her for who she was, not what she looked like.

Jacqui looked around, trying to look through the older man still staring her down. *I can see your wedding ring,* she thought. And then a flash of familiar stripes made her sit up a little straighter. Was it? No way . . . there was no way. But it was worth a shot. She stood up, pulling her underwear-completely-optional-low-rider jeans up with her, and walked off to follow the lanky guy wearing a very familiar-looking rugby shirt.

Back at the beach, Mara gets blown off so Eliza can blow out her hair

MARA COULDN'T BELIEVE THEY'D PULLED THIS ON THE first night. She packed up the picnic basket, trying to keep an eye on the one-two-three-four (thank God they were all there!) kids. 'All right, everybody, follow me.'

'Don't want to go! Want to stay play ou'side!' Zoë whined.

'Can we go over there? There's ice cream,' Madison said, pulling at Mara's hand.

'Why you want ice cream for? Porky Pig Porky Pig!' William jeered. He started snorting and making noises with his armpit.

'William!'

'William!'

'WHAT???'

'STOP MAKING THAT . . .' Mara clapped. 'Arrrghh!'

William, who was clearly enjoying torturing his sister, cackled. Madison was nearly in tears.

'Hey, buddy, that's not nice.'

Mara looked up to see Ryan Perry standing next to her, holding a death's-head skateboard in one hand. He wore a faded Groton sweatshirt over his frayed shorts. He smiled at Mara, then put a hand on William's head and turned the kid around. 'Apologise to Maddy.'

'Erm sorry.' William sniffled.

Madison stuck a chocolate-covered tongue out at her brother.

'I saw Eliza and Jacqui back at the house. I figured you might need a hand,' he explained.

'Oh – that's so nice. Really, though, it's all good,' she said, just as William wrestled Madison to the ground and the two of them began rolling down the hill towards the ocean.

'No – no – no – come back!' Mara cried.

'Don't worry, they won't get far,' Ryan promised as he picked up the picnic basket. 'Hey, cool, you brought the Scrabble,' he said when he spied the board game among the Tupperware.

'I thought it might be fun, you know, to teach Zoë about letters.' Mara shrugged. 'I found it in the closet in our room.'

'You any good?'

'I'm not bad.' Mara smiled.

'Bet I can beat you.'

'Oh, I don't know – I do a mean triple-triple. I know all the words that begin with *x*.'

'All of them?' Ryan cocked an eyebrow.

'Try me.'

'I'll take you up on that challenge.'

'Deal.' Mara smiled even more broadly.

Ryan tucked the box under his arm along with his skateboard and began to push Cody's stroller. He lifted Zoë on his shoulders.

'Giddyap, Ryan!' Zoë said.

'Hang on, Zo.'

The four of them walked down the hill towards the mini death-match.

'WILLIAM ADDISON PERRY! MADISON ALEXANDRA PERRY!' Ryan roared.

William and Madison immediately froze.

'That's enough of that!' Ryan scolded.

'You're not really mad, are you, Ryan?' Madison asked, releasing her hold on William and getting up to take his free hand.

'Me! Me! Me!' William whined, trying to find something of Ryan's to hold on to. With no available hand in sight, he grabbed the edge of his big brother's T-shirt.

'Easy, big guy,' Ryan said.

They headed back to the Range Rover. Ryan stashed his skateboard in the back and they drove the half mile back to the house.

'Sorry they're so out of control. It's really not their fault. No one's ever taught them any boundaries.'

'The kids?' Mara asked. 'Don't worry, I've taken care of worse.'

Mara told Ryan about the neighbourhood nightmare – eight-year-old Tommy Baker, who was famous for locking himself in the bathroom for hours, only to emerge as his parents were pulling back into the driveway. He'd pee on the floor just as they were walking in.

'It happened every time I babysat him and his parents never even tipped!'

'Bastards,' Ryan said.

'Look,' Mara whispered, turning to look at the backseat, where the children were all sleeping. 'Like angels. You'd never think –' But she cut herself off – they *were* still his siblings.

Ryan glanced at them from the rearview mirror. 'Angels with dirty faces,' he surmised, giving Mara a warm smile.

They pulled up to the driveway. Mara carried Cody to his crib, and Ryan walked the rest of the sleepy trio back to their rooms.

'I've got to make a couple of calls, then I'll be in the kitchen,' he said. 'Think you're up for a game later, Madame X?'

'Yeah, sure,' Mara agreed.

'Don't stand me up, now,' he teased.

'I won't,' she promised, flushing a little.

She tucked the kids in, and after she was satisfied the four were safely in dreamland, she tiptoed down the stairs towards the kitchen.

'Hey, they're totally out – do you want to bust out the Scrabble? Ryan? Ryan?' she called, a little short of a stage whisper. But he was nowhere to be found. She wandered in and out of the darkened rooms for a while, thinking he might magically pop out of one.

But he wasn't anywhere. Mara felt her good mood deflate. A wave of homesickness hit her in the middle of the perfectly spotless kitchen when she saw a Post-it on a French cabinet that she could only assume was hiding the fridge:

M: Sorry, duty called. Scrabble another time? – R

Of course he had better things to do. *Someone to do, more likely,* Mara thought with a tiny twinge of jealousy. She pulled out her mobile phone and dialled.

'Jimmy? You still up? It's me, Mara.'

Back at resort, Jacqui certainly has an eye for fabrics

JACQUI WALKED FAST THROUGH THE CROWD, NOT LETTING those rugby stripes out of her sight. Her heart was beating quickly; she was short of breath. There was no way, was there? This was fate. Kismet. This was meant to be. It was what she had been dreaming about since the day she woke up alone in her room in São Paulo. . . . Those broad shoulders, the fine, baby soft hairs on the neck . . . She had kissed that neck many times . . .

With trembling fingers she put her hand on his back. 'Luca?'

Jacqui couldn't believe her eyes. It was him! Luca, with his pale, freckled skin, glossy honey-coloured hair, and beautiful green eyes behind those nerdy-but-hip eyeglasses.

'Luca?' she choked.

'Excuse me.' Luke van Varick smirked, turning to face her. His eyes widened and he blinked for a minute, unsure of what to do. Then he broke into a lopsided grin.

'Jacarei!' Luke said as he leaned down to kiss her forehead. 'What the HELL are you doing here?'

'I work here!' Jacqui laughed, so happy she was almost screaming. *Luca! Here! In the Hamptons!*

'Here?' he asked, motioning to the floor with the straw from his gin and tonic. He was swaying a little and Jacqui smelled the alcohol on his breath.

'No, up the road. I'm an au pair.'

'How cool is that?' Luke laughed. 'I didn't know you worked with kids. I thought you were just a shopgirl.'

This is making no sense, Jacqui thought. *We haven't seen each other in two months and all he wants to do is chitchat? What about all the stuff we did in São Paulo?*

'Listen, you wanna get out of here?' Luke asked as his eyes roamed around the room.

'*Sim,*' Jacqui replied. That was more like it. She took his hand. She loved him. Her Luca! He could lead her anywhere.

A few minutes later Jacqui hung on as Luke sped down the Montauk Highway to his parents' home in Bridgehampton. The place was as expansive as the Perry homestead, and Luke showed her his private entrance and the four-bedroom suite in his 'wing'. It was a classic bachelor pad, with a vintage Foosball table, a Miss PacMan game console, dartboards, a basketball hoop, and dirty laundry strewn around the carpet. He pressed a button on a remote, and a sixty-inch television materialised from the floor.

Jacqui sat on the edge of his bed, looking around at all of his things – his soccer trophies, his G4 computer, his bulletin board studded with photos from his travels around the world. So this was where he lived. This was where he slept. She drank it all in – intent to know as much as she could about the guy who'd finally opened her heart and made her feel all jittery inside.

Luke stood in front of her, holding an open bottle of Absolut in one hand. He took a swig. His other hand was underneath his shirt, scratching his stomach. He stared at her hungrily. 'You know, you're even more beautiful than I remembered,' he said, putting down the bottle and reaching for the light switch.

'What else do you remember?' Jacqui asked with a playful lilt.

With the lights snuffed out, Luke splayed himself spread-eagle on top of the goose-down comforter. Jacqui curled up next to him. He tossed an arm around her and she snuggled on his chest. She listened to him breathe, happy to be so close to him again.

'I remember this,' he said, tracing a finger on her cheek.

Soon she felt his hand move down towards her breast, cupping it over her shirt, then slowly inch its way down underneath the neckline. She wasn't wearing a bra, and his fingers were cold on her skin.

'Oh . . . Luca,' she said, turning to kiss him fully on the mouth.

He pulled her up on him, holding her close so she could feel him getting excited.

They kissed, slobbering with open mouths, so quickly and

urgently that Jacqui could barely catch her breath. All the while Luke tugged at her top. Finally he pulled it over her head and threw it to the corner of the room.

She realised she was trembling a little – she'd missed him so much. It was everything she ever wanted and everything she had been yearning for when he left her in São Paulo.

She sat up, looking down on him. They held hands and stared at each other.

A trick of the moonlight lit up a photograph on his night-stand.

It was her Luca, smiling, with his arm around a girl.

Huh?

Jacqui stopped and released his hands. He reached up to touch her face, but she pushed his hand away. 'Who's that?' she asked, pointing.

He craned his neck to see what she was talking about.

'Oh. Nobody.' He shrugged, gently laying the photo down. 'Just someone I knew before I met you.'

Jacqui felt a little better. But somehow the moment had passed. She rolled off him and slid underneath the sheets.

He joined her, spooning her so that her back was pressed against his chest. He began to kiss between her shoulder blades, her most sensitive part. His hand awkwardly unbuttoned her fly. His fingers reached south.

'Not tonight. Okay, baby?' Jacqui asked, grasping his hand right above her waist.

'Uhmmmm?' Luke asked sleepily. 'Are you sure?'

'Uh-huh.'

'Mm-kay.'

They were quiet for a moment, and Jacqui listened to his soft breathing.

'Luca? I love you,' she whispered. It was something they never had time to say to each other during their two weeks in São Paulo.

But Luke was already snoring.

Eliza is red, white, and definitely blue

'ELIZA – WE'RE GOING . . . ,' SUGAR CALLED OVER, interrupting the conversation. She stood outside the circle, tapping a kitten heel.

'We'll meet you out front,' Poppy said, ignoring the fawning looks from the throng. The sisters stalked off, fully aware that all eyes were on their perfectly sculpted backsides.

'Sorry, guys. See y'all later?' Eliza asked.

'Where are you staying?' Lindsay asked, miming a phone call.

'My uncle's place – uh, in Sagaponack. He's not listed – but don't worry, I'll be in touch,' Eliza said, putting down her drink. 'Sugar! Poppy! Wait up!'

She ran after them, catching up just as the twins stopped to pose for the paparazzi stationed outside the entrance. She waited hesitantly just out of flashbulb range.

'Hey – how 'bout one with your friend?' a photographer asked, noticing Eliza and shooing her into the picture. Eliza found herself wedged between the twins, giving them apologetic smiles.

'Beautiful! Three of a kind!' The photographers wolf-whistled their approval.

'That's enough,' Poppy decided when the valet pulled up with their Mercedes SUV. He held open the door and handed her a ticket stub. 'Oh no . . . I left my wallet at home,' she said patting her purse and looking around expectantly.

'Don't look at me,' Sugar said. 'You know I never carry cash.'

'Here, I got it,' Eliza offered, rooting in her Louis Vuitton Epi pouchette. 'How much?'

'Forty dollars, miss.'

Holy . . . That was, like, half a day's salary. Eliza paid the parking fee while Poppy slid behind the wheel.

'Shotgun,' Sugar called.

The girls piled into the SUV and Poppy started poking at the GPS screen. 'I can never figure this thing out,' she muttered to herself just as Justin came blaring through the speakers. Sugar had dated him for a minute, and she liked to say this song was for her, even if it wasn't true. Sugar stuck her hands through the sunroof and whooped loudly as they made their big exit.

'That was fun!' Eliza yelled over 'Rock Your Body', feeling drunk and giddy and happy to be back. After spending the spring locked in her room because she couldn't bear another cold night in a wet field drinking Natty Light – the only thing that passed for a social life in Buffalo – Eliza finally felt like her old self again.

'That place was great!' she said.

'Are you serious? It was packed with nobodies.' Poppy sniffed.

'Did you see that troll in last-season's Gucci?' Sugar agreed. 'Totally D-list.'

Eliza surreptitiously tugged on her not-exactly-new mini. She vowed to hit the shops as soon as she got her fat cash-filled envelope in three weeks.

'So, what are we going to wear to P. Diddy's party?' Poppy asked, zooming past a stop sign. 'Oberon said it's strictly red, white, and blue attire only.'

'That's so corny.' Sugar yawned.

'It's at the PlayStation2 House, isn't it?' Eliza added.

'Isn't that the place where J.Lo had her birthday party last week?' Sugar mused. 'I don't think it's even open to the public.'

'Apparently even Brad and Jen RSPV'd.'

'Awesome!' Eliza leaned forward between the front seats. She was dying to see some real celebrities again. Back when she was still living on 63rd and Park, she hardly ever noticed them. Spotting Julia Roberts hailing a taxicab or Sarah Jessica Parker pushing a stroller was just kind of the backdrop for her life. Good luck catching anyone *US Weekly*-worthy in Buffalo.

'This is your street, right?' Poppy asked, pulling into a private driveway a few blocks from the club.

'Uh . . . actually . . .'

'You guys rented out your house?' Sugar asked, eyes wide.

'Well . . . um . . .'

'What's the deal? Spit it out,' Poppy ordered.

'I'm kind of staying with you guys,' Eliza said sheepishly.

'What?' Poppy exclaimed as Sugar nudged her sister hard in the ribs. Sugar turned around with a sweet smile. 'Excuse my sister, she doesn't know how to mind her manners. Of course you can crash with us tonight. You can borrow something. You're a size zero like me, right?'

'No – it's not that. I'm kind of . . . well . . . Kevin called my dad the other day. He asked me if I could help out Anna with the kids this summer,' Eliza finished lamely. 'It's no big deal.'

Except that it was. The twins remembered their father telling them about the Thompsons' troubles, not that they had paid much attention back then.

'Oh,' Sugar said, putting two and two together.

'Excuse me?' Poppy asked, turning around in shock. The SUV jumped over a speed bump and the three of them flew up from their seats.

'Ow! Watch the road!' Sugar said, glaring at her sister.

'Sorry!' Poppy said. 'You're one of the au pairs?' she asked disbelievingly, looking at Eliza in the rearview mirror.

'Kind of,' Eliza admitted.

There was an ominous silence.

'Huh. Well, that's gonna be fun, right? All three of us together again!' Sugar said cheerfully.

The SUV pulled up to the Perry homestead. Poppy pulled into the driveway and cut the engine. 'We're home,' she said brightly.

'So, I'll just run in and put on something patriotic and I'll meet you guys back here?' Eliza asked, swinging her door open.

Sugar and Poppy exchanged a quick glance.

'You know what, I'm soooo pooped,' Sugar said, yawning.

'Me too,' Poppy agreed. 'God, it's been a really long night.'

'Yeah,' Eliza conceded.

'I think we're just going to go to bed. We have tennis really early tomorrow, right, Pop?' Sugar asked. 'We'll see you later, Eliza.'

'Night,' Eliza said, unsteadily slipping out of the car onto the crunching gravel underfoot.

'Night,' the twins called, already halfway into the main house.

Eliza made her way down the stone path and opened the door to the au pairs' cottage ever so slowly. She was trying to be quiet. Really, she was. But she snagged her stiletto heel on the rug and went sprawling. She crashed into a bedside table with a loud thud.

The light clicked on.

'What the hell?' Mara asked, blinking like an owl without her contact lenses. She put on her glasses and glanced at the digital clock on the nightstand. 'Eliza, it's two in the morning!'

'So what?' Eliza asked, heaving herself up from the floor and falling backwards into her bed. 'It's early!'

'For you, maybe,' Mara snapped. 'Some of us actually worked today. What's the deal with cutting out? Hey, are you drunk?'

'God, Mara, get a grip.' Eliza moaned. 'I don't know how to break it to you, but we're in the *Hamptons* – hello? *The Hamptons.*'

'I know that,' Mara snapped.

But clearly she didn't, thought Eliza.

'Where's Jacqui?' Mara asked.

'I don't know. Probably still having a lot of fun, unlike some people,' Eliza said pointedly. 'You missed a great party.'

'I wasn't invited,' Mara replied.

Right. Eliza looked uncomfortable. She had forgotten about that part. That was kind of mean of her, she realised, and she wasn't a mean person – really. Just careless. But someone had to watch those bratty kids.

She peeled off her tank top and struggled out of her skirt, pulling on her favourite silk camisole and a pair of Brooks Brothers pyjama bottoms. She was still feeling high from her night and caught a glimpse of the pool reflecting in the garden pathway lights. It gave her an idea . . . the six-pack Jacqui had found was still in the cooler.

'Hey, Mar, what do you say we . . . ,' she started to say, turning to her roommate. But Mara was already back asleep. Boy, Mara was one lame goody-goody.

Eliza hopped into bed, hitting her pillow just as an all-too-familiar rumble geared up outside. *No, it* can't *be,* she thought, bolting upright.

'Get in!' she heard Sugar's scratchy voice call.

She scrambled to the window and watched as Poppy ran out

of the main house, wearing a red, white, and blue tank top and white jeans, looking furtively over her shoulder towards the au pairs' cottage. Eliza's stomach dropped as the car backed stealthily away, the headlights sweeping the road only after they'd made it out of the driveway without the lights. *I invented that trick,* thought Eliza.

They were going to the party after all.

It was all well and good to hang out with her at a VIP room or two – but when it came to hitting the *real* action, she was just deadweight.

The truth hit her hard, and for a minute she was back in her bedroom in Buffalo on yet another lonely Friday night. No one had asked her to be on prom committee even if it was obvious she had more style than anybody else in the class. They'd all thought she was such a snob when she turned up for her first day of school in a mink chubby. But hell, it was *cold* up there.

This summer was supposed to be different – she was supposed to be back with the old posse, back in the limelight, back in the lap of luxury, where she belonged. She thought Sugar and Poppy were her *friends*.

She thought back over the evening, looking for clues. So much had happened and she'd had so much to drink. It was mostly a fun, loud, Gucci-Envy-scented blur.

But she did remember one thing: they hadn't even thanked her for paying the valet.

A blistering day
at the beach

MARA SHOOK ELIZA'S SHOULDER. IT WAS ALMOST NOON
and she was annoyed. Jacqui was nowhere to be found and Eliza
had slept in all morning. Only Mara had shown up to feed the kids
their breakfast in the main house (a grapefruit for Madison, gluten-
free pancakes for Zoë and William, mashed rice cereal for Cody).

'What time is it?' Eliza asked sleepily.

Mara told her. 'Hurry up. Anna wants us to take the kids to
the beach. They're already in the car.'

Eliza grumbled as she hoisted herself up against her pillows.
She blinked at the tiny attic room. *Where on earth am I?* Then she
remembered. *The Hamptons. Working for the Perrys. As an au pair.
God, it was depressing.*

'Where's Jacqui?'

Mara shrugged. 'I don't think she came home last night,' she
said with a hint of disapproval in her voice.

Eliza yawned. 'Good for her.' She padded to the bathroom to
get ready, just as Jacqui walked into the room.

'Olá meninas!' Jacqui greeted, a blissful expression on her face. She was glowing and fresh-faced, although Mara noticed she was still wearing last night's clothes.

Mara frowned. 'Anna's on a rampage. I suggest you guys meet me and the kids in the main house in five minutes if you all don't want to get in trouble.' Mara was irritable from their little stunt the night before, and determined not to let them get away with it again. She stormed off, and Eliza and Jacqui exchanged dismayed expressions.

'What crawled up her butt and died?' Eliza asked. Jeez. She hadn't bargained on having to spend her summer with some hick from the sticks, who was so obviously a little tattle-tale, as well.

Jacqui shrugged. That morning, she and Luca had more than made up for their months apart, and she was still in a romantic daze. She was also sporting a few red hickeys on her neck from their passionate reunion. 'She needs *um amante*. A lover,' Jacqui decided. That was Jacqui's solution to everything. Jacqui had had one boyfriend or another ever since she turned thirteen and it was the only way she felt totally comfortable.

'Don't we all,' Eliza sighed.

They changed into their shorts and swimsuits and met Mara and the kids by the driveway. William was jumping up and down in the gravel driveway, the baby was bawling in his car seat, and the little girls sat in the very back of the SUV with bored faces.

'William! Please get in the car!' Mara pleaded.

'C'mon,' Eliza said, picking up William and shoving him in the car. 'You better behave or I'm enrolling you in ballet with your sisters.' That sobered him up. Mara wished she'd thought of that.

Eliza walked to the driver's seat. 'I'll drive, I know how to get there.'

Mara nodded, thankful for the help. They piled in and Eliza drove to Georgica Beach. They dropped Jacqui off to go grab lunch at the snackbar and Eliza gave her instructions on where to meet them. It was a struggle keeping all of the kids together, but Eliza finally chose a spot on the sand that was far from where her old crowd hung out. She shook out the towels and reclined on a beach chair. She still had a pounding headache from the night before, and the kids' whining wasn't helping any, but boy did it feel good to be back at Georgica.

Mara affixed a floppy sun hat on Cody's head and began to slather sunscreen on the girls. When Zoë and Madison were good and covered, she tried her luck with William. 'Sit still! Wait! I still have to do your back!' Mara pleaded, but William kept jumping and wriggling away.

'I give up!' Mara sighed. She looked around. Eliza was asleep on her towel. They'd dropped Jacqui off almost an hour ago, but she was still missing. What a surprise.

'What happened to him?' Eliza asked, horrified, hours later, when she woke up and noticed William's red, puffy face.

'What do you mean?' Mara said. She had been so busy playing with the girls and Cody that she hardly noticed how red William had got. Mara had been so grateful when he'd finally got out of the waves and splayed out on a towel that it didn't occur to her that lying down might be a tad uncharacteristic for the boy.

'I don't feel too good,' William said. His entire body was an angry crimson, with a couple of pale handprints where Mara had succeeded in slapping on a smear of sunscreen.

'Haven't you heard of sunblock?' Eliza asked Mara accusingly.

'I tried to put it on him,' Mara said weakly. 'But he wouldn't sit still!' She put a hand on his forehead. 'He's burning up!'

'Sunstroke. I've seen it happen to tourists. It's bad. We should get him to the doctor,' Jacqui said, surveying the damage with a critical eye.

The girls panicked. William began to hyperventilate. Mara's heart began beating hard against her chest. She scooped William up in her arms and ran to the car. Eliza and Jacqui packed up the remaining kids and the bags in helter-skelter fashion and scrambled after them.

At the hospital, they deposited an unconscious and feverish William in the arms of a gentle nurse and a kindly doctor, and handed the other three kids off to Laurie, who'd met them there. 'I won't tell Anna. For now. But call if you need me,' she said sternly before driving off.

'It's my fault,' Mara said quietly. She felt terrible for neglecting him. It didn't even occur to her that he had been Eliza and Jacqui's responsibility as well.

'Well, he really wouldn't stay still,' Eliza conceded. That was as close to an admonition of guilt as Eliza would get. Still, she was really worried about the kid – and not just because they might get fired.

Jacqui murmured a short prayer. She felt a twinge of guilt for sneaking out to meet up with Luca for lunch.

They waited in the little outdoor room, debating whether or not to call Anna. Mara said yes. Eliza said no. And in the end, it was Jacqui's deciding vote for *what she doesn't know won't hurt her* that finalised their decision not to call.

When the doctor emerged, the news was good. Minor sun stroke. Nothing ice packs, fluids and bed rest wouldn't cure. They almost cheered when William ran out, just as spastic as ever.

Eliza tousled his hair. 'You gave us quite a scare!'

'Next time will you sit still?' Mara asked.

William only grinned. Jacqui hugged him.

'What's that on your neck?' he asked her.

Jacqui blushed.

They returned home hoping not to run into Anna. No such luck. She had just returned from the salon and pulled up to the house at the same time.

'Anyone care to explain?' She demanded when she saw William.

'Um, it was the sunscreen. I don't think it was strong enough,' Eliza said smoothly.

'But he's fine,' piped in Jacqui. 'Right, Will?' William just smiled and pointed at her hickey. He was *definitely* fine.

'Drugstore brands are really ineffective,' Eliza said, playing up to Anna's snobbishness. 'There's a really good one from Zurich that is divine.'

'Order some for tomorrow,' Anna allowed, and turned away without even saying hello to any of the children.

The three breathed a sigh of relief. And then William ran off, as though nothing had happened at all.

The girls have finally learned how to locate the fridge under all that French cabinetry

TWO WEEKS AFTER THE TWINS DITCHED HER BEFORE the PlayStation2 party, Eliza stood by the washbasin in the laundry room, trying to get the mud off Sugar's Escada tennis whites. This was so not what she had prepared for when she told Kevin Perry she would 'help out with the kids' this summer.

Poppy and Sugar's snub had hit Eliza hard, but she still managed to claw her way back into the scene through her old friends Taylor and Lindsay, who had instant access to every guest list event in town, from store openings to movie premieres. The three of them hit a different nightclub every night, strategically avoiding the Perry twins. It was harder to pretend they didn't exist back at the house, where the blonde brats kept her busy with countless mundane tasks. Eliza didn't mind so much since it appeared Sugar and Poppy had failed to mention her diminished status to anyone in the clique. Were they being forgetful or just indifferent? Eliza couldn't hazard a guess, but she was thankful for the reprieve in public, at least.

'There,' she said, holding the soiled cloth up to the light. 'That should be good enough.'

She had ruined her manicure in the process, but at least she wouldn't wake up in the morning to hear Sugar's hoarse voice asking her ever so sweetly why her tennis skirt wasn't hanging in her closet. She walked out to the kitchen, where Mara was sitting in front of a bowl, her forehead knit in concentration as she carefully balanced a small green object on her fingers.

'What are you doing?' Eliza asked.

'What does it look like I'm doing? I'm peeling Madison's grapes,' Mara explained, as if it were the most normal thing in the world.

'Hell no.' Eliza still couldn't believe some of the things they had to do for these kids.

Mara gingerly took an edge of the grape and peeled off its skin. The bowl in front of her held about two dozen similarly skinless specimens.

'Where's Jacqui?' Eliza asked.

'Feeding Cody dinner. It's her turn.' And for once Jacqui was actually there to do it.

Eliza made a face. Talk about a thankless undertaking. The girls had learned not to stand in the line of fire when Cody hurled after every meal. Two words: projectile vomit.

'MERDA!' Jacqui stormed into the kitchen from the dining room. A river of green-coloured puke ran down the length of her cotton dress. 'Why does everything he eats have to be hand

the au pairs

chopped?' she ranted. 'Has this woman never heard of baby food? This makes his stomach *enjoado!*'

They grunted in sympathy.

Madison walked in and helped herself to a grape. 'Bleh,' she said, spitting out a chewed-up mess.

'What's wrong now?' Mara sighed.

'They're not cold enough. And that one still has its skin on a little bit.'

Mara wanted to throw her hands up in despair. Madison's grapes were never cold enough or peeled properly or else could not be eaten because they were deemed 'funny looking'. Mara knew the kid was just rebelling against the strict diet her step-mother had put her on, but it was seriously making her own life difficult.

'There's nothing wrong with them,' Eliza said, taking one and popping it into her mouth. 'Yum. I wish I had somebody to peel my grapes. You're a lucky girl.'

Madison looked at Eliza doubtfully but began to eat the grapes without complaint. A miracle.

The door swung open again and this time Anna walked into the kitchen. The three au pairs froze, wondering what was wrong now.

'Has anyone seen the mail?' she asked.

They shook her heads. Laurie had told them that Anna was desperately waiting for an invitation to a dinner party at Calvin Klein's house. Unfortunately, it had yet to arrive.

'Anna? Could we ask you something?' Mara assayed.

'Yes?'

'The kids keep talking about these other girls – who, um, used to take care of them? Do you know what they're talking about?'

'Some girls named Camille, and Tara, or something,' Eliza added.

Anna scowled. 'Yes. They used to work here. But we don't talk about them,' she said sternly. 'Do you understand?'

They nodded. Obviously, the former au pairs were a sore subject. But the girls' curiosity was doubly piqued. What had they done that was so bad? If only someone would tell them. It obviously hadn't been letting one of the kids fry like a potato chip. They'd done that and they were still here. But they had to find out, because as all three of them agreed, they couldn't afford to make the same mistake.

After cleaning up the kitchen and putting the kids to bed, the au pairs staggered back to their dingy room.

'God! What a week!' Eliza said, flopping into the only armchair. Between the cooking and the cleaning and the scrambling out of a VIP room whenever she spotted any sign of the twins' blonde heads, Eliza was exhausted.

'Seriously,' Mara agreed, thinking about the week spent catering to the whims of four adorable but very spoiled children.

Jacqui had disappeared into the bathroom to change. She was meeting Luca for dinner at The Laundry, a romantic French restaurant.

Eliza looked at the clock. It was nine. Too early to hit the clubs yet. 'You know what? We deserve a little break.'

'What have you got in mind?' Mara asked.

Eliza smiled mischievously. 'Look what I found.' She grinned, holding up an antique key that just happened to unlock the Perrys' liquor cabinet. It was about time they had a little fun.

The best way to find out a secret? a bottle of Grey Goose and a game of TRUTH

AN EMPTY VODKA BOTTLE ROLLED DOWN THE THREADBARE carpet.

'Here's another one.' Eliza hiccupped, grabbing another bottle from her bag.

'No thanks – I'm done,' Mara said.

'No way, if I'm having another, everyone else is, too.'

Jacqui held up her glass. She wasn't one to argue with that.

Stealing a couple of bottles from the Perry stash seemed totally appropriate, given how they had been slaving away. It was sort of like a bonus, Eliza had told herself.

'Let's play truth,' Eliza decided, and spun the bottle around.

It stopped in front of Jacqui.

'What do you want to ask me?' Jacqui asked. Plus Luca had called earlier to say could they meet at eleven for drinks at Turtle Crossing instead, so she had lots of time to kill with the roommates.

'Have you ever been in love?' Eliza asked, thinking she would start it off easy.

Jacqui blew out a puff of smoke and considered the question. 'Of course.'

'Are you in love now?' Mara asked.

'Maybe,' Jacqui hedged.

'The game is called TRUTH!' Eliza said.

'Okay, okay. Yes. I'm in love.' Jacqui giggled. She told them about Luca, the guy she had come all across the globe to be with, and how they had got reacquainted very, very quickly. It was the same as it ever was. Or was it? She didn't tell them, but Luca never took her out on proper dates. Instead they spent an awful lot of time in his bedroom or in dingy, out-of-the-way crab shacks on the North (known by most as the 'Wrong') Fork.

'I'm just not digging the scene this year, Jac,' Luke had explained one evening when they were getting ready to drive all the way to some ramshackle bar on Shelter Island for what he called 'the best hamburgers in the Hamptons'. Jacqui didn't think the burgers at the Dory were anything to write home about, but she had found her man and as long as they were together, she was happy.

Jacqui spun the vodka bottle, which pointed towards Mara.

'Shoot,' Mara said. 'Ask me whatever you want.'

'How many guys have you slept with?' Eliza asked with a grin. She wanted to shake Mara up a little. The girl was so uptight sometimes.

To Eliza's surprise, Mara merely rolled her eyes. 'One.'

She told them about Jim, her boyfriend back home, not that

it had escaped her roommates' notice that all Mara seemed to do after work was log on to her laptop to send him e-mails or else max out her mobile minutes to chat to him every night. As if it was doing her any good. Even Jacqui could see that every time Mara set her eyes on Ryan Perry, she got all flustered.

'So how was he?' Eliza giggled.

'I don't believe you guys get follow-up questions!' Mara huffed.

'Not that good, huh?' Eliza teased. She was in a good mood after three vodka tonics.

'How many guys have you slept with?' Mara demanded.

Eliza blushed. 'It's not my turn!'

'C'mon, how many?' Jacqui asked, curious.

'I'm not telling.'

'TRUTH! TRUTH! TRUTH!' Mara demanded.

'All right – fine. None,' Eliza said challengingly.

'Wow.' Jacqui and Mara raised their eyebrows. Now things were getting interesting.

'I almost did once. With my boyfriend Charlie.' Eliza's face softened. 'It was our six-month anniversary, and he'd just given me these earrings,' she said, touching her ear. 'I had bought this really cute little outfit from La Perla.'

'What happened?'

'He'd rented a room at the Carlyle, but when we got up there, he fell asleep from all the wine at dinner,' Eliza said. 'Then we broke up the next week, so we never got a chance.'

'What happened?' Mara asked.

'Things got – uh, complicated,' Eliza said. 'I had to go away.'

'Were you in love with him?' Mara asked.

'Yeah – I think so,' Eliza said. She had certainly loved *being* Charlie Borshok's girlfriend, if not Charlie himself. There were so many perks that went with the title. The gifts (always hand-delivered by special messenger). The vacations (weekends in Locust Valley, skiing in Telluride, surprise jaunts to St. Bart's). The flat-out envy of everyone in the sophomore class.

'Do you guys keep in touch?' Mara asked.

'Not really. But he's in the Hamptons this summer,' Eliza said. 'I'm sure I'll bump into him one of these days.'

'Maybe you guys will get back together,' Mara suggested. She couldn't help it; she was a romantic at heart.

'We'll see,' Eliza said. 'I heard he's already dating someone else.' She looked at her mobile phone for the time. 'I've got to get ready!'

'Where are you going?'

'There's some benefit for baby-teeth testing at Trupin Castle. It's this huge mansion this guy built in Southampton; he broke, like, all the zoning laws to do it. I heard he paid six million in fees. Anyway, it's never been open to the public and the new owner just got it renovated.'

'How do you keep getting into all these things? Don't they card?' Mara asked.

Eliza took a puff from her cigarette and placed it on a makeshift ashtray (an upside-down Bumble and Bumble styling wax top). 'I've got a fake ID. And it's a private event. As long as you're on the list, it doesn't matter. It's two hundred bucks a head, but Kit gave me three tickets. You guys wanna come?' The tonics and secret-sharing were making Eliza feel surprisingly benevolent. *Maybe these other girls aren't so bad after all,* she thought.

'No, I'm meeting Luca,' Jacqui said.

'I told Jim I'd call.'

'Suit yourselves,' Eliza said, pulling on a pair of skinny jeans and an off-the-shoulder top. She gave her blonde mane a shake and took one last look at her reflection in the mirror. 'Later,' she said, disappearing in a cloud of smoke and perfume.

It was eleven o'clock. By Hamptons standards, it was early. The evening had just begun.

Mara's got something special about her: it's called being nice

PROMPTLY AT MIDNIGHT THE ALARM CLOCK IN THE AU pairs' room emitted an angry screech. Mara banged the snooze button down in confusion. She blinked. She had been asleep for less than an hour. What was the deal?

Then she remembered.

Zoë.

She hauled herself out of bed and put on her robe and fuzzy slippers. She trudged all the way back to the main house and disabled the burglar alarm after only a few attempts. The house was eerily quiet. Mara walked up the stairs to the second landing and to the room in the corner. She opened the door and walked quietly towards the small form huddled on the bed.

'Zoë, get up,' she said.

'Huh?'

'Time to go to the bathroom.' Mara yawned.

One morning Mara had discovered Zoë drenched up to her neck in her own pee. No one in the household seemed to know or care – least of all her stepmother – that the six-year-old was still wetting the bed. The kid was ruining five-hundred-thread-count Frette sheets by the day. She had also developed an itchy rash on her legs from her nightly emissions. Mara couldn't believe that the girl hadn't been potty trained. So after picking up a well-thumbed copy of Dr. Spock from Bookhampton, every night at midnight Mara stole into the kid's room and walked her to the bathroom. Zoë still couldn't believe it when she woke up in the morning to dry sheets. Mara was a miracle worker.

'I'm done, Mara,' Zoë called from the bathroom. She flushed the toilet and walked back to her bed.

'Maybe next time you won't need me to wake you up,' Mara said hopefully.

Zoë nodded. Whatever Mara said, Zoë was starting to believe.

Mara closed the door and walked out to the landing just in time to see Ryan Perry walk out of his room, fully dressed to go out. His hair was still wet from the shower, and he smelled like Ivory soap and cologne. He was wearing a linen sweater and dark jeans. Mara thought he could not look any cuter.

'Hey,' he said. They hadn't seen much of each other since the first night. He had apologised about missing the Scrabble game, citing a friend in a broken-down Jeep as his excuse.

'Hi,' Mara said, wishing she was wearing something other than a plaid robe, bunny slippers, and a ragged nightshirt that read I ONLY SLEEP WITH THE BEST! in big pink bubble letters.

'Cute shirt.' He grinned. 'Is it true?'

'My sister gave it to me for my birthday when I was eleven,' Mara said, embarrassed.

'Kids being a pain?' Ryan asked.

'No, I thought Zoë buzzed the intercom. But she's asleep. What are you up to?' Mara didn't want to blow up Zoë's spot, even if she was only six.

'My friends are dragging me out,' he said, cracking his neck. 'Some party to save babies; I don't remember.'

'At Trupin Castle?'

'Yeah.' His face lit up. 'You going?'

She laughed, looking down at her slippers. 'Does it look like I am?'

His smile faded a little. 'Do you want to come? I'm sure it won't be a problem.'

She shook her head. 'No, I'm fine, really.'

'Next time, then.'

'Sure.'

Mara walked back to the au pairs' cottage, wondering if she should have taken Ryan up on his offer, and found Jacqui sitting on the front steps, looking dejected. 'What happened? Where's Luca?'

'He cancelled,' Jacqui said. 'I sat out there in front waiting for him for an hour, and he just called and said he was too tired.'

'I'm sorry.'

'I feel like going out, though. *Está uma noite bonita.* Don't you?'

'I'm in pyjamas,' Mara pointed out.

'You could change.'

'I dunno . . .'

'C'mon. I called Eliza and she said she'd put us on the list if we changed our minds.'

Mara thought about it. In two weeks she hadn't even set foot outside the Perry estate after dark. And Ryan was going to be there, too. Maybe it was time to see this 'other side of the Hamptons' that Eliza was always talking about.

Jacqui looked at her hopefully.

'Oh, sure, what the hell, we'll go.'

And with that, Mara and Jacqui bounded back to the cottage to change.

There's never a dress code
if you're cute enough

NOT FOR THE FIRST TIME SINCE SHE ARRIVED, MARA wondered why everything was so *crowded* in the Hamptons. For a so-called weekend retreat, it was certainly packed with enough people.

She and Jacqui had taken a cab, and they barely had enough between them to pay the meter. They were aghast at the price, but they were still leery of taking full advantage of the 'take any car that isn't being used in the lot' rule – plus, the Grey Goose had made them both a little tipsy. When they arrived at the castle gates, Mara was sure they were never getting inside. The people at the door of Trupin Castle couldn't understand Jacqui's accent, and when they did, they couldn't find Eliza's name on the list. Then even *after* they found it, one of the guards shook his head at Mara's shoes. 'There's a dress code here, ladies,' he scolded. Jacqui had told her not to wear her Reeboks, but then when she saw Mara's totally-in-need-of-a-pedicure toes, she acquiesced. Closed toes were a must. Luckily the other bouncer took a shine to Jacqui and decided to let them in anyway.

'You made it!' Eliza said when she spotted them by the bar. 'What do you want? I know the bartender,' she added, signalling. They told her, and two drinks were promptly passed over. 'Check out the live shark tank,' she said, pointing to the middle of the room, where six-foot-long hammerheads were on display.

Mara tried not to gape. Was there no end to all this excess?

'I got Mara out. Can you believe it?' Jacqui laughed.

'Where's Luca?'

Jacqui shrugged. 'He was busy.'

'Jacqui, you've met Lindsay and Taylor,' Eliza said, motioning to her two friends, who were giving the newcomers not-so-subtle once-overs.

'Yeah – the exchange student,' Lindsay said, giving Jacqui a fake smile. Lindsay didn't like girls that looked like Jacqui. They were way too much competition at a game she could never win.

Exchange student? Mara wondered. *Huh?*

'And this is Mara, another new friend of mine,' Eliza said.

'What *is* that?' Taylor asked, pointing to the Amstel Light in Mara's hands.

'Beer?' Mara replied.

Taylor made a face. 'Ugh, how can you drink that?' she asked. 'So foul.' Mara sipped her drink and cautiously looked around. Everyone else was holding brightly coloured cocktails in martini glasses. Couldn't she do anything right? And where was Ryan?

She couldn't see him anywhere, but there were so many people, it wasn't that surprising.

'Taylor – drinks?' Lindsay asked, even if her glass was only half empty. The two took that cue to make their exit. They'd had enough of Eliza's 'new friends'.

'Don't look now, but Charlie's walking over,' Taylor warned before she stalked off, motioning to a short guy in a blue blazer who was making a beeline their way.

Eliza turned around to show her best side and slouched down a little – in her heels she was taller than he was, and she knew he never liked that.

Charlie Borshok was a classic trust fund kid. Rumour had it his family had already spent half a million dollars on restructuring his face. He'd received a nose job, ear tuck, chin lift, cheek implants, forehead lift, and who knows what else to approximate some sort of attractiveness. There had been a documentary made about the lives of super-rich kids that had caused a big mess a little while back. Rumour had it that he was supposed to be one of the stars. 'Prenup! Prenup! Prenup! It's been drilled into my head since I was three!' he'd told the cameras. 'And if she won't sign, she's a disgusting gold digger anyway.' But the Borshok family had filed enough court injunctions that the director finally gave up on Charlie, and the material was left on the cutting room floor. Of course, everyone heard about it anyway. Eliza knew half a dozen kids who had been interviewed for the film whose parents had tried to do the same thing.

But none of that mattered to Eliza. Charlie was still the great guy who gave her a pair of two-carat Harry Winston diamond earrings on their six-month anniversary. Now that was love.

'Hey, handsome,' she said, still smiling down at him despite the slouching.

'Hi, Eliza,' Charlie said, a little coldly. He was still pissed that she had dumped him last semester. What was up with that? Hadn't he given her a pair of two-carat Harry Winston diamond earrings on their six-month anniversary? Wasn't that love?

'Long time no see,' Eliza said with as much warmth as she could muster. She and Charlie were good together, she was sure of that.

He shrugged. 'Heard you were shipped out to Farmington.'

Eliza tried not to look uneasy. She'd been very careful not to mention exactly which boarding school she was supposed to be attending, lest someone in her circle knew someone who prepped at the same school. But somehow word had gone out that she was supposed to be at Miss Porter's, an elite finishing school for girls in Connecticut.

'Tell me about it. Charlie, I want you to meet my friends, Mara and Jacqui. Guys, this is *Charlie*,' Eliza said triumphantly.

'Nice to meet you. How do you know Eliza?' Charlie inquired, to be polite.

'Oh, we wor – ' Mara began.

'She's my roommate!' Eliza interjected, thinking quickly.

'How do you like it?' Charlie asked.

'It's not too bad. The kids can be a pain, and our room is really small, but otherwise it's all right,' Mara said. 'Our boss is kind of demanding, though.'

'That's what we call our house mistress.' Eliza laughed shrilly. She gave Mara frantic warning eyes. '*Boarding school* is *très* lame.'

Boarding school? 'Uh . . . right,' Mara said hesitantly. 'Yeah. Boarding school. The uniforms suck.' What was going on here? 'But, um. Eliza's the most popular girl there,' she was inspired to add.

'Well, that's not a surprise,' Charlie said, looking keenly at his ex-girlfriend. Charlie looked at women the way he measured Thoroughbreds – the flanks, the teeth, the shoes – and Eliza passed with flying marks on all counts. He was still smarting from their breakup. The Charlie Borshoks of the world didn't take too kindly to being dumped out of the blue. But Eliza Thompson was easily still the prettiest girl in East Hampton.

'We should get together sometime,' he said to Eliza, giving her a kiss on the cheek.

Eliza's eyes misted at his touch. Was she being forgiven? Was Charlie going to let her back into his life? Was everything going to be perfect again? Would he rescue her from that roach-infested attic and book them a suite at the Bentley Hotel?

'Looks like you guys are gonna get back together after all,' Mara said after Charlie had left.

'God, I hope so. Charlie's parents have the *biggest* yacht!' Eliza said, oblivious to how shallow she sounded.

'But what was THAT all about – us being friends from school?' Mara asked. 'And why is Jacqui an exchange student?'

'It's like this . . . ,' Eliza said, biting her lip. Should she tell them? Could she trust them? They had covered for her so far. Who knew Mara could lie like that? They had made her look good in front of Charlie. Maybe she owed them the truth, even without an empty vodka bottle pointing in her direction.

Eliza pulled them to the quietest corner she could find – behind the column, near where several glassy-eyed club kids passed a suspiciously fragrant rolled-up cigarette. She told them the whole story – Buffalo, bankruptcy, and the boarding school fiction.

'I just don't want my friends to know, especially Charlie, that I'm working here this summer . . . you know? As an au pair . . .'

Mara and Jacqui looked at each other. What was the big deal?

'I know it's stupid, but I just want to have fun this summer. Is that okay?' she pleaded.

Jacqui yawned. Eliza's confession meant nothing to her. Let the girl tell everyone she was the Queen of England, what did it matter to her? Mara found it harder to understand. There was no shame in living in Buffalo. Hey, she was from Sturbridge. Eliza obviously had some issues, but Mara knew it wasn't her place to tell her that.

'So you guys won't tell anyone?' Eliza asked.

They nodded. Her secret was safe with them.

You call this progress?

IT WAS FINALLY TIME FOR THE FIRST WEEKLY PROGRESS report, even if the girls had been working at the Perrys for almost three weeks. Laurie assured them this time Anna and Kevin would expect them in the screening room at ten o'clock Sunday morning. The girls were nervous as they left their attic room and walked over to the main house.

They had good reason to worry. The kids were getting on their nerves, constantly comparing them to their predecessors. 'Astrid made us spicy tuna rolls.' 'Camille always let us stay up till ten.' 'Tara was so much prettier than you.' The little girls had been late for ballet twice because Mara was the only one who got up early enough to take them and she was always getting lost in the side streets.

Plus they were all a little on edge ever since one of the house-maids confirmed that the original group of au pairs had worked at the Perry house since June but had been let go abruptly without any notice. They still had no clue what had gone down.

'Quick, what was the last book we read to Cody?' Eliza asked.

113

'*Hop on Pop?*' Mara ventured.

'What's that? Sounds like a porno.'

'You have a dirty mind! It's Dr. Seuss!'

'Riiiight.'

'No, I think it was *Pokey Little Puppy,*' Jacqui said.

'*Hop on Pokey.* Got it.' Eliza nodded.

'What did Madison have for breakfast?' Mara asked frantically.

'What else? An ice cream cone and a tub of Oreos,' Eliza said, rolling her eyes. 'Like she does every day.'

'Noooo – she's on that macrobiotic raw food diet! Eliza, I left the recipes on your bed. You were supposed to take care of that while Jacqui and I brought the boys to krav maga!' Mara groaned. Anna had enrolled her sons in the Israeli martial art, even though the youngest was still awfully prone to falling when he walked. Apparently karate classes just didn't cut it.

'What are their names again?' Jacqui asked.

'Are you kidding me?' Mara demanded.

Jacqui shook her head. There were so many of them, it was hard to keep track. Plus it wasn't like she was around all that much – every minute she could find, she stole off to be with Luca. 'Uh – Villiam. And Manhattan?'

'MADISON.'

'*Sim.* Zooey . . . and . . . Cory?'

'Cody.'

'Zoë. Tell me about Zoë,' Eliza said. 'Is there something I should know about her?'

114

'What's to say? She's still sucking her thumb and acts like a three-year-old rather than a six-year-old. Her yoga teacher complained that she kicked someone in class the other day.'

'*Coitada,*' Jacqui muttered.

'What else do you think they're going to ask?' Eliza said, wringing her hands. She didn't want to mess up the good thing she had going. Mara basically took care of the kids while she and Jacqui spent every night partying and every day nursing their hangovers.

'It'll be fine,' Mara said, even though her heart was pumping hard in her chest. Cody hadn't even stuck a toe in the water. Madison had gained two pounds. William had taken to ramming his head against the walls. Zoë barely recognised the alphabet.

'Well, here goes.' Eliza shrugged, opening the door to the basement screening room the Perrys had installed over the spring. A large sixteen-foot-long and eight-foot-tall screen was set up at the far wall, and each girl took a seat on a black leather Barcalounger.

They waited for ten minutes. Fifteen . . . half an hour . . .

Jacqui fell asleep. Eliza read a copy of *Vogue*, happy to have a bit of quiet time away from the little devils. Mara looked at her watch anxiously.

Finally Esperanza, the Perrys' full-time housekeeper, appeared at the door. '*Meu deus,* I forgot to tell you. Laurie say Miss Anna out shopping and Mister Kevin playing tennis.'

Oh.

Tanning is Eliza's favourite sport

'MAR, PASS THE SUNTAN OIL,' ELIZA ORDERED FROM behind her wraparound shades. The sun was blinding, but that wasn't the reason she hadn't taken off her sunglasses all day.

Earlier that morning the Doublemint twins had found her wiping up Cody's daily spill in the sun-filled breakfast room. They were dressed in matching skimpy satin nightgowns and cashmere bathrobes. 'Ew, gross,' Sugar had said, daintily stepping away from the mess.

'How can you even touch that?' Poppy asked.

Eliza's cheeks burned as she scrubbed the floor on her knees. She hadn't counted on the twins getting up so early.

'Did you call Kit?' Poppy asked her sister. 'What time is he picking us up to hit Sunset Beach?'

Sugar gave Poppy a warning look, not so subtly motioning towards Eliza, who could hear them perfectly even if their backs were turned to her.

'I don't know; let's check later,' Sugar said, taking a banana from the fruit bowl. 'Hey, Eliza, did you remember to call Jean-Luc to make us a reservation?' Poppy asked.

'Yeah, you're booked for eight-thirty,' Eliza mumbled, picking up the baby from his high chair.

'You made sure we got the corner table, right?'

'That's what they told me.'

'Huh. Well, if we're seated anywhere else, I'm so not going to be very happy,' Poppy threatened.

Sugar shrugged, gave Eliza a half-scornful, half-pitying look, and followed her sister out of the room.

After they were gone, Eliza had quietly sobbed into Cody's Diaper Genie. It just wasn't fair. It just wasn't fair . . . She was a good person, underneath the fading five-hundred-dollar high-lights, and she hadn't done anything in her life to deserve being treated that way. Cody watched her in fascination as she sniffed and blew her nose loudly.

'One day, when you grow up and come into your trust fund, promise me you'll try to get them disinherited,' she told him, cuffing his chin.

Her eyes were still red and puffy from her run-in with the two wicked stepsisters when she went out to join the others by the pool. But that was what big Gucci sunglasses were made for.

'Mara – the suntan lotion, please?' Eliza snapped, still holding out her palm.

'Oh, sorry,' Mara said, looking up from the side of the

Infinity Edge pool, where she was trying to coax Cody into the water. She was a little annoyed that both Eliza and Jacqui acted like they were getting paid to laze about and sunbathe in their skimpy bikinis. The two of them had been comatose on their lounge chairs all afternoon, hardly lifting a finger to help – even when William fell in and pretended to drown. 'Psych!' he'd yelled when Mara dove in after him, still in her shorts and T-shirt. And Madison was stuffing her face, but no one had the energy to find yet another of her junk food hiding places.

The only time the two had shown any motivation was when Kevin Perry passed through on his way to his golf game. Eliza had jumped to help William with his scuba mask, and Jacqui had assumed interest in the book Zoë seemed to be reading out loud to herself. Unfortunately, the little girl wasn't actually reading any words, just pretending to by repeating the instructions her mother gave to their housekeeper every morning. 'Make sure you alphabetise the spices in the pantry.' 'When my trainer arrives, tell him to meet me in the studio.' 'Please make sure you are using the environmentally safe tile cleaner I bought from Amsterdam.'

'So how are our girls doing?' Kevin had asked, his gaze resting on Jacqui's spectacular MTV-rocks-Cancún body, barely covered by two seashell-trimmed crochet triangles and a matching thong.

'You missed a spot,' he said, coming over to wipe a smudge of white sunblock goop on Jacqui's shoulders. He rubbed it in with his thumb. 'There, that's better.'

Mara and Eliza blanched. But Jacqui didn't flinch from his touch and returned his stare with an impudent smile of her own. With her luck, maybe she wouldn't need to do anything this summer except keep the kids' dad's imagination well occupied. Besides, nothing could put a damper on her blissful state. Luca had promised he would take her to the very charming and quaint Farmhouse restaurant later that evening. And it was actually just down the street in East Hampton and not an hour away.

When Kevin departed, Jacqui and Eliza flopped down on their lounge chairs again. Mara sighed. She didn't know what to do about her two coworkers. She had expected them to be closer after William's sunstroke accident and the night of truth, but no such luck. Jacqui was completely preoccupied with Luca, and Eliza was acting aloof and distant. So the three were only really speaking when they were dealing with the kids or complaining about the Perrys. Although there really wasn't that much to grouse about – Anna and Kevin were hardly ever home. It wasn't as if she had no troubles of her own. Lately Jim had been pressuring her to take a weekend off, get on the New London ferry, and get her behind back to Sturbridge.

'Here,' Mara said, getting up and slapping Eliza's palm with the orange bottle.

'Thanks.'

Eliza massaged the oil into her skin, all the while exorcising the twins' insults from her memory. She counted herself lucky because unlike Sugar and Poppy, she didn't freckle or burn but browned to an even golden colour.

She didn't have their money, but at least she could do one thing they couldn't.

She could tan.

Eliza gives the gardener a free show

THE SOUND OF CLIPPING SHEARS STARTLED THE GIRLS, and they all turned around to see a very cute dark-haired guy in a holey T-shirt and weathered jeans trimming the hedges. Eliza looked up questioningly, and the guy met her gaze for a second before dropping his eyes back down to his task.

He's checking me out, Eliza thought, a little annoyed but also a little intrigued. She stretched her legs and arched her back as she slowly rubbed her chest and bare flat stomach with SPF 4 carrot juice.

When she turned on her back and untied the strings, she caught him looking again. Ugh. How rude. She rolled her eyes. But a minute later she peeked at him from behind her lowered Gucci wraparounds.

Broad shoulders, blue eyes underneath that icky fishing hat. Hmmm . . . possibly even cute?

As if she would ever be interested.

Let him look, Eliza thought. *It's probably the highlight of his life.*

'C'mon, Cody, it's just the kiddie pool, it's just water, it won't hurt you,' Mara said, trying to soothe the trembling child.

'YES, IT WILL! HA HA HA!' William said, splashing his baby brother as he cannonballed in.

'Ignore him.'

'Ah, just throw him in,' a jovial voice joked. The girls looked up to see Ryan Perry – bare chested and wearing faded jams, stretching his legs to get ready for his afternoon laps.

'Hey, dude, are you heading over to the thing at Sunset later?' Eliza called. *What was it about Ryan Perry?* Eliza wondered. He was superhot, but somehow she was never interested. Maybe because she'd known him since they were babies. And seriously, could she ever even think of dating those wretched girls' brother? She'd pass. But it didn't mean she didn't enjoy lording it over Jacqui and Mara that they had a somewhat more special relationship. Her being an old friend of the family and all.

'Maybe.' Ryan nodded, but his attention was focused elsewhere. He knelt down to where Mara was wrapping Cody in a towel.

'Hey, when do you want to get together for that long-delayed Scrabble game?' he asked.

'What? Oh . . . sure. Anytime,' Mara said, smiling.

'Cool.'

They grinned at each other, and Ryan dove headfirst into the pool. Mara missed Jim, but it was hard – every time she called, he was either drunk in Andrus Field with his boys or helping customers (who happened to sound awfully young and female) at his

122

uncle's car dealership. And Ryan was so nice to her. If she'd let herself think about it, she'd have already realised that Ryan was nicer to her than Jim had ever been.

'I forgot to tell you guys – Anna said we get to take the kids to the polo match next week,' Jacqui said. 'She left instructions on how to get in the VIP tents.'

At the mention of 'VIP', Eliza's ears pricked up. 'No way – you guys got a box this year?' she yelled to Ryan.

Ryan nodded from the deep end.

'Oh my God! But I have nothing to wear!' Eliza shrieked, sitting up and accidentally flashing the gardener in her excitement. 'Oops,' she said, pulling her straps up and retying her top.

The shears tumbled to the ground.

Eliza blushed but resumed her poise.

'What's the big deal about a polo match?' Mara asked.

'It's the Mercedes-Benz Polo Match Championship,' Eliza said, in the tone of, 'It's the Presidential Inauguration'. 'Everyone will be there. It's like a really important weekend.'

'Is just game, *sim?*' Jacqui asked, shrugging. Polo. Horses. Mallets. Big deal. Give her the World Cup any day.

Eliza shook her head. You couldn't really *explain* the Hamptons social scene – you either had it or you didn't, and you either got it or you didn't. And sadly, Jacqui and Mara just didn't have it *or* get it. They didn't even realise how lucky they were to be in East Hampton – they could have been stuck in Montauk, for heaven's sake.

'It's not about the game. Nobody really cares who wins. It's about the champagne in the tents. And between the third and fourth chukker everyone goes out to stomp on the divots! It's, like, tradition. Stephanie Seymour always comes out in five-inch heels that sink into the mud! One year Prince Harry rode with one of the teams.' Eliza caught her breath, remembering how much fun she'd had last summer.

'Anyway, everyone gets really dressed up. But casual. Kind of like LA.' She fretted, 'But I don't have anything new. I need to go shopping.' Eliza was itching to spend some of her hard-earned money.

After the cancelled progress meeting, the girls were given a handwritten note from Anna and three envelopes stuffed with cash ($3,334 exactly). *Thanks for all the hard work. So sorry we couldn't meet today. Giorgio couldn't reschedule my appointment. Try not to spend it all in one place. XOXO, Anna,* read the thick embossed card.

'Yes . . .' Jacqui said wistfully. 'At Daslu, I always had new outfits every week. I saw this great dress from Gucci with a snake belt in *Vogue*. It would look perfect with my new Alain Tondowski slides.'

They both looked so bummed, Mara almost laughed at them. 'Hey, if you guys want to go shopping, I can stay here and watch the kids.'

'Are you sure?' Eliza yelped.

'Fantástico!' Jacqui exclaimed. The two began gathering their

towels and beach bags, delighted at this unexpected turn of events.

'You guys taking off?' Ryan asked, pulling himself out of the pool, dripping fat drops of water on the limestone.

'Just them,' Mara replied. 'They wanted to go shopping, so I offered to stay with the kids.'

'You should go, too. I'll watch 'em,' Ryan offered.

Mara was floored. 'Seriously?' she asked. Shopping did sound tempting – and she was feeling kind of frumpy around those two fashion butterflies. It wouldn't hurt to get a little something – maybe a new skirt or a pair of those big sunglasses with the *G*s on the side that everyone seemed to own. Plus she could probably stop by the bank while she was in town to make a deposit.

'Yeah, Mar, c'mon, leave them with him. He's got nothing to do all day,' Eliza said, giddy at the prospect of an afternoon of her favourite pastime. So giddy that she almost liked the idea of Mara coming along.

'Oh, okay. All right, but we'll be back in, like, fifteen minutes,' Mara promised.

Fifteen minutes? Eliza and Jacqui eyed each other. Obviously Mara had never been shopping with girls like them before.

Main street, East Hampton: that is why they invented credit cards

THE GIRLS LINGERED OVER SARIS AND 'SUMMER weight' satins at Calypso, where Jacqui picked up another Eres bikini to add to the fifteen bathing suits she had already brought with her, then they hightailed it to Tracey Feith to take a look at the new sundresses, passing by Steven Stolman because Eliza wanted to check if the rainbow-coloured Jelly Kellys were in. Sadly, they weren't: they were on a waiting list and out of stock. At Jimmy's the selection of beaded corset gowns took their breath away.

Next stop: Scoop on the Beach.

'This is my *favourite!*' Eliza said, walking by the racks of terry cloth Juicy tube dresses, pastel-coloured Marc Jacobs camisoles and tanks, rows of candy-coloured cotton minis, and shelves of James Perse baby T-shirts and shrunken Joie hooded sweaters – the unofficial Hamptons uniform.

The store was filled with emaciated twenty- and thirty-year-old women trying on Petit Bateau T-shirts (made for French toddlers). Duelling mother and daughter tag teams abounded.

Mara noticed two distinct breeds – mothers who dressed younger than their daughters in Von Dutch tank tops and terry cloth sweatpants while their daughters wore vintage Chanel jackets, and mothers who dressed exactly like their daughters, both generations in sleeveless black Lacoste dresses and espadrilles.

'Can I help you?' asked a bubbly salesgirl, about their age, in a T-shirt that read JUICY across the chest. 'Looking for something in particular?' she asked Mara, who looked a bit hesitant, while Eliza and Jacqui went through the racks with feverish passion.

Mara shrugged. 'Not really.'

'Just let me know if I can help you in any way!' the salesgirl chirped, and left Mara alone to wait on more savvy customers.

Mara noticed most of the shoppers clustered around several tables stacked with folded jeans and decided to follow their lead. There were blue jeans, dark blue jeans, pin-striped jeans, coloured jeans, and 'dirty' jeans. Bell-bottom. Low rise. Super–low rise. Flared. Slim. Boot leg. Jeans with cargo pockets in the front, on the butt, or on the thigh. There were so many permutations of infinitesimal difference. Yet everyone around Mara was discussing which ones they already owned and which ones they still had to buy. Mara turned over a price tag. $175! For a pair of blue jeans that didn't look too different from her own trusty Levi's.

'Mom, what do you think?' a sylph of a girl asked, walking out of the dressing room wearing a nude chiffon slip dress with a plunging neckline.

Her mother, a knockout with toned Linda Hamilton arms and a taut midriff, shook her head. 'Don't you think it's a little too much for someone your age?' she asked.

'I'm twelve!' her daughter argued.

A thirty-year-old woman walked out of her dressing room wearing the same exact dress. She looked at the girl and sighed. 'I would kill to have your waist.'

The energetic salesclerk helped Jacqui and Eliza as they both disappeared into the dressing rooms underneath a humungous pile of clothing. Mara hung behind, her eyes widening at the prices. She found a cute bandanna-printed sleeveless blouse but immediately put it back when she saw how much it cost. $250! For a cotton top? Was there nothing in the store under fifty bucks? Yup – a pile of cotton belts in a bucket by the door. Eliza emerged from the wooden shutter doors in a slinky bias-cut Diane von Furstenberg wrap dress.

'Omigod, that is totally adorbs on you! Reese bought the same one yesterday,' the salesgirl gushed. Dropping a celebrity name was just the thing to ensure a quick sale; even Mara knew that.

'You don't say?' Eliza asked. 'I'll take it!'

The salesgirl grinned. Mara knew that smile: it said *sucker*, but Eliza was too pleased with her new dress to notice.

'Find anything?' Eliza asked Mara as she tugged at the under-fifty-dollar belt and critically appraised her figure in the mirror.

'No, uh, I'll just wait for you guys. Maybe I should get back,' Mara said.

'What are you talking about!' Eliza said, marching over. She pulled out a body-hugging red strapless Shoshanna dress that came with a pair of matching red lace underwear. 'Try this on. With your dark hair, this is going to look perfect on you!'

'I don't know . . . ,' Mara said.

The mother and daughter who were arguing about the sexy chiffon dress walked up to the register. 'Get out of my way, Mom, I'm getting it,' the daughter said, holding the hanger and brandishing her Visa card. 'It's perfect for Tiffany's bat mitzvah!'

Her mother sighed and gave Mara a look that said: *Kids, what can you do?*

Mara didn't return a sympathetic glance. She wasn't sure she approved of twelve-year-olds in lingerie chic, but she was from Sturbridge, so what did she know. She had already spotted girls Zoë's age wearing Porn Star T-shirts on the beach.

Jacqui walked out of her dressing room in a mini Polo shirt and the briefest striped denim shorts. 'What do you guys think?'

'That is to die!' Eliza screeched. 'Those look insane on you. Jac, don't you think Mara should try this on?' Eliza asked, holding up the dress.

'Is *perfeito*. You must. We insist,' Jacqui agreed. The two of them pushed Mara into a dressing room.

'Oh, all right, but just for fun,' Mara said. Jeez, it was so tight, how did anyone get their hips into this thing? She zipped it up in the back and looked behind her at the mirror. It barely covered her butt! So that was what the matching underwear was for.

'Hey, guys, what do you think?' she asked, stepping gingerly out of the dressing room.

'*Muito bonito,*' Jacqui pronounced.

'What did I tell you?' Eliza asked. 'But you need shoes. Sorry, but those Reeboks aren't going to cut it and don't you dare think you can wear your cowboy boots with that.'

Jacqui nodded and picked out a pair of matching red plastic Sigerson Morrison high-heeled flip-flops. 'Here, put these on,' she said, slipping them on Mara's feet.

The extra height lengthened Mara's legs, which were getting good and brown from their daily excursions to Georgica Beach. 'Perfect!' Eliza crowed. 'Except for the hair. Have you always worn it that way?'

'Why? Is there something wrong with it?'

Eliza tut-tutted. 'We're going to have to let Pierre have a hand in it.' She punched some numbers on a mobile phone. 'Pierre? It's Eliza. Do you think you could come and visit me later? I've got a friend who really needs your help.'

'Jim would never let me wear this in public,' Mara said, scrutinising herself in the mirror.

'Who's Jim?'

'My boyfriend,' Mara reminded them. The two of them seemed to have some kind of amnesia whenever Mara told them anything about her life back home. 'He's kind of pissed at me already for leaving him this summer.'

'Right. Mr Numero Uno,' Eliza teased. 'Why? Can't he visit? Aren't you from Boston? That's only four hours away.'

'Sturbridge. And yeah, it's not that far, but Jim's kind of a homebody.'

'God. What a baby,' Eliza said. 'If I were him, I'd want to keep an eye on you!'

'And who cares about Jim? *Esquece ele.* That's going to blow Ryan's mind!' Jacqui said.

'What do you mean?' Mara squeaked.

'Don't tell us you don't notice the way he looks at you. And he's supernice to you all the time.' Eliza smirked. Shopping always made Eliza more magnanimous.

'He's nice to all of us,' Mara said stubbornly.

'Have it your way.' Eliza shrugged.

By habit Jacqui began putting away the sweaters they had disturbed. She was enjoying herself as she folded the cardigans into perfect squares. But as she laid them on the shelf, she looked out the window and almost dropped the whole load. Outside was Luca! Her heart started to beat. They almost never saw each other during the day anymore. He always had some sort of excuse – he had to go back to the city for a family event or he had to go on a fishing trip with his dad.

'Luca! Luca! *Um momento!*' she said excitedly, heading for the door, still wearing all of the store's clothes. She scrambled out to say hello, and just as she hit the sidewalk, she was pulled roughly back into the store by the ever-vigilant Scoop salesgirl.

'Whoa! Miss! Where do you think you're going?' she said with a viselike grip on Jacqui's elbow.

'Hey! Jacqui! It's great to see you! Nice Polo!' Luke hollered from across the street without slowing his pace.

Huh. Jacqui reluctantly followed the salesgirl inside. Maybe he didn't want to spoil the romantic dinner they'd planned that evening? Somehow that didn't feel likely, and making all these excuses for Luca was starting to wear on her.

'Seriously, I can't buy this. I can't wear it and I can't afford it,' Mara said.

'What are you talking about?' Eliza asked. 'I get 25 percent off at this store. VIP discount, hello. That dress was made for you. And didn't we just get paid?'

Jacqui paid for her outfit, and Eliza put her purchases on the table. A Marc Jacobs Stella handbag, several C&C California T-shirts, four pairs of Jimmy Choo sandals, and a new Theory dress. The whole thing amounted to five hundred dollars more than she had actually made. 'Put the rest on my Visa,' she told the salesgirl.

Mara hesitated, but she did need a new dress, and those flip-flops were so cute.

'All right, I'll take it,' she said reluctantly.

Shopping bags in hand, Eliza led them to her *second*-most favourite shop in East Hampton, Scoops – with an *s* – where they all ordered chocolate parfait sundaes.

Contrary to *queer eye* logic, not all gay men dress well

THAT NIGHT, WHEN ALL FOUR KIDS HAD FINALLY BEEN put to bed, the three au pairs hung out in their room and made plans.

'You coming out, Mara?' Eliza asked. 'Don't say no again!'

Mara was reluctant, but it wasn't as if she had anything better to do. She had already walked Zoë to the bathroom, so she didn't have to stay home for that. And Jim was giving her the cold shoulder after she had told him she couldn't take the weekend off to visit. She had even sent him a care package from Barefoot Contessa, complete with scones and muffins, as a guilt present, but it had done nothing to thaw his temper.

'Oh, okay. But we're not going to stay long, right? The girls have ballet in the morning.'

'Yeah, we'll stay for, like, a minute,' Eliza said, winking at Jacqui.

Mara pulled out her new red dress.

'WHAT are you doing?' Eliza asked, taking it from her and putting it back on the hanger.

'Um, wearing my new dress?'

'Sweetie. This is for the polo match. It's all wrong for Jet East. This is a day dress. Also, you don't want to show up at polo wearing something everyone's already seen.' Eliza sighed. 'Here – put this on,' she said, handing Mara one of her own shirts – a clingy, black jersey halter with a plunging neckline. 'You can wear it with your jeans; those are cool. And your new flip-flops.'

Jacqui came out of the bathroom wearing a black lace top and silk cargo trousers that she had bought especially for her date with Luca that night. She stood in front of the cracked antique mirror with Mara.

'Don't pull your hair back; wear it down,' Jacqui said. Pierre, Eliza's hairdresser friend and self-proclaimed 'Queen of Hair', had come over that afternoon to give all the girls a haircut gratis, in exchange for posing with their new styles for his portfolio. Jacqui started to brush Mara's hair expertly. 'See, you keep the flip here, and kind of smooth it down here – but shake it out and make it all messy-messy.'

Jacqui brought out her twenty-pound, professional make-up artist's trunk and began to apply foundation, powder, eyeliner, eye shadow, and lipstick on Mara.

When Jacqui was done, Mara looked at herself with the hand mirror Jacqui provided. 'Don't you think it's too much?' She'd never worn this much make-up in her life, not even counting the spring formal she had gone to with Jim last year.

'You look almost better than me!' Eliza said, a little enviously. '*Almost* being the operative word,' she joked.

Mara laughed.

They said goodbye to Jacqui, and Eliza pumped her fist in the air when she saw the twins hadn't left yet. Their Mercedes SUV was still parked in the driveway.

Eliza clambered into the front seat. 'Get in,' she told Mara.

'What about the twins?'

'Anna and Kevin said we could take any car in the lot.' Eliza shrugged. 'The Volvo's still available.' She grinned wickedly.

A line of paparazzi stood in front of the red carpet, hollering at various people. Eliza walked slowly, hoping they would snap some shots, but they were distracted by blonde pop starlet Chauncey Raven and her crew of bodyguards. The eighteen-year-old most famous for baring her toned midriff all the way down to her pelvis and declaring her virginity while sucking face with a crew of Hollywood hotheads was the latest tabloid phenomenon. 'CHAUNCEY! CHAUNCEY! OVER HERE! CHAUNCEY!' the photographers screamed in desperation, but the star stayed completely hidden behind her seven-foot-tall army of former linebackers.

Eliza and Mara entered the club after her without any fanfare. Inside, Eliza began scanning the place for her friends and disappeared into a back room, losing Mara in the crowd. Mara stood by the wall, holding a martini glass and feeling a little out of place. She put down her drink and hit the ladies' room, where she found a chubby Chinese guy stuck halfway through the back window, his arms dangling helplessly over the porcelain sink.

'Excuse me?'

'Help! You, there, in the two-hundred-dollar top and the Jennifer Aniston haircut! Help me!'

Mara took one of his hands – the one not holding an enormous Nikon camera – and pulled him inside.

'Oh, good Lord!' the guy said, wiping his brow. 'I should really stay away from the buffet table next time. Too many free meals are not good for *moi!*'

The man in front of Mara was a pint-sized Chinese guy with an enormous belly and a double chin. He wore a leopard-print jacket over a paisley shirt and shiny, polyester trousers. Everything was too small and too tight – as if he had been caught off guard by some sudden expansion of his girth.

'Lucky Yap!' he said, holding out a hand for Mara to shake.

'Mara Waters.'

'My saviour! I need to get a shot of Chauncey Raven or my boss is going to have my ass. The little tart didn't even stop for photos outside the club. And they wouldn't let me in even though I'm on the list.'

'Wow, they can do that?'

'Honey, they specialise in that! Her PR guy is a total prick. But then, they weren't too happy with the shot we got of her last week.' Lucky sniggered. 'Girlfriend passed out at Tavern and had to be carried off the dance floor. *Star* magazine paid a hundred grand for the exclusive.'

Mara sniggered. 'C'mon, I think I saw an alternate entrance to the room back there.' They headed to the hole between the curtains that separated the VIP tables from the rest of the riffraff. Inside, Chauncey was straddling her latest paramour with great gusto. 'Keep it sexy!' Lucky said, angling his camera for a shot. 'That's right, baby, grind it! Woo-hoo! Show me the money!' His flashbulbs barely made a dent in the laser strobe light that shone to the beat of the music.

'Thank God her thong was showing. They always pay more for undie shots,' Lucky said, putting his camera away. 'You're a lifesaver.'

'No worries.' Mara smiled. Meeting Lucky was the most fun she'd had so far that evening.

'I'm going to do a lap to check if there's anyone else worthy of being plastered all over the party pages with spinach on their teeth. Do you know if the Perry twins are here? Sugar and Poppy?' he asked.

'Um . . . not sure.' Mara giggled, wondering if the twins would hazard the Hamptons nightlife in the crappy Volvo. *Crappy?* Apparently the Hamptons really were getting to her.

She said a warm goodbye to the prickly paparazzo. But now that their little adventure was over, she didn't know whether to go or stay. She was still deciding when she felt someone brush by her.

'Hey, you,' Ryan said, bumping her shoulder with his fist lightly.

'Ryan! Hi!' she said, so happy to see a familiar face that she impulsively gave him a hug and a kiss on the cheek.

'Wow, you look great!' he said, stepping back to take a good look.

'Because for once I'm not covered in baby drool?' Mara teased.

'No, no, I mean, you always – er, look good. I mean, I . . . ,' he said, uncharacteristically fumbling for the right words. 'So, uh, I thought you said you were staying in tonight,' Ryan finished lamely, trying to change the subject.

'Can't a girl change her mind?'

'I'm glad she did,' Ryan said, a little more seriously than was necessary. 'Anyway, Eliza said you were here. Come on back and meet some of my friends.'

'Sure.'

He took her hand and led her to the far corner of the room, where a bunch of guys were lounging on velvet couches, smoking stogies, their girlfriends perched daintily on their laps.

'Hey, everybody, meet my friend Mara,' Ryan said. 'Mara, that's pretty much everybody.'

His friend! Mara thought, elated at the introduction. *He didn't say meet the au pair! Or meet the girl who's working for us this summer! His friend!*

The tall guy with the shaved head sitting nearest to Mara

made as if to kiss her hand. Mara laughed as Ryan swatted his pal's hand away. 'Enough of that,' he said. 'Can I get you a drink?' he asked her.

'Sure, why not?'

As they turned to the direction of the bar, Lucky Yap walked by. 'Hey! Mr Perry!' he said, blowing Ryan a kiss.

'What's going on, Lucky?' Ryan said, laughing. 'How's Frederic?' Like everyone in the Hamptons, Ryan knew Lucky Yap was über-party-photographer Frederic O'Malley's right-hand man.

'He's all right. In Cannes for the festival. Leaving me with the B-listers! There's no one here! I haven't even seen your sisters all night. Let me get a photo of the two of you instead!' Lucky ordered.

Ryan and Mara looked at each other questioningly, then Ryan put his arm around Mara's shoulders and they both turned to the camera.

'Perfect! Marvellous! Sexy!' Lucky enthused. Afterwards he let them take a peek at the results on his digital viewfinder. Lucky whipped out his notebook. 'Ryan Perry and Mara Waters, right?' he said, scribbling their names.

Ryan raised his eyebrows at Mara, impressed that the town's most social shutterbug already knew her name.

Mara only smiled mysteriously.

Somewhere in the sticks (aka Hampton Bays), Jacqui gets in touch with her feelings

JACQUI VELASCO WAS . . . WHAT WAS THAT WORD that Mara used? Bummed? Yes, bummed. Really, truly bummed.

She should be really, truly, totally, completely happy at being reunited with Luca. In fact, she had spent the last month telling herself how perfectly happy she was, how glad she was that everything was working out just like in her wildest dreams. But that was the problem – Jacqui knew that if she really felt happy, she wouldn't have to keep reminding herself how happy she was. As the weeks dragged on, miserable seemed like a more accurate description of her feelings. Yes, miserable, Jacqui decided.

Luca had negged on the romantic dinner again. Instead of taking her to the Farmhouse, he'd suggested a 'romantic' clambake on the beach. They had driven an hour to a small, run-down restaurant where Luke had bought two soggy oyster po'boys and picked up a six-pack of beer. They weren't even alone. His friend Leo had met them on the beach.

At least the boys had made a roaring campfire, or else Jacqui would have frozen in her silk and lace. She shivered under her thin cotton sweater and wondered when she would be able to go home.

The other thing that was making her miserable: Luca wasn't even paying her the least bit of attention. That was the heart of the problem. She wouldn't have minded at all – they could eat at Burger King every night and she wouldn't care, but she was beginning to realise that maybe he wasn't quite the guy she had met in Sao Paolo. In fact, all he'd done all night was roll a couple of fat stogies filled with tobacco and pot and smoke them by himself. He'd offered Jacqui and Leo a few puffs, but pot made Jacqui's head ache, and Leo had declared himself fine with the beer.

'I'm out of rolling *papiere!* Nobody panic!' he said, laughing hysterically at his own joke.

Jacqui watched him silently. He was the love of her life, but when he was like this, she had to face it, he was kind of a jackass.

Luke got up from the blanket and ran down the beach to where he'd parked the car behind some sand dunes.

'You having a good time this summer?' Leo asked, propping himself up with his right arm and looking up at her. He didn't have Luke's startling blue eyes or fine, Roman nose, but he had a kind face.

'Yes. Is been nice,' Jacqui said politely, hugging her knees to her chest.

'Don't mind Van Varick. He can cut up kind of rough sometimes,' he said gently.

Jacqui nodded, not really sure what he'd said.

141

'So what's Brazil like?'

Jacqui thought about it. What a question. But soon enough she was telling Leo all about her life back home – her two younger brothers, who still lived at home in Campinas, her life in the big city with her grandmother, who was sending her to the prestigious Santa Anita convent, where the president's daughters were educated, how her family wasn't rich, so she had got a job at Daslu to help pay her tuition.

Leo was an avid and interested listener, asking her all the right questions and prodding her for more details. Jacqui found herself feeling so much better just to have someone who was actually interested in what she had to say.

The two of them were laughing at some particularly funny soccer play-by-plays she was recounting when Luke rounded up the hill.

'What's so funny?' he asked suspiciously.

'Nothing – nothing,' Jacqui said, still chuckling at the David Beckham fumble.

Luke looked pointedly at his friend, who shrugged and turned away. Jacqui knew that look. It said: *Easy, man.*

Luke crouched next to Jacqui. 'Hey, babe, you wanna go for a walk? So we can get a chance to talk without this clown around?' he asked, winking lasciviously.

Jacqui nodded and let Luke help her up.

'Just going to take Jacqui for a moonlight stroll,' he said to Leo.

Luke led her to a secluded spot near the bushes. 'Come down here with me,' he said, patting the sand.

'Look at the moon,' Jacqui said as she sat down beside him. 'Remember how you told me that poem about the stars?' she mused.

'Mmm,' Luke said, not having any idea what she was talking about.

'Walt Whitman. You read it to me when we were camping outdoors. "The Astronomer" . . . "the Astronomer" something?'

'"When I heard the learn'd astronomer",' Luke said impatiently.

In São Paulo, Luke had recited this poem to her when they were looking up at the night sky.

Yeah, Dalton had taught him something, but he wasn't about to repeat that poem – or that moment – with her now. He had other things on his mind, and before she could ask him another question, he was on top of her, slipping a hand up her shirt. She flinched as he stuck his wet tongue in her ear. He smelled like shellfish.

'You know how pot makes me so horny . . . and you look on fire tonight, babe. God, you don't know what you do to me,' he said, slobbering all over her neck and shoulders.

Jacqui blinked up at the fat, white moon and the perfectly silent stars. It wasn't romantic and it wasn't making her happy, but somehow, she wanted her Luca all the same.

Ryan finds out Mara is full of surprises

THE PARTY WAS OVER. CHAUNCEY RAVEN AND HER thirty-person entourage were long gone. The only people left at the club were desperate single people who were still hoping to go home lucky, hard-core alcoholics, and a stray cocktail waitress or two. Even the publicists and the gossip columnists had gone to bed. Eliza had taken the Mercedes SUV, though, so Mara was still there, sitting alone in the back room with Ryan.

'I guess we should go,' Mara said as the overhead lights blinked on and off.

'You think?' Ryan grinned.

They walked out to where he had parked the Aston Martin convertible, one of the few cars left in the lot. Even the valet guys had punched out. Ryan opened the door and Mara stepped inside. 'I didn't realise it was so late,' she said.

She rubbed her eyes, smearing her eye make-up all over her face.

'God, I look like a mess!' she said, pulling down the visor to check out the damage in the mirror.

Ryan turned. 'You make a pretty cute raccoon.'

She wiped her face with tissues, amazed at how much make-up came off. Jacqui had really outdone herself.

They drove back to the house in comfortable silence. The night air smelled fresh and a little wet, and in the quiet of the night Mara could feel what made this place so special. Yes, all that posturing all the time was a little much, but it was beautiful.

'Well, good night . . . ,' Ryan said, helping Mara up the steps.

'Good night.' She smiled at him sleepily. She walked down the garden path towards the servants' cottage.

Ryan lingered at the doorway, his forehead knit in a frown. 'Hey, are you going to bed?' he called after her.

'I was . . . ,' Mara said tentatively.

'I thought maybe I'd build a bonfire on the beach. It's a nice night, and, well, I've got some sleeping bags.'

Mara smiled into the dark. 'That sounds great. Just let me change.'

A few minutes later Mara watched as Ryan dug a hole in the sand and filled it with firewood and kindling. She was wearing a T-shirt and pyjamas and had scrubbed off all the make-up.

He struck a match. The newspapers flared up, but the firewood didn't catch.

'I think they're a little damp.'

'Here, let me help,' Mara said. She was an expert at building fires. Her parents liked to heat their house with their woodstove through the harsh New England winters; they thought it was quaint, even though Mara knew there wasn't much quaint about their single-story ranch. 'You just need a little more kindling . . . and blow on the smoke . . .' She arranged the sticks into a teepee over the newspaper, and when the initial blaze died down, a few red embers remained.

'Blow, blow!' she told Ryan, and the two of them huffed and puffed on the small sparks. The sparks became larger and finally the wood caught fire. Mara and Ryan cheered.

'I found some marshmallows in the pantry,' Ryan said, opening a bag. He grabbed a long stick from the cattail bushes and stuck one on. He handed it to Mara. She held it over the fire, watching the sugar melt into a brown glaze.

'When I was little, I always left the marshmallows in too long and they would burn and fall off,' Mara said; taking a bite.

'But you have to leave them on for a long time! That's when they taste best!' Ryan argued.

He left his stick in the fire, and the marshmallow sizzled and fell into the flames.

'See, I told you!' Mara laughed at his dismayed expression.

Ryan speared another marshmallow. 'This time you're not getting away!' he said sternly to his food.

They sat in companionable silence for a while. Mara dug her bare toes into the cold sand until it started to feel wet a few inches down. She could see the smallest orange reflection of their fire as the waves rolled in again and again. Behind them were the biggest houses she'd ever seen, but it was the beach that impressed her the most.

'I always thought I'd stay here forever,' Ryan said, breaking Mara's silent reverie.

'What do you mean?'

'Growing up, when we used to come out to the Hamptons, I never wanted to leave come September. I promised myself that when I was older, I would live here year-round.'

'It must get so cold, with the ocean right there.'

'Oh, it's awful,' Ryan said cheerfully. 'But there's no one here. That's what's so great about it.'

'But now?'

'I don't know. The house isn't the same.'

'I'm sorry.' Eliza had told her once that the house used to be different – more comfortable, less like a big showpiece.

'Don't be. It's not a big deal. I mean, what would I do here anyway?' He shrugged. 'What about you – what did you think you wanted to do when you were little?'

'I wanted to be a scientist,' Mara said. 'When I was nine, I was sure that's what I wanted to do. I thought that would be cool, wearing a lab coat, looking in microscopes.'

'And now?'

'Well, I kind of suck at science! And I hate maths. So no, I don't think I'm going to be a scientist.'

'What do you want to do, then?'

Mara thought about it. What she really wanted to do was

become a writer. She wasn't sure what kind, maybe a journalist. Or maybe the kind that wrote books. But it seemed like such an impossible thing. Like saying she wanted to win an Academy Award. It just wasn't going to happen. Besides, her parents always said if she made it to college, she should be a lawyer or a banker, someone who made a lot of money. She couldn't afford her dreams.

'I don't know . . . maybe a writer,' she whispered. For some reason, she felt comfortable telling him. Maybe it was because he was so easy to talk to or maybe because she knew he wouldn't ask her to explain herself.

'Cool.' He nodded.

They ate a few more marshmallows and kept talking on and off. Mara liked the silent time between the talking as much as she did their conversations. She never mentioned Jim because for once it was nice to not just be 'Jim Mizekowski's girlfriend'. To Ryan she was just Mara, and for once Mara felt pretty good about just being herself.

As the sky started to show signs of a new day, they zipped themselves into their sleeping bags like beach caterpillars. And then, in a quiet moment, while they listened to the waves crashing, Mara and Ryan fell asleep.

The next day Page Six ran two photos. One of Chauncey Raven straddling the current Wimbledon champ in the VIP room. The other was of Mara and Ryan, under the headline 'Has the Perry Heir Found Love?'

Eliza's postmortem brunch of pancakes and Page Six

'OH. MY. GOD. I AM STILL SOOO WASTED,' LINDSAY rasped, chasing down a Bloody Mary with an unfiltered Camel. 'I am, like, hoovering these,' she said, alternately blowing smoke and smashing her face with a handful of french fries.

'Jesus, you should have seen me last night,' Taylor said. 'I totally threw up all over Kit's mom's bathroom.'

'Oh, man, at least you guys had people to drive you home. I basically woke up in a ditch!' Eliza hooted. 'I was, like, excuse me, how did I get here exactly?'

The three were playing drunken one-upmanship, where whoever was suffering from the most severe case of hangover won. They were at their usual table at 75 Main Street, a cute corner café in Southampton, checking out the scene from behind dark sunglasses.

'Psst. Check it out.' Lindsay nudged her friends as a famous comedian's comely wife passed by with a double stroller.

'And isn't that . . . ?' Taylor asked, looking over her shoulder at the bleary-eyed star of the latest romantic comedy flop.

'Uh-huh. Check out that face-lift. She can't fool anybody. My mom said she's, like, fifty-two.'

'No way!' Eliza hissed, loving every minute. '*People* magazine said she was thirty-eight!'

'The morning sun ain't too kind,' Lindsay decided.

They attacked their pancake- and french-toast-stacked plates, feeling young and superior.

'I brought the paper,' Taylor said, digging into her bag for a rolled-up *New York Post*. She flipped straight to their favourite section: Page Six.

'Linds, there's a photo from your party!' Taylor crowed, showing them.

HAS THE PERRY HEIR FOUND LOVE? the headline blared, over the picture of Ryan and Mara.

'Oh my God! Don't tell me Ryan Perry has a girlfriend already!' Lindsay cried. 'I'm so pissed! And at my party, too!'

Technically, Ryan and his friends were just hanging out at the club. He hadn't even known about the party. But Eliza and Taylor wisely didn't correct their friend's assumption.

'Give me that!' Lindsay said, grabbing the paper from Taylor's manicured fingernails. 'Who IS she?'

'She's gorgeous, whoever she is,' Taylor observed.

'Lucky bitch!' Lindsay hissed.

'And she's wearing the Chloë top I wanted last season, but they sold out!'

'Why does everyone have to be so much cuter than me?' Lindsay complained. 'It's so not fair. She's like a total babe and, of course, she gets, like, the hottest guy.'

'Mara Waters . . . Waters . . . I wonder if that's Tobin Easley's cousin? You know, I think I've seen her around somewhere.'

Eliza said nothing, feeling a tiny twinge of realisation at how superficial this all was. If only these girls knew Mara was an au pair, they would never talk about her like this. She wouldn't even register on their radar. As she examined the picture, Eliza also felt a rush of pride. Mara did look awesome, and it was all because of her . . . and Jacqui, of course, but Eliza liked taking most of the credit.

'I dunno, guys. I mean, I think she's a little high waisted, don't you think? Her legs are, like, up to her chin!' Eliza said. As if that could be in any conceivable way a bad thing.

'Yeah, you're right,' Lindsay agreed all too eagerly.

Soon the three are dissecting all of Mara's 'flaws'. Her eyes were too big. Her nose was way too small. Her smile, too wide. She was practically Quasimodo when they were through with the virtual dissection.

'And I don't think she's Tobin's cousin. I heard she's *working* for the Perrys,' Eliza said, whispering the scandalous news. 'She's practically the help!'

'Oooh . . .' Lindsay and Taylor were breathless with excitement. This was called hitting pay dirt.

'I heard it from Sugar and Poppy, and they would know,' Eliza said. Sure, she was selling Mara out – but she also wanted to know what her friends thought of the whole deal.

'Ryan Perry's dating – the maid?' Taylor asked, wide-eyed.

'No, she's, like, the au pair or something,' Eliza explained, backtracking.

'Au pair!' Lindsay snorted. 'Is that what they're calling them now? Isn't that just a euphemism for foreign sex slave?'

Eliza wanted to tell them that only one of them was foreign and that most of their duties were 100 percent real and dealt with four children under the age of twelve, but she bit her tongue.

'Ryan's dating the housekeeper! That's hilarious!' Taylor cackled loudly.

'So he's, like, slumming,' Lindsay said smugly. 'We should inform the *Post*! Tell Page Six we have a bigger scoop!'

Eliza had a difficult time keeping the smile plastered to her face.

After the girls were done, they threw down the newspaper. 'So, like, what's up with boarding school? Are you staying there next year, too?' Lindsay asked.

'Yeah, I think so. Hey, are you guys going to the polo match?' she asked, changing the subject.

'Of course,' Lindsay said. 'You?'

'Charlie and I are sort of going together,' she confessed with a smug smile.

'So what's up? You guys back together?'

'Not really,' Eliza said. 'Not yet, anyway.' But he did ask her to be his date at the polo match, and she had told him she would meet him there. She was also supposed to be working at the event, taking care of the kids. But that was fine since Charlie was actually playing on one of the teams and wouldn't be in the tents much. He hadn't exactly said anything about getting back together, but she was hoping that was all about to change at the polo match. Thank God she had bought that hot little wrap dress. Charlie wouldn't be able to resist.

'Anyway, ladies, this was hella fun. But I got to go.' A little of the California talk that was so big in Buffalo right now snuck in as she threw down a twenty on the table.

Lindsay waved it away. 'I have my dad's Visa. Why do you have to leave so early? I thought we were going to go shopping after brunch.'

'Nah, I told my aunt I'd go to some art exhibit in Water Mill with her today,' Eliza lied. In fact, she was due to pick up Mara, Jacqui, and the kids at Fifi Laroo, where Anna had booked the kids for massage treatments.

As she drove down the street, her friends' words rang in her head. 'Au pair is just another word for mistress on the payroll!' 'He's dating THE MAID?'

God help her if they ever found out the truth about her.

Prima Donna's got nothing on these girls

MADAME SUZETTE WAS A FORMER PRIMA BALLERINA.
She had danced for Balanchine and Baryshnikov, and was once
the star of the American Ballet Theatre. She'd been linked with
many rich and famous men, and earned the adulation of the cul-
tured elite. It was one of the reasons why her studio was one of
the most sought-after in the Hamptons.

On a bright Saturday morning, a group of little girls in black
leotards and pink tights and ballet slippers stood in order of
height against the mirror.

'Plié, plié, grand plié, plié,' Madame ordered briskly, walking
up and down the barre. 'Pointe tendu,' she directed, inspecting
the girls' outstretched toes.

'Szzt! Madeeezun!' Madame called. '*Arretez!* Toes point out!
Like theez!' Madame stretched her foot to show Madison how
her toe was arched out in a sharp point. Madison fumbled and
tried to imitate it. Madame sighed.

'Allez! From the top! Plié, plié, grand plié . . . '

During the course of the lesson, Madame returned to Madison's place several times to correct her posture, her arm movements, her awkward *rond de jambes*.

'Toes in, ankles out! What do you not understand?' Madame asked, as she forced Madison's feet into fourth position. Several girls sniggered. Madison's cheeks burned.

'Isn't that your sister?' someone asked Zoë.

After the grueling hour, the studio assistant set out milk and cookies as treats for the students, and Madame handed out performance grades on embossed note cards.

'Madison, you must *améliorer*. Improve. This is an art. A practice. You are not cut out for ballet. Perhaps you should take the jazz dance.' Madison lowered her head and reached for a cookie.

Madame clucked her tongue. 'No cookies for you. You have not the ballet shape.'

When Mara, Eliza and Jacqui came to pick up the girls, they found Madison crying softly and Zoë trying to hold back tears. 'What happened?' Mara asked, immediately coming around to give Madison a hug.

Madison shook her head.

A few of the other students walked out of the studio to meet their parents and nannies. 'Madeeezon! No cookies! You no have ballet shape!' one pretty little girl jeered. The other girls laughed.

'Excuse me?' Eliza snapped. 'That's not a very nice thing to say.' A nanny gave Eliza an apologetic look and gathered the little girl into a Mercedes.

Jacqui began wiping Madison's wet face. 'Ignore them.'

'What's this?' Mara asked, after Zoë handed her the report cards. Mara read them, appalled at the notes.

'Check this out. *I strongly recommend Madison try another dance form. She is not cut out for ballet. It is a waste of time.*' Mara read aloud.

Eliza nodded. 'Madame Suzette's pretty harsh.' She too, had endured summers in the upstairs studio, and remembered the ballet mistress's baleful glare.

'This is totally unacceptable,' Mara said. 'She's only ten years old!'

Jacqui noticed that Zoë was munching on madeleine cookies, but Madison didn't have any. 'Did you eat yours already?' she asked.

'Maddy didn't get any,' Zoë replied.

'Shut up, Zoë.' Madison snapped, humiliated.

'What do you mean she didn't get any?' Mara asked. 'Why not?'

'Madame Suzette said she was too fat,' Zoë said matter-of-factly.

Mara was so infuriated she couldn't believe her ears. Madison was a healthy child, and so what if she still had a little baby fat around her middle. What kind of person – what kind of *teacher* – would talk to her students that way?

'I'm going to give that witch a piece of my mind!' Mara said wrathfully.

'Don't – she's like, French.' Eliza said. 'She's mean. That's why they send us to her.'

'You went here?'

'Yeah. Everyone does. She's famous. She used to date Onassis or something.'

'I don't care. You don't treat a kid like that! Look at her!'

Madison was sitting on the floor, hunched over her ballet bag. Mara knew that slouch. It said: *No one notice me, please. I'm not worth looking at.* Mara had been a little chubby as a kid. She knew what this was like.

'It's not right, Eliza.' Jacqui agreed. 'Ballet should be fun.'

'And Madison loves ballet, don't you?' Mara asked.

'Uh-huh,' Madison nodded. She did like it. Other than Madame Suzette, everything else about it was great. The music, the pianos, and every year they put on a recital and got to wear make-up and tutus and everyone came to the show to see them.

'Excuse me? Madame Suzette?' Mara asked.

'*Oui?*' The sixty year old former ballerina appraised Mara from behind *pince-nez* glasses.

'I'm Madison's, uh . . . guardian,' Mara decided. 'And about what you said this afternoon? I don't appreciate you talking to her like that.'

'*Excusez-moi?*' Madame asked. In all her years teaching

spoiled brats how to plié, this was a first. Usually the mothers were so intimidated by her resume and background, no one ever uttered a squeak of protest. But Mara didn't care if the *New York Times* had once called Madame 'the most exquisite dancer this side of Pavlova'.

'She might not be very graceful, but she's trying very hard. Doesn't effort count for anything?'

'*Non,*' Madame replied. 'This is about performance. If you cannot perform, you cannot be part of my class.'

'C'mon Mara,' Eliza said, pulling her away.

'This is such bull!' Mara cried.

'Let's go,' Jacqui said.

They hustled the little girls down the rickety steps. Mara was still so annoyed. 'That woman should not be allowed near children!'

'There's a great Pilates studio that just opened up. I met one of the teachers at Scoop the other day. Really sweet. Anyway, they have a kids' class.' Eliza suggested. 'I'll tell Anna about it.'

'I used to do pilates, it's so much better than ballet,' Jacqui told the little girls. 'More fun and more relaxed.'

The next day, it was settled. Zoe and Madison were enrolled in Pilates, and the au pairs took them shopping for cute new outfits, to make up for the loss of the black leotards. They all agreed pink tights were for babies anyway.

At the Mercedes-Benz polo match, not all the cute boys are loaded

ON THE FIELD THE HORSES' HOOVES SOUNDED LIKE roaring thunder. A loud, sharp THAWK filled the air as the red-shirted team whacked the ball with mallets and sent it flying to the opposite end, tying the score 1–1. The star centre, a dashing nineteen-year-old Argentine, raised his hand in victory.

'How hot is he?' Eliza marvelled.

'Who's that?' Mara asked.

'Nacho Figueroa. Charlie's dad stole him from Peter Brant's team this year.'

'He's gorgeous,' Mara said, admiring Nacho like a fine oil painting.

'Saw him first!' Eliza teased.

The girls giggled. Having a crush on Nacho was like having a crush on Orlando Bloom. Gisele and that other Brazilian model from the Victoria's Secret catalogue were cheering for him on the sidelines. He wasn't someone Mara or Eliza could really take seriously as a romantic possibility. Still, it was nice to look.

Nacho scored another goal, and the crowd – especially the girls – went wild.

In the VIP tents no one paid much attention. The guests filled their plates with beluga, guzzled magnums of champagne, and gossiped about each other's new outfits. Mara and Eliza turned back to where Jacqui was trying to find a table for all four kids. Ryan pulled an empty chair towards the table. He'd been hanging out with them all morning trying to help.

'Mr Perry! The Hamptons' answer to Brad Pitt! And Miss Waters! In a four-hundred-dollar dress bought on sale for two hundred dollars at Scoop!' Lucky Yap said, giving Mara two air kisses on each cheek and shaking Ryan's hand vigorously. 'Let's get a shot!'

Mara posed prettily in her new red dress. She felt a little awkward in it, and every once in a while she would grab the end of the too-short hemline and yank it down over her butt, but only when she was certain Ryan wasn't looking. She felt a little self-conscious, but looking around, she could see that her tiny dress and high heels were perfectly appropriate for the Hamptons.

Ryan excused himself to rustle up two more flutes of champagne. Every once in a while he would look back just to sneak a peek at Mara's legs in that dress. When she had walked out to the car wearing it earlier, he had almost fallen out of the driver's seat. She was such a babe, and the best thing was, she didn't even realise it.

'Hey, Lucky. Good to see you again,' Mara said.

'Oh, you'll be sick of seeing me soon. I'm everywhere. Honey, did you see your picture in the *Post*?' he asked.

'No! I didn't!' Mara said, shocked.

Lucky nodded. 'Check it out. It's still online. Gotta run, I see Lara Flynn Boyle with a huge ice cream cone!' he said, bouncing off towards his prey.

Ryan returned with the goods, clinking glasses with Mara. He was about to tell her how pretty she looked when her phone began to chirp.

'Oh, sorry,' she said nervously, balancing her glass and flipping open her mobile phone. 'Hello? Jim! Hi! How are you?'

Ryan backed off. *Jim? Who the hell is Jim?*

'Who's Jim?' Ryan mouthed. He couldn't help himself.

'My boyfriend,' Mara replied, holding the phone to her ear and turning away.

Boyfriend? What? She'd never mentioned that before. Not even the night when they had fallen asleep on the beach together. He watched her walk away.

'Ryan?' a voice called behind him.

He turned around.

'Hey, remember me?' asked a pretty redhead in curvy black Lycra. She smiled at him disarmingly.

'Camille Molloy!' He smiled. 'How could I forget?'

He wandered over to her side, and they were soon in animated conversation.

*   *   *

Meanwhile Mara was having trouble with the reception on the other side of the tent. 'Can you hear me now?' she yelled.

Jim Mizekowski was cute like a bulldog, stubborn, with small-town boy written all over his John Deere hat and his rusted Nissan four-by-four pickup. In the background Mara could hear Dave Mathews playing – Mara knew that Jim liked to play Dave when he was feeling 'deep'.

'Are you there? Is that better? God, I feel like I haven't spoken to you in ages,' Mara was saying just as Madison began tugging at her skirt. 'What, honey? No, not you, Jim . . . I'm working . . . It's not really a good time right now.'

'Mara, I feel sick,' Madison complained, looking a little green around the edges.

'Hold on, sweetie . . . Jim, I'm sorry, but one of the kids is . . . No, please don't hang up on me!'

'Gurrrgle,' Madison said, clutching her tummy. She had had one too many cucumber sandwiches from the buffet table and started spewing green-and-white chunks all over the grassy floor.

Mara gave Eliza a pleading look. She didn't want to hang up on Jim. Not when he hadn't called her in so long. 'Liza, please,' she mouthed.

Eliza sighed and took Madison by the arm. 'I told you not to have that last one,' she scolded.

'I want my mommy,' Madison whimpered, white spittle flying from her chin.

Eliza knew Madison's real mommy was probably a million

miles away, so she chanced a look at Anna, who was greeting friends and looking untouchable in a new Valentino sheath and a massive ostrich-feathered hat. She guessed the last thing Anna wanted was to be bothered by a vomit-covered stepchild, so she carted Madison away to the parking lot to clean her up by the restrooms.

'Madison, if you have to go again, just make sure you don't do it all over my new shoes, okay?' Eliza asked, kneeling down to wipe away the puke from Madison's embroidered French blouse.

Eliza grimaced at the smell. 'Ugh! I'm out of tissues!' she complained, and looked up to see the cute gardener from the Perry house who'd been giving her eye the other day, standing next to her, holding a towel.

'I thought you might need this,' he said, offering it to her. His dark curly hair fell over his eyes, and he was wearing a blue one-piece work suit with *J. Stone* scripted on the left-hand pocket.

'No thanks, I've got it under control.'

'Suit yourself.' He shrugged.

'Don't you have, like, a tree to prune or something?' Eliza asked superciliously, still wiping the front of Madison's shirt and rubbing the mess into the fabric instead of the other way around.

'I'm off today. I do the landscaping for the field; I thought I'd make sure they didn't ruin my top seed,' he said. 'I'm Jeremy.'

'I know who you are,' she snapped.

He put away the towel and began to walk off, and right then

Madison blew chunks all over Eliza's shoes. 'Noooooo! I told you!' Eliza wailed, standing up in shock. 'I just bought these!'

Jeremy ascertained the damage. 'They're leather. It'll come off,' he said, kneeling down and taking a shoe off Eliza's foot. 'Let me.' He began to clean off the ick.

'Seriously, you just can't leave a girl alone, can you?' Eliza said, softening a little. He really was cute.

'Not if I can help it.' He grinned.

'You know, it's really okay. I'm totally fine. It's not that I don't appreciate all this . . . ,' she said, hopping on the other foot as Jeremy cleaned the other shoe. 'Could you get – er – that part?' she asked, pointing towards a smudge.

Jeremy gave her an are-you-kidding look, but Eliza only smiled sweetly. 'I guess this means I can't ignore you anymore.'

'In some cultures we're practically married,' he joked, standing up. 'See you around . . . Eliza.'

'How'd you know my name? And where do you think you're going?' she demanded in mock annoyance.

'I'm off now. Getting beers with the guys,' he yelled back. 'I didn't know you cared so much!'

'I don't!' she yelled back, but she was still smiling. 'C'mon, Madison,' Eliza said, holding her hand. 'Don't sniffle. You're okay, aren't you? Will you be good now and listen to what I say?'

The two headed back inside the tents. Mara was still engrossed in an intense mobile phone conversation with Jim, and Jacqui was still MIA. Zoë, Cody, and William were seated at the table, scarfing down platters of raw clams, which they recognised from their high-protein-low-carb-diet. Eliza spotted Taylor and Lindsay smoking in the roped-off section and shooed Madison towards the other kids under the tent. She walked over to them so they could admire her outfit.

'Charlie was looking for you,' Taylor said accusingly.

'He was here?' Eliza asked. 'Where is he?'

'He's gone. He looked kind of mad,' Lindsay added dramatically.

Eliza's shoulders slumped. All the time she was in the parking lot up to her ears in barf and flirting with the gardener, her ex-boyfriend was inside looking for her.

'I'm sure he'll call me later,' Eliza said, trying to sound confident.

The minute they turned their backs, Eliza rushed over to the kids' table for a quick head count. William, check. Madison, check. Cody, check. But where was the other little girl? Oh, there she was, underneath the table, picking up a scallop from the floor.

Thank God. They were a lot of work, but she was actually starting to warm up to the pukey little brats.

There is some pain even Bacardi 151 can't numb

MADISON HAD ASKED FOR ANOTHER HELPING OF shrimp, so Jacqui, thinking it was probably allowed on the little girl's diet, had gone to fetch her some. It was seafood after all — how fattening could that be? As she spooned a few plump pink specimens on a porcelain plate, she glanced up across the lawn. It was divot-stomping time, and the game had stopped to let the spectators pound the clumps. Ladies in *peau de soie* and gentlemen in navy blazers and pressed khaki trousers paraded out to toe at the clumps of grass unearthed by the quick stops and starts of the ponies. They patted the earthy patties back into the ground, grass side up, of course.

Across the field a familiar mess of blond hair and glasses caught her eye. *But Luca hadn't mentioned anything about attending the match!* She put down the plate, all thoughts of feeding the child promptly fading from her memory.

Wait — what? Luca — holding some girl's hand? Someone who looked familiar? But why would he be holding her hand? Or —

gulp – kissing her? On the lips? Like that? She stormed over, all the hurt and misunderstandings she'd been keeping in check for the last month boiling in her brain.

'Luca!' she shrieked.

But Luke had seen her clear across the way and was ready. 'Jacqui!' he said smoothly, kissing her on the cheek. 'Good to see you!' He put an arm around her. 'I want you to meet my *girl-friend*, Karin. Karin, this is Jacqui. We met in São Paulo last spring break. And now she's working for the Perrys! Small world, huh?' He glared at Jacqui, warning her not to give him away.

'Hi, Jacqui,' Karin said pleasantly. She was a mild-faced blonde with soft, rounded features and a small button nose. She was wearing a floral calf-length Laura Ashley dress that looked more like a sack.

Jacqui shook Karin's hand automatically. 'Pleased to meet you,' she mumbled.

It wasn't this girl's fault, Jacqui knew that. But just as she was trying to find the right English words to say, Luke turned and started to walk away, taking Karin along with him.

'Um, nice meeting you!' Karin called back.

Too hurt to run after him, Jacqui walked away, catching her high heels in the dense thick mud. Several South American polo players returning to the field walked by her, chattering to each other in Spanish and Portuguese.

'Cuidado,' one said, catching her as she tottered.

'I know where I'm going!' Jacqui hissed. She brushed by them, completely oblivious to their appreciative stares.

'*Bonita!*' yelled Nacho Figueroa, the handsome team captain. So what if she was gorgeous? She was miserable.

Jacqui walked off in a daze and found herself in front of a white linen table manned by a tuxedoed bartender.

'Bacardi. 151. Straight up. Double,' she ordered, and downed four shots in quick succession.

She returned to the Perry table, where Eliza and Mara were in the middle of arguing about whether it was time to take the kids home yet.

'I swear, they won't mind!' Eliza pressed. She wanted to high-tail it out of there before Taylor and Lindsay spotted her playing Mary Poppins. 'Look how tired Zoë is.'

'But Anna and Kevin didn't say anything about it,' Mara said doubtfully.

'Do you really think they care if the kids see the end of the game? Look around you, Mara, everyone's leaving!'

It was true. Now that the TV cameras and the photographers from the society rags had departed, many of the guests decided they'd had quite enough themselves.

'Hey, Jacqui, where've you been?' Eliza snapped, then instantly regretted it when she saw the look on Jacqui's face.

'What's wrong?' Mara asked, concerned. They had never seen their self-possessed roommate so unnerved. Jacqui was shaking, her eyes were red, and she looked like she was about to cry. And she smelled like a rum distillery.

Mara put a hand on Jacqui's shoulder. 'You're so cold!' she said.

'What happened?' Eliza demanded.

'It's . . . Luca . . . He . . . he has a girlfriend . . . He's been lying to me . . . ,' Jacqui choked out.

'What?!' Eliza exclaimed.

'That's terrible!' Mara said.

'I just saw him . . . across the field . . . He said it was someone he used to date . . . but it's not . . . *nossa* . . . that's why he never wanted to take me out anywhere . . . I was just . . . a fling . . . *fácil*, and I thought . . . I thought . . .'

'What a dickwad!' Eliza declared.

'Don't,' Jacqui said. She felt even more depressed by their sympathy. 'He's right behind you.'

Eliza turned around and saw Luke van Varick with Karin Emerson.

'That's your Luca? Jacqui, you should have told me earlier! That's Luke van Varick. He's like the biggest player in New York. A total jerk. I've known him for years. He and Karin have been dating since eighth grade, and he's been cheating on her the whole time.'

Jacqui nodded and bit her lip. She had known something like this was coming; she just hadn't wanted to believe it. Now she was stuck in some godforsaken place in the States when she could have been in Rio with her friends.

'There was no way you could have known that,' Mara consoled.

'He always plays that whole nerdy thing, like he's not interested, but it's all a ploy. He's totally cocky and arrogant. Ugh.

He's the worst,' Eliza said. 'You're better off without him. Good riddance!'

'*O que quer que*, I'm going to get another drink,' was all Jacqui said.

Eliza and Mara looked at each other helplessly, and then they did the things that came most naturally to them in times of crisis. Mara took a tissue and wiped the mascara from under Jacqui's eyes, and Eliza handed Jacqui two half-drunk flutes of champagne. For now, it was the best they could do.

Jacqui knows that the best way to get over somebody is to get under someone else

AN HOUR LATER JACQUI STOOD UNDER THE SAME TENT, nursing her drink. The bartender had put a cheerful umbrella on her mojito, but the sight of the jaunty little paper parasol just made her feel worse. She rested her drink on a nearby table and fished in her purse for a cigarette.

'Excuse me,' a guy said, placing an empty glass next to hers. He'd been heading towards the parking lot before he stopped. 'Jacqui?'

She looked up to see Leo – Luca's sweet friend Leo – standing there with a goofy grin on his face. He was wearing a similar seersucker jacket to the one Luca was also wearing that afternoon, with the sleeves scrunched to the elbows, and baggy blue jeans with the top of his flannel boxer shorts showing. It was very hiphop Wasp, a big look in East Hampton that summer.

'Good to see you – hey, something wrong?' he asked when he saw the look on her face.

'Nothing,' she said. She didn't want anything to do with him, especially anything or anyone who reminded her of Luca.

'C'mon, you can tell me,' he said gently, placing a hand on her bare shoulder.

'Seriously. *Não é nada.* Maybe I'm a little homesick,' she said. She realised once she said it that it was true. She missed home. The Hamptons were fun and all, but without Luca it was just another overpriced American city. She missed her grandmother, a stubborn old lady who worked long hours as a manager of a textile factory to keep her only granddaughter in school.

'You want to get dinner somewhere?' Leo asked. 'There's a place not too far that has the best fish tacos.'

'I don't know. I should probably get back to work,' Jacqui said, scanning the emptying tent for the Perry kids and her roommates.

'C'mon, seriously, it will make you feel so much better. C'mon,' Leo said, taking her arm.

By then she was too drunk to argue.

He drove her to a taco stand in Amagansett, where they shared Baja fish tacos underneath a rickety straw roof. Leo was right, the food did make her feel better. She was still numb, angry, and hurt in a way that she didn't even want to think about – she felt stupid and embarrassed on top of feeling lonely and miserable.

There had been signs, of course. The picture. His weird aversion to hanging out in the Hamptons proper. His constant excuses and absences. She was being played for a fool. Jacqui should have known better than that.

She looked at Leo across the table as she chewed on the spicy, delicious mahi-mahi taco. He kind of looked like Luca, with that same glossy honey-coloured hair. He even smelled like him – like Chanel Egoiste and aftershave. He dressed so much like Luca that Jacqui even made a mental bet that those were Tartan boxers underneath the baggy Fubus. He even talked like Luca. In fact, if she closed her eyes, she could almost pretend she was still with her Luca.

So when they stumbled out of the restaurant and Leo suggested maybe she might want to, um, hang out a little more, see his, um, guitar collection or something, she didn't say no. And when they got there and his guitar collection consisted of two wimpy Fenders and he tried to kiss her instead, she kissed him back. And when he lifted up her shirt and unzipped his jeans, she didn't protest. In Brazil they had a saying: The best way to get over somebody was to get under someone else.

'So, it's really over between you guys?' Leo asked when it was over and they were lying in his bed watching Jimmy Fallon needle the hapless host on *SNL*.

She nodded.

'Good, because I don't want to get in the way of that, you know what I mean?'

'Sim.'

'You know, I was so into you the moment I saw you,' he said.

'Me too,' she lied.

173

He squeezed her tighter.

She was about to tell him that this was a mistake, that this was all wrong. That they shouldn't see each other again. It would hurt Luca's feelings if he knew she had hooked up with his best friend.

Wait.

It *would* hurt Luca's feelings. Or at least, put a huge dent in his pride.

Jacqui had an idea. Suddenly, being with Leo didn't feel like a mistake after all.

Mara finally gets a backbone

THE NEXT MORNING MARA WOKE UP TO THE INTER-minable refrain of her mobile phone melody.

'Herrhhhoo?' She wiped the sleep from her eyes. 'No, I'm awake, I'm awake. Hi, Jim.' Mara held the phone to her ear with a hand across her eyes. Jim's enthusiasm was unbearable at such an early hour.

'Enough is enough. I've got a great plan – you'll love it! My parents are going away for the weekend, so I've got the home-stead all to my lonesome. Anyway, I was thinking, you know, I really want my girl – my Mara to be there, you know? Coz it's going to totally rock! I'm going to have a party for sure. And you know, I'm going to need someone to help me clean up after-wards!' He laughed at his joke.

But Mara was beginning to realise Jim wasn't really kidding. 'Jim, I'd love to, but I can't,' she told him.

'What do you mean you can't?'

'I can't. I have to work. It's not like I get the weekends off, you know. This job is full-time, twenty-four hours a day.'

'That's what you always say,' Jim grumbled. 'I don't believe it, Mara. Those rich losers you work for won't even let you take one stupid weekend off? What are you, some kind of slave? That's ridiculous!'

'It's not ridiculous. You always think what I do is stupid, and it's not. It's really important. I'm making a lot of money here, and you know my parents can't cover my whole college tuition.'

'Whatever, Mara. Something's up. I can just tell. You're, like, different now, and I don't think I like it.'

'What do you mean?' Mara propped her head up against her pillows.

'I dunno, it's like you're all hoity-toity all of a sudden . . .'

'Excuse me?'

'You're acting kind of selfish, you know? It's like all you think about is yourself. It makes me sick, really it does.'

Mara sat up at that. 'I'M SELFISH? *I'M* SELFISH?' she yelped, suddenly very angry. 'Oh, and I suppose when I hand-washed your football jersey for the big game instead of studying for my English final, I was just thinking of myself? And what about when I gave you *my* hamster when Bobo died, that was selfish? Or the time I let you and your stupid friends into Ye Old Tavern so you guys could see what nineteenth-century ale tastes like? Or the time I had to go to the ER when you had to get your stomach pumped and I had the SATs the next day?' Mara could keep going like this for hours. 'Or, I don't know, Jim, what about the time I sold my antique dollhouse so you could buy new hub-caps for your car?'

'Oh, right, sure, Mar – '

But Mara had had enough. 'You know what, Jim? You're right – I have changed – and I'm not going to do this anymore!' And then, with as much force as she could muster, she pressed her thumb on the end button of her phone. It didn't have the same drama as slamming a receiver down, but that's technology for you.

'Arrggh!' Mara screamed at the empty room.

Ryan isn't exactly having breakfast in bed, but . . .

MARA RAN DOWN THE STAIRS AND OUT THE DOOR OF the au pairs' cottage, slamming the door behind her. *What the hell was wrong with Jim? Selfish? Selfish?*

Mara scurried across the lawn towards the main house. It was almost noon – *God, they'd been out late last night!* – Ryan usually got back from his morning surf right about now.

He was probably in the kitchen making one of his favourite double-decker submarine sandwiches – the housekeeper always made sure to pick up fresh mortadella, prosciutto, bologna, and salami from Papassini's just for him. He and Mara had shared a big fat hoagie every Saturday morning now, so her timing was probably going to be about perfect.

She walked quickly up the stone pathway to the glass-enclosed kitchen. Sure enough, Ryan was there – still wearing one half of his wet suit (the other half he'd peeled down from the heat). In his right hand he wielded a dinner knife thick with yellow mustard and in the other hand . . . he was holding the waist of a very pretty girl in a matching folded-down black wet suit and red string bikini top.

Mara was certain she had seen that girl somewhere, and with a sick twist in her stomach she realised it was the girl from the polo match. The redhead Ryan was talking to while she was arguing with Jim on the phone.

'Ryan – stop – no!' The girl squealed, giggling as Ryan pretended to flick mustard on her cheek.

'You love it.' He grinned.

He popped a cherry tomato in her mouth and chased it with a kiss.

Oh.

Mara stood in front of the kitchen window, completely taken aback and unsure of what to do. She was so surprised to see him with *someone*.

Someone *else* – that is – but she tried to ignore it. *C'mon, it wasn't as if I was expecting him to . . . It wasn't as if I thought of him as . . . And there's Jim, although . . .*

But just as Mara's face was beginning to contort with some strange understanding of what was really going on here, Ryan looked up.

'Mar – '

But Mara was already halfway down the back stairs, more embarrassed and confused than ever.

Eliza is learning a lot this summer, like the Atkins diet isn't worth it

IN THE FRONT YARD ELIZA THOUGHT SHE HAD THINGS under control. She had got all the kids in their beach clothes without too much of a struggle. William was already strapped in and Cody was in his child seat, which left only Zoë and Madison to go.

'Where are we going?' Zoë asked, holding a raggedy copy of *Where the Wild Things Are* to her chest.

'Same place we always go,' Eliza replied, checking the seat belt.

'I'm hungry,' Madison said.

'You're always hungry.' Eliza sighed.

'Hi, Jer'my,' Zoë called from the backseat.

Eliza turned to see Jeremy carrying a hose and a rake, walking out from the rear shed. He tipped his cap.

'HI, JEREMY!' William mimicked.

'Come get ice cream with us!' Madison said.

'Yeah, come get ice cream!' Zoë agreed.

William took up the call, and soon all the kids were begging Jeremy to come to the Snowflake with them.

'You guys getting sundaes?' Jeremy asked. 'Which ones are your favourite?'

'Hot fudge,' William said promptly.

'Good choice, my man.' Jeremy nodded.

'Butterscotch,' said Zoë.

'Even better.'

'Can you? Can you? Can you?' Zoë asked. 'Come with us?'

'If it's okay.' Jeremy asked. 'I'm done for the day.'

'I don't mind.' Eliza shrugged. 'I was going to wait for Mara, but I heard her fighting with her boyfriend on the phone, so I figured she might need a break.'

'Then it's just us.' Jeremy smiled.

The Snowflake was a cute retro-fifties-style diner on nearby Pantigo Road, famous for its juicy hamburgers and vats of home-made ice cream. Eliza eased the Range Rover into the parking lot next to the creepy statue of a six-foot-tall hot dog squeezing ketchup on itself. It was famous in the Hamptons as 'the weird hot dog'.

The Perry kids lined up in front of the ice cream counter, peering into the freezer.

'I want Tasti D-Lite,' Madison decided. 'Poppy and Sugar always order it.'

'They don't have nonfat ice cream here,' Eliza said patiently. It was one of the reasons the Snowflake was so popular. 'And anyway, it's not really that good for you, sweetie. It has more sugar than regular ice cream so you'll be hungry again in an hour, plus it doesn't taste as good!'

Eliza felt bad for the kid. Sugar, Poppy, and Anna, with their fickle, macrobiotic diets, food phobias, and addiction to laxatives, weren't the best examples of healthy nutrition. Lately Madison had been mimicking their food indulgences – not eating for hours and then gorging herself, which made it even worse. But at least she hadn't learned the twins' trick of post-meal excursions to the bathroom to throw up. Not yet, that is.

'Eating healthy is all about moderation,' Eliza said. 'Why don't you have one scoop of butter pecan instead of the whole sundae that you usually do? You'll feel better and you won't crave sweets later.'

If there's one thing Eliza knew about, it was the Zone, the South Beach Diet, Atkins, Sugar Busters, and portion control. Mostly she thought it was a bunch of hooey – *who can give up carbs for good?* – but she'd taken the major tenets to heart years ago.

Once the kids were properly sated, they piled back in the car. Eliza backed out of the lot and wheeled the car to their usual destination.

'Have you ever been to Two Mile Hollow Beach?' Jeremy asked.

'Isn't that the gay beach?'

'Yeah, but only on the far side. On the other side it's all families. And it's great. It's so empty and doesn't have the scene of Georgica. We should go there.'

'Are you sure?'

'Yeah, just take this next right and it's straight down.'

Just as Jeremy had predicted, Two Mile Hollow Beach was paradise compared to the towel-to-towel congestion of Georgica. Down beyond, Eliza spied groups of handsome gay men arrayed around lavish picnic spreads, complete with champagne and caviar, while several random lesbian couples sunned underneath golf umbrellas.

'This is great!' Eliza said, unzipping her Juicy Couture hoodie and taking off her shorts. She was wearing a sleek black bandeau bikini with boy-cut briefs monogrammed with the letter *E*. She looked like a throwback to one of those Vargas pinup girl calendars, with her long blonde hair in a high ponytail with a thick black headband.

'I always come here. It's the best beach in the Hamptons – it's so private,' Jeremy said.

The kids seemed to agree. Already William was engrossed in building the largest sand castle he could imagine – he always had to fight for space on the other beach. Madison had taken off her shorts – she was always too self-conscious to be seen in her bathing suit, but since there was no one else around, she didn't seem to care. Zoë just snuggled next to Eliza, who seemed a lot nicer when she wasn't trying to hide from her friends.

Eliza pulled out a glossy magazine from her tote bag. Zoë

had forgotten *Where the Wild Things Are* at the ice-cream parlour, but Eliza was determined get her reading. She flipped through the pages. Maybe the reason Zoë wasn't learning was because she was reading all those boring books about puppies and flowers. Maybe if they gave the kid something more interesting to read . . .

'Here, Zoë, let's start with this,' Eliza said, finding a promising page. 'How to blow his mind in twenty-six ways.' Eliza pointed down the column. *It was alphabetical! So educational.* 'A is for Always Be Ready.'

'Always be ready,' Zoë repeated, her eyes wide at the picture of a woman in a tiny camisole lying on silk sheets.

'For what?' She asked Eliza.

Eliza didn't quite know how to answer that one. 'Hmm . . . let's try something else,' she said, paging through to a fashion spread. 'Here we go. Packing for a weekend in the country.'

Jeremy, who had been silently appalled the whole time, burst out laughing.

'I dare you to kiss her,' Zoë turned to Jeremy.

Jeremy blushed. 'A dare is a dare,' he said solemnly, and brushed Eliza's cheek with a quick kiss.

Eliza was flattered. She was surprised at how much fun she was having. It was always such a hassle finding parking, getting a space, and making sure no one from her old high school spotted her with the kids. This way she could actually relax. And that kiss wasn't too bad either . . .

'What are you doing later?' Jeremy asked. 'My friends are having a bonfire in Montauk tonight.'

Just as Eliza was about to ask what time, her mobile phone rang with a piercing shrill.

'Sorry – let me just take this,' she said. 'Oh, Lindsay, hi! Charlie's having a party? No, he didn't tell me. Tonight? Oh my God, I've been dying to get in there. Sure, I'm not doing anything! What time should I meet you guys?'

She clicked off, a happy smile on her face.

Eliza noticed when Jeremy turned away and scowled at the ocean. *Did I really just make other plans right in front of him after he asked me out?*

'About tonight . . . ,' Eliza said hesitantly. 'Something just came up for later. But maybe we can still do dinner or something?'

'Sure.' Jeremy nodded. He wouldn't normally have said okay, but there was something about Eliza that made guys agree to lots of things they normally wouldn't.

Jacqui is still testing out that Brazilian saying

MEANWHILE, SOMEWHERE IN BRIDGEHAMPTON WAS A bedspread with two lumps underneath. Jacqui and her new boyfriend were spooning, and she was happy to feel the warmth of another person next to her. It was the most comfortable she'd felt in weeks.

'Oh . . . Luca . . . ,' Jacqui whispered.

A tousled head shot up. 'What did you say?' he asked Jacqui. 'What did you call me?'

'*Leo* . . . Leo . . . I said, "Oh, Leo",' Jacqui explained, peppering his face with kisses. 'I said, "Leo . . . *meu amor.* . . ."'

Leo settled back down next to her, even though he wasn't quite sure that Jacqui was thinking about him. Jacqui lay there, thinking of how Leo was a bad idea she couldn't shake. Jacqui couldn't help herself. She was the type of girl who always had a boyfriend, and she needed to do something to stop herself from crying all the time, and finding solace in Leo's skinny arms seemed to do the trick.

After the scene at the polo match Jacqui hadn't had the heart to continue working. Who could work when your heart was stomped on and thrown to the dogs? Instead she holed up in Leo's room, watching bad television and raiding the fridge. She had gone back to the Perry house to pick up clothes when she knew Eliza and Mara were out with the kids.

She didn't want to face them. They had been so nice to her at the match, but she just wanted to be alone, or at least alone in the only way she knew how to be. She knew she was going to get in trouble, but she was in a foreign country, in a place that only meant something to her because of the guy she loved, and somehow everything that she knew was *actually* important – like her job – just . . . faded away. She thought about maybe just getting on the next plane back to São Paulo and forgetting all about the Hamptons. She hadn't even spent any of the money she'd made so far. That morning, she'd looked up ticket prices on Leo's laptop. But right now, she didn't even have the energy to leave the shelter of Leo's bedroom, and she had a feeling that feeling wasn't going to go away anytime soon.

Anna would probably fire her when she got back, but Jacqui was too far gone to care.

How silly of her to think that anyone could really love her. Their two weeks in São Paulo were nothing but a mirage. What had Eliza said? He was a 'player'. Someone who pretended to be in love with her, but he was really only in love with her body. Just like every other guy on the planet. No one ever got past her looks to bother with the real person inside.

Leo seemed different, though. Yeah, he was always telling her how beautiful she was, but he was also always mentioning how lucky he felt. When she looked at him, she didn't feel any butterflies, and when he kissed her, she didn't close her eyes and see fireworks. But she could pretend. She was good at that.

He was sweet. He was a nice guy. And right now, he would have to do.

Mara finally orders the right kind of drink

SHE COULD GET USED TO THIS LIFE, MARA THOUGHT AS SHE sipped on her second frozen star fruit margarita. The cool, sweet, and tart concoction tasted like liquid heaven, and she was getting a nice buzz from the pure agave tequila. Better yet, Ryan had asked her to come with him to the party – as friends of course – it wasn't a date or anything. But Mara had been flattered enough that she was trying very hard to put the weirdness of that morning behind her.

The two of them shared a prime outdoor table with an ocean view, underneath a heat lamp. Lucky Yap had swished by and taken yet another photo of the two of them. By now it was such a common occurrence, Mara knew how to pose to show off her best side.

Ryan explained it was some party for an old friend of his. Whoever it was, he must be really important, Mara decided. Around them assorted glitterati mingled and table-hopped. Mara had already spotted the teenage star of the summer's hit movie, the game-winning shortstop of last year's World Series, and a slew of quasi-famous reality TV stars, from the twenty-something socialites who had shipped themselves off to boot camp to a couple who had met and married on a dating show.

If Megan could see me now, she thought, feeling a little home-sick at the memory of her funny older sister, who worked at the local beauty shop and spent her days giving the local clientele her approximation of the latest Hollywood looks. Mara promised herself she would remember every detail so she could tell her sister all about it.

But her mind kept wandering back to the scene in the kitchen. So Ryan had a girlfriend, so what? She kept reminding herself that she had a boyfriend, too.

And so what if Ryan liked redheads? Who didn't? Mara thought as she unconsciously pulled on her own dark locks. The girl was cute, Mara would give her that. Too cute. She could surf, too. Mara was a flop at athletics. Always the last picked on any team. Cute and could surf. And blessed with a hot little body that filled out her string bikini top. Speak of the devil . . .

'There you are!' the girl said breathlessly, giving Ryan a quick kiss on the lips before she sat down.

Mara tried to curl her lips into a smile, but they wouldn't obey.

'Hi! I'm Camille!' she said, sticking her hand in Mara's face.

'Mara.'

Camille leaned forward to whisper something in Ryan's ear.

The two of them started to laugh, and Mara felt extremely uncomfortable.

'Sorry! We're being so annoying, aren't we?' Camille asked.

'How did you two meet?' Mara asked. She and Ryan had avoided talking about this – her – until now, but Mara was above all that. At least, she would try to be.

'Oh, I used to work for Ryan!'

'How do you mean?'

'She was, uh, one of the au pairs . . . before you guys came,' Ryan explained, a little apologetically.

'Yeah, getting fired was, like, the best thing that happened to me! I got a job at Bamboo and I'm staying at my friend's place in North Haven. And now I don't have to feel guilty about dating the boss's son!'

Ryan laughed nervously.

'So! Mara, you replaced me!' Camille joked. 'How are the kids doing?'

'They're fine. We take them to Georgica every day,' Mara said.

'GEORGE-i-cuh,' Camille said, batting her eyelashes.

'What did I say?' Mara asked.

'George-EEE-cah.'

'Oh.' Mara couldn't tell the difference.

'Accent's on the first syllable, not the second,' Camille explained. 'Lots of newcomers do it. Where are you from? New Jersey?'

Mara had been in the Hamptons long enough to know when she was being insulted. She didn't reply.

191

'Ryan, let's go dance! Can we dance? Please . . . ' she whined, pulling Ryan up to the dance floor, leaving Mara at the table alone.

Mara ordered another drink, determined not to feel abandoned. She couldn't tell exactly why she was so irritated. A breathless Eliza rushed in and took the empty seat.

'I'm so sorry I'm late! Jeremy and I went to Lunch for dinner and we got lobsters and corn bread. I'm SO fat from the carb bloat!' Eliza giggled as she kissed Mara hello.

'Jeremy with the clippers? You went out with Jeremy?' Mara asked. She'd met him the first week. He'd been really nice about helping her navigate the estate. Mara looked at Eliza with a new perspective. Jeremy was a real good guy – a solid guy – she didn't think someone like Eliza would ever be interested in someone like him.

'Yeah, we spent the whole day together. It was awesome. Oh, look, there's Lindsay. Hiiiii!' Eliza said, waving.

'So why didn't you bring him? Didn't you have a plus one?' Mara had learned that anyone who was anyone had their name 'plus one' on the guest list.

'Oh, he would never fit in here,' Eliza said between getting up and saying hello to her friends.

'What do you mean by that?' Mara asked.

'You can't just bring someone like Jeremy into this world,' Eliza explained. 'Oops! Watch it!' she snapped as an overeager birthday well-wisher spilled his whiskey on the rocks onto her dress.

Eliza wiped off the stain, a little annoyed. 'People can be so rude,' she griped.

'What world?' Mara asked stubbornly. Her good feeling towards Eliza had vanished. Jeremy was from the same background as Mara – his dad was a carpenter, her dad was in construction. His mother was a teacher, Mara's mom was a social worker. In fact, back home she was a lot more like Jeremy than Eliza.

'You know, all this,' Eliza said airily. 'Oh, there's Charlie. Hey!' She got up and ran after him. She wanted to make it up to him for missing him at the polo match.

What the hell did Eliza think she was doing, chasing after Charlie when she just had dinner with Jeremy? Mara frowned. She was already in a bad mood from meeting Camille, and now she was totally offended by Eliza's breezy generalisations and insouciant snobbishness.

Mara had started to really like Eliza, too, even if she was kind of princessy and prone to flake. Eliza had a natural charm about her that Mara had gravitated towards, and she was still grateful for the makeover. Her hair had never looked this good. But now this . . .

Her mobile phone blared the familiar chords. *Oh, oh, oh, sweet child o' mine . . .*

Mara checked the caller ID.

JIM M flashed.

Ugh.

She shut it off. Ryan might have a girlfriend, but that didn't mean she was ready to make up with her boyfriend. Yet.

Ryan gets schooled

AT THE END OF THE EVENING THE REST OF RYAN'S friends trooped to Charlie's after-party at the nearby American Hotel, and Eliza went with them. Mara had pleaded exhaustion, and Camille had left, so Ryan took Mara home.

'You know, we never did get to have that Scrabble game,' Ryan said as he pulled into the driveway.

'Yeah, I guess we both got kind of busy,' Mara said, a little more cutting than she'd meant it.

Ryan gave her a sidelong glance. 'Do you want to play?'

'Sure.'

They set up the board in the kitchen, and Mara counted out the tiles. She adored board games. She knew it was really dorky of her, but she couldn't help it. In seventh grade she had won a Trivial Pursuit tournament, and she was addicted to the Game Show network.

They played a heated battle, but Mara kicked his ass, spelling *sacristy, temptation,* and *gigolo* to Ryan's *cat, mop,* and *yam.*

Finally Ryan placed his tiles down and spelled *'Xer.'*

'Xer?' Mara asked. 'Prefixes aren't allowed.'

'No, it's like Generation X-er.' Ryan explained. 'A member of Generation X. You know, those people who are a little older than us and sold out the grunge thing for five-dollar cappuccinos.' He smiled at her. 'Let's see. I'm on a triple-word tile . . .'

'Xer isn't a word.'

'Yuh-huh.'

'No way. It's slang.' Mara shook her head.

'Are you saying you challenge?'

'It's not a word!' Mara laughed.

'You're killing me!' Ryan said.

'I'm not going to challenge, but it's not a word. Go ahead, leave it on. There's no way you're going to win anyway.'

'Oh, look who's cocky now.'

'That's right.' Mara grinned.

'I'm not going to take your pity,' Ryan huffed, collecting his tiles.

'Leave it! Leave it! I was only kidding.' Mara laughed.

They put away the board game and Ryan opened a bottle of wine, which they drank while looking out at the view from the porch. But their silence wasn't as comfortable as it had been all those times before.

'So, what happened with Camille?' Mara finally asked.

'She wanted to go to some fund-raiser in Wainscott. I didn't have it in me to hit another party.'

'She's very . . . um, cute,' Mara offered.

Ryan shrugged. 'She's nice,' he said, almost defensively.

'Have you guys been seeing each other for a while?'

'Not really,' Ryan said. 'What about you and Jim? How long have you guys been dating?'

'Since freshman year, officially. Unofficially, probably since third grade,' Mara said, as if this conversation wasn't unbelievably awkward.

'Mmm,' he said. 'It's Camille's birthday next week. What do you think I should get her? Is jewellery too much? It's always so hard to figure out what girls want.'

'Mmm,' she said. Mara didn't want to hear any more of Ryan's plans for his girlfriend's birthday. 'It's so gorgeous out here,' she said, changing the subject. 'You don't know how lucky you are.'

'Actually, I do,' Ryan said.

'I'm sorry – I didn't mean it that way.'

'No, no, it's fine.' He smiled a little.

'It must be nice – being rich, I mean,' Mara said, a little shocked at her candour.

'My dad's rich. It's his money, not mine,' Ryan said. 'I don't confuse the two. But I don't fool myself about it either.'

Mara wasn't sure exactly what he meant by that, but by now they'd covered two of the most awkward conversations they could – significant others and money – and Mara was trying not to push her luck. She was also trying really hard not to let the hurt

196

she felt about Camille and her New Jersey comment show through. Combined with Eliza's take on Jeremy's 'status', Mara was feeling more out of place than she had in a while.

'What do you want to do with your life?' Mara asked. 'Surf the Big Ten in Hawaii?' *Oops, that didn't sound so nice*, Mara realised.

'Nah – that's just a hobby.' He paused. 'I have an uncle in Paris. I think a lot about moving there and helping him with his business.'

'That sounds nice. What's he do?'

'He owns a gallery. My mom's brother. Not Anna's. My real mom.'

'Where is she?'

Ryan looked sad for a moment. 'Honestly, I don't know. She said she was going to check out some ashram in Tibet. Or maybe she's in South Africa, getting a face-lift on safari. I never know. The kids miss her. She was a lot of fun when she wasn't crazy.'

'Why? What did she do?'

'Oh, one night she came home and she'd spent basically their entire bank account on a car and a couple of furs and she drove up Fifth Avenue wearing nothing but her underwear in the snow. The doctors said she was manic-depressive. I could have told any-one that. She would bake chocolate cakes and throw an impromptu birthday party and have us all wearing fun little paper hats and the next moment she'd be sobbing in the corner, threatening to slit her wrists.'

'That's terrible. I'm so sorry.'

Ryan sighed. 'It's good to talk about it sometimes. Dad just pretends nothing ever happened and Anna's been in the family forever. What's your family like?'

'We're so boring.' Mara shrugged, feeling bad for being so testy earlier.

'Boring sounds perfect.'

'My dad's in construction. He builds, like, developer houses, and he always complains about the shoddy jobs they do. He always tries to do his best, but no one ever wants to pay for it. They put, like, plastic windows in their houses. He's a good guy. My mom's a social worker. She works with autistic kids, home-schools them. I'm the youngest. My sister Molly is married and lives in South Boston with her husband. She has two kids. My other sister, Megan, is a hairdresser. She's a riot. She makes all her own clothes and she looks like Julia Roberts.'

'You guys sound close.'

'We are,' Mara said, her eyes misting a little. She really missed them. 'Every summer we go out to Gloucester for a week. It's nice. Nothing like this, though.'

'What made you decide to take this job?'

'I needed the money,' Mara admitted. 'And talk about boring, nothing ever happens in Sturbridge.'

'Well, I for one am glad you decided to make it,' Ryan said, leaning down to look in her eyes.

Mara was a little drunk, and for some reason, she didn't look away. He was gorgeous – but more than that, he was smart – and funny – and just adorable. She lowered her lashes. She felt his breath on her cheek. She raised her lips to meet his.

And pulled away when she heard the patio door bang open.

Poppy stood in the doorway, holding a cigarette and an open bottle of beer. 'Ryan! I didn't see you there! You scared me!'

'Hey, sis,' Ryan said, easing back into his seat.

'How was Charlie's?' Poppy asked, leaning on the glass door. 'Oh, hey, you're, like, one of the au pairs, aren't you?' she said, turning to Mara.

Mara nodded.

'That's Mara. Mara, you've met my sister Poppy, haven't you?' Ryan asked.

'I think I'll go to bed now,' Mara said, jumping up and saying good night.

'Good night,' Ryan said, trying to catch her eye, but Mara refused to look at him.

Poppy shrugged. There were so many people going in and out of their house, it was hard to keep track. 'Ry, you got a light?'

'You shouldn't smoke,' Ryan told his younger sister on his way inside. 'It's bad for your skin.'

'Screw you,' Poppy sneered. Her older brother was such a killjoy.

These girls aren't as predictable as they look

'CODY! YOU GET BACK HERE, YOU HEAR? CODY!' Eliza yelled in despair.

The two-year-old streaked out of the main house completely naked, chortling to himself.

Inside, William was gleefully lobbing soggy Cocoa Puffs onto the floor, and Zoë and Madison were bickering over who ate the last blueberry scone.

Eliza made a last-ditch effort to try and tackle the baby. With Jacqui nowhere to be found and Mara nursing a killer hangover (mixing star fruit margaritas and cabernet was a very bad idea, it turned out), Eliza was the only one available for kid duty.

'Need some help?' Jeremy asked, picking up Cody by his elbows and swinging him into Eliza's arms.

'They never listen to me,' Eliza lamented.

With Jeremy's help Eliza got all the kids, the picnic basket, the Hokey Pokey Elmo, the Limbo Elmo, the Chicken Dance Elmo, two Bratz babies, colouring books, and buckets and spades into the car.

'I had a really nice time last night,' she said as Jeremy leaned into the window.

'Me too.'

Impulsively she gave him a quick kiss on the lips.

'Eliza and Jeremy sitting in a tree. *K-I-S-S-I . . . ,*' Madison began to chant.

'Shush!' Eliza said, putting a hand on the girl's mouth. But she gave Jeremy a warm smile.

'I'll see you later,' she said with a lopsided grin.

'Later.' He bowed a little at the waist and walked back towards the garden.

Eliza hustled the kids to their usual spot on Main Beach near the lifeguard section. They didn't have proper bathrooms at Two Mile Hollow, and that had ended up being a bit of a problem the other day. The kids were running wild, and Eliza was so bummed to be on solo babysitting duty today.

But just a few paces ahead was Mara. Good old Mara. She was wearing awfully big sunglasses and nursing a Gatorade, but she was there. Lord be praised.

'About time you guys got here,' Mara said, taking Cody out of his stroller and giving him a little tickle.

'What happened to you! You looked like you were at death's door this morning,' Eliza said.

'I was, I was. But Ryan made me this great hangover remedy – Worcestershire sauce and egg yolk.'

Eliza made a face. 'Ew.'

'I know, but it worked. I don't have a headache anymore, but I'm still so dehydrated,' Mara said, taking another gulp.

'How'd you get here so fast?'

'Ryan drove me.'

'Of course,' Eliza wanted to say, but held her tongue. Mara was so weird about the whole Ryan situation, and Eliza didn't want to make her feel self-conscious about it.

Mara took the baby to the shore, and Eliza and the others followed.

'C'mon Cody, just a few more steps. It won't hurt, c'mon, I got you.'

Cody followed Mara tentatively, but screamed and ran away as a wave rolled in.

'It's no use. The kid is never going to learn to swim,' Mara sighed. 'Cody! Come on! Look, it's fun!' she said, splashing the water.

'I saw Jeremy this morning – he was so cute! He helped me put all the kids in the car. And we were looking all scruffy . . . ,' Eliza said dreamily. *Since when do I say things like 'scruffy'?* she wondered dreamily. 'He was wearing the cutest overalls. Did you see?'

'Enough! I'm already about to vomit,' Mara joked. She was in a lot better mood after seeing Ryan that morning – they'd acted like everything was normal, which made it feel pretty, well, normal. She could even forgive Eliza's indiscretions last night. No one was perfect, and Mara was sure Eliza didn't really mean half the things she said. Look at how she glowed whenever she said Jeremy's name.

'You're so mean!' Eliza pouted. 'I finally find a guy I really like and I can't even tell you about all the cute things he did!'

'What about Charlie?' Mara asked.

'Oh, I don't know.' Eliza shrugged, 'Jeremy is just so perfect, and, I don't know, he's so good with the kids . . .'

'Seriously, Liza, I'm going to yak if you don't get out of here,' Mara said with a smirk.

'Out of here?'

Mara waved her doubts away. 'Totally. Go see him. You saved my butt the other day at the polo match. Go ahead! Really, just go!'

'I owe you one!' Eliza squealed, wrapping her arms around Mara and giving her a kiss.

She ran down the dune, hoping to catch Jeremy before he went home for the day.

Poor little
not-so-rich girl

ELIZA TIPTOED BACK INTO THE ESTATE, DUCKING BEHIND the statuary as she observed Kevin Perry heading off for the yacht club. He was taking out the schooner today and had even invited Jacqui to come with him. Kevin stood in front of his Ferrari Spider, checking his watch. But when it was clear Jacqui wasn't going to appear anytime soon, he drove off in a snit.

Eliza crept through the back entrance and found Jeremy planting hyacinths near the croquet hoops.

'Guess who?' she asked, covering his eyes with her hands.

'Sugar? Is that you? I'm awful tired out right now,' Jeremy joked. 'Or is it Poppy, hoping for some action?'

'That's so not funny,' she said, walking off, a little hurt. She didn't think anything to do with the twins was in any way entertaining.

'I'm sorry, I'm sorry,' Jeremy said, running to catch up with her. 'I'm just goofing around.'

He nudged her in the midsection and Eliza smiled. She couldn't really stay mad at him for long.

'C'mon,' she said, taking his hand and leading him to the au pairs' cottage. They snuck inside the attic room, which was still mercifully empty. (Hell, it wasn't too often no one was there, after all.)

'Nice digs,' Jeremy said, checking out the small, eight-by-ten room.

'It's not the Four Seasons, that's for sure.' Eliza sighed, sitting on the edge of the bed. She looked at him expectantly. Now that she had ditched work to hang out with him, she wasn't sure what they were going to do.

She tried her hardest to look endearingly innocent, sitting there in her pink sundress and canvas espadrilles, waiting for him to make the first move.

Jeremy took a seat next to her. 'So.'

'So.'

They turned to each other, and the next thing Eliza knew, he was kissing her. Softly at first, on the lips, light little trembly things. She closed her eyes. He smelled like the dark, warm earth with a hint of sweat and the sun. One of his hands was tangled in her hair, the other caressed the small of her back.

She returned his kisses eagerly, exploring the taste of his mouth. He tasted like mint and Dr. Pepper. He thought she smelled like coconuts and vanilla.

He pulled her onto his lap, and she buried her face in his chest.

'That's nice,' she said.

'Mmm?'

'Last night, did I tell you I live in Buffalo now?' she asked.

'No, you just said you grew up on Park Avenue.'

'I did.' She sighed, resting her face in the crook of his neck and liking the way his stubble felt on her skin.

'My dad used to be a big deal on Wall Street. You might have heard of him. He was kind of famous. There was some scandal with the accounting stuff, and he lost his job and we had to leave our apartment. My parents had to sell everything – their art collection, the house here . . . and we moved to Buffalo.'

'Buffalo's not so bad.'

'No, it's worse.' Eliza moaned. 'It's awful. All the kids think I'm a total snob and no one talks to me. And the thing is, I don't even do anything. I don't have anything to be snobby about. My dad's on unemployment, and my mom got a job at Kinko's to make ends meet.'

Jeremy was silent and stroked her hair. 'It's going to be okay,' he whispered, holding her close.

It felt good to talk about all this. Eliza had never really told anyone what happened to her – what her life was really like. She was so comfortable around him, knowing that he wouldn't judge her, somehow knowing she could tell him anything, anything at all about herself, and he would still like her.

'I never realised I was so spoiled before. I used to charge my lunch at this fancy restaurant in the city every day – like, thirty-dollar hamburgers and stuff – and I never gave it a second thought. And I would go into Barneys and Bergdorfs and buy whatever I wanted. Sometimes I'd even harass the salespeople to find things at other stores if they didn't have it in my size.'

She paused, remembering those heady, halcyon days, when she had her own Town Car at her beck and call and her AmEx didn't have a preset limit.

'I know this sounds really shallow, but I really miss it. I miss it more than I ever thought I would. Before, I could walk into any room, and everyone thought I was so special just from looking at me. Sugar and Poppy used to be in my clique in high school. They were part of *my* group. My clothes were always the coolest, the newest, the most expensive. My hair was always the blondest. I had it highlighted every thirteen days. I was thinner than everybody. Even the building we lived in – it was the hardest one to get into in the city. I just had IT, you know? But now I can't afford to have IT anymore. I just look like everyone else.'

She looked at him, afraid she would find him laughing at her. Eliza knew they were stupid, silly, material things. But it practically broke her heart when the strap of her Mombassa handbag broke. She knew she would never be able to afford another one.

'I know it's kind of funny. I mean, please, I know people are starving somewhere. But I'm really kind of . . . sad,' she said.

'You have every right to be,' Jeremy soothed. 'But Eliza – you have nothing to worry about. The first time I saw you, I couldn't take my eyes off you. And it had nothing to do with whatever 'IT' is or whether you have the latest Dolce and Gambino or whatever; you just have this glow about you.'

He took her face in his hands again, cupping her chin. 'You're absolutely beautiful. And I know we're just getting to know each other, but I think you're beautiful inside and out.'

It was the nicest thing anyone had *ever* said to her.

She kissed him long and hard. One day she was going to show him just how much he meant to her.

The only good thing
Anna Perry has ever said

ON MONDAY MORNING ANNA CALLED AN EARLY MEETING in her office. Mara and Eliza walked to the third floor, the only level they hadn't yet explored. They found their boss inside a magnificent, book-lined room, sitting in front of a dainty writing desk, dictating a memo to Laurie, who had her pen poised in readiness.

'Thus I feel it is in everyone's best interest that I chair the fund-raiser this year,' Anna said crisply. 'I expect my choice of lead designer to bring in thousands in guaranteed contributions.'

Anna looked up and raised a finger so Mara and Eliza wouldn't interrupt. 'All best, Mrs Anna Farnsworth Perry. The number is on the fax machine.'

She waved the girls to sit down. They sank into the velvet-upholstered armchairs. Mara looked around at all the beautiful hard covered books on the walls. She wondered if Anna even bothered to read them. Eliza had a shy smile on her face. She was still thinking about Jeremy.

'We have to take the kids back to the city this week to meet with their independent private school admissions counsellor,' Anna said. 'So we'll have to skip this week's progress report. You don't mind, do you, girls?' She smiled.

Mara and Eliza shook their heads. Not at all. They didn't mind one bit. Especially since they had yet to have a weekly progress meeting anyway, and they were already more than halfway through the summer.

'By the way, I haven't seen that – Jacqui – around very much. Is she ill?' Anna asked, concerned.

'No, she's, uh – giving Cody his bath,' Mara improvised.

'Yeah, she's been working on his water treatment,' Eliza agreed. 'Some kind of South American theory.'

'Good. Good idea.' Anna nodded crisply. 'Can you please excuse me for a moment, girls?' Anna teetered in her Manolos towards the hallway.

'I'm so sick of covering up for her all the time!' Mara complained when Anna left the room to check on the fax she'd asked Laurie to send. She and Eliza had noticed some really strange clothes coming in and out of their cottage, but they hadn't seen their third roommate in the flesh since . . . well, since the polo match, come to think of it.

'Where do you think she is?' Mara asked.

'Beats me. Maybe she has a new boyfriend. She's certainly not sleeping here.'

'I'm worried about her,' Mara said.

'She's fine. Jacqui's a big girl. She can take care of herself,' Eliza said.

'I hope so.' Mara frowned.

'Don't stress yourself over it; she's not worth it. I mean, she obviously doesn't even care to tell us where she is, so why should we bother?' Eliza had nothing against Jacqui except to begrudge her getting out of a fair share of the work. Another pair of hands would have been sorely appreciated the day William decided to try out his krav maga training on his sisters.

Mara sighed. 'I just hope she knows what she's doing.'

Anna returned to the room, looking a little ruffled and arguing with her hapless assistant. 'I told you to type it up on my personal letterhead, not just a blank piece of paper.'

'I'm so sorry; I didn't check.'

'Well, send it again. They might not even look at it! I know the committee is meeting today.'

'Yes'm.' Laurie bowed, skittering out of the room.

Anna looked surprised to find Eliza and Mara still sitting in front of her desk. 'That's it, girls. You can go. And don't worry, we'll be back for Super Saturday, and if you need anything . . . Ryan is in charge.'

It was like music to their very tan ears.

Ryan calls a very important meeting in the hot tub

THE REST OF THE WEEK FLEW BY IN A FUN-FILLED BLUR.
Without any kids to look after, Eliza and Mara spent the entire
time perfecting their tans and discovering new shopping streets.
On Wednesday they hit the Saks in Southampton, Thursday was
the Tanger Outlets in Riverhead, and on Friday they bought
matching vintage Lilly Pulitzer dresses at Colette. They were also
spending a lot time with the boys. Eliza and Jeremy had explored
the vineyards on the North Fork, and Mara had been taking surf
lessons from Ryan, sans Camille, thank goodness

Friday night Ryan called a house meeting in the hot tub.

'So I was thinking . . . it's about time we had a little party,'
Ryan said, grinning from behind the bubbles. 'You know, just a
small party – only close friends,' he suggested.

'That sounds awesome!' Eliza cheered.

'Sure, it sounds like fun.' Mara nodded.

'Okay, so tomorrow night, then. Mara, you'll come with me
to get the food. Eliza, you have the best ID, so I'll put you in

charge of the booze. And Jacqui, hey, where the hell is Jacqui?'
Ryan asked, his face furrowing. 'Has anyone seen her lately?'

Mara and Eliza shook their heads a little guiltily. They knew
something was up with Jacqui – but both of them had been so
wrapped up in their own lives, they barely paid attention to anything else.

The next evening Mara and Ryan set off to Barefoot Contessa to
amass party treats. They were picking out smoked salmon platters
and choosing between canapés when Mara's phone started ring-
ing incessantly.

'Who's trying to get ahold of you so bad?' Ryan asked, balancing several baguettes in one arm and holding a jar of caviar in the
other.

'Jim,' Mara explained. They hadn't talked about Jim or
Camille since their almost-kiss the week before, but they also
hadn't come close to anything like that again, so Mara was ready
to chalk it up to the cabernet (and the margaritas, ahem). 'I just
kind of need a break from us for a while. I really can't deal with
him right now.'

'Mmm,' Ryan grunted.

'But it's not, like, permanent or anything,' she added hastily,
for no good reason.

Mara looked sidelong at Ryan while she pretended to pick out tor-
tilla chips, and she couldn't help but notice that maybe, just maybe,
he looked a little down when she'd said it wasn't 'permanent'.

Eliza always gets what she wants, even if she doesn't want it anymore

'I THOUGHT I SAID CLOSE FRIENDS ONLY,' RYAN GROUSED as he surveyed the fully packed living room, dining room, ballroom, game room, pool area, patio, and sundeck. Everyone under the age of twenty-one in the Hamptons was present and accounted for, including several rock star offspring and the cast of various MTV reality shows.

Sugar and Poppy had done what they did best – spread the news – and keeping things 'small' was in no way part of their agenda. They had even hired a publicist, who had secured a party permit and made sure there was valet parking for guests.

'Great idea, bro!' Sugar hooted at Ryan as she was carried, sphinx-like, by an army of admirers toward the back cabana.

Ryan shook his head. Oh, well, might as well enjoy it. He turned up the stereo so that the rafters shook to the beat of the Hamptons' perennial 'It's All About the Benjamins'.

Already all the bedrooms were occupied, and the smell of pot was strong in the air. A clique of British teens was huddled around the glass dining room table, and a fedora-wearing dealer (a Bennington alum on his summer vacation) was making the rounds.

Ryan found Mara standing to the side, sipping a glass of white wine.

'You having fun?'

'Who are all these people?' she asked in astonishment.

'Beats me. They must all be my sisters' friends.' Ryan laughed. 'C'mon, I see my boys down by the patio.'

Eliza kept an eye out for Jeremy. He was supposed to be here by now. He had promised he would be there by eleven, after he got off his second job as a waiter at TGI Friday's in Hauppauge. She fluffed her hair in the mirror and made herself another vodka tonic. Things were going so well between them, every time he left her side, she missed him instantly. She didn't know she could feel this way about anyone.

She spotted Kit in the crowd and raised her glass hello. He and Taylor had broken up the week before, and Eliza had been trying to cheer him up. As much as she was friends with Taylor, she had always thought Kit deserved better. A lot of her old friends were at the party, but every time one of them waved her over, she just shook her head and smiled.

'Where do you think you're going?' a voice called as she stepped out to check the driveway for Jeremy's pickup again.

She spotted Charlie Borshok leaning on a pillar, completely wasted.

'Nowhere.'

Charlie took a few steps over and wrapped his arms around her. 'Oh, Liza, you smell so good. I missed you, baby.'

'That's really nice, Charlie,' she said, twisting her body away.

It was what she had wanted to hear all summer. That he wanted her back. That they were the golden couple again. That she was still the same girl who had snagged the richest boy in New York. But now she was looking for Jeremy.

A half hour later, Jeremy's pickup truck pulled into the driveway. He was still wearing his uniform T-shirt and apron. Eliza ran out and leapt into his embrace.

'Hey, baby.' He grinned at her.

'I MISSED YOU!'

She hugged her legs around his waist tighter and whispered, 'Let's go find somewhere we can be alone.'

Jacqui has always been smarter than you'd think

NOW, THIS WAS A PARTY! JACQUI THOUGHT, WALKING into the Perry mansion, momentarily forgetting that she was employed there.

She'd been drinking all afternoon. She felt *fantastic* – except for the wooziness and the dizziness and the slight double vision, that is. But who cared? She snuggled up to Leo. Leo, nice, faithful Leo, who made her forget, well, almost everything.

So what if they had zero chemistry? Not to mention that his parents' three-bedroom shack in Bridgehampton was nothing compared to Luke's corner wing on the Van Varick estate. And so what if he was slightly cross-eyed and had an irritating laugh? None of it mattered. He was Luke's best friend. And as every girl knows, there's nothing a guy hates more than sharing.

Jealousy was a terrible thing, and Jacqui knew exactly what she was doing. She wanted Luke to feel as bad as she did when she found out about his girlfriend. She wanted him to squirm. She wanted him to *suffer*. Maybe she wouldn't be able to break his heart – but she could damn well try to shatter his ego. It was time for her to go public with her latest conquest.

'Where's the bar?' Leo asked, yelling in her ear.

'Over there!' she screamed, pointing to where Ryan was mixing frozen daiquiris in a blender.

They picked their way past a group playing Twister and several clumps of people dancing on the sofa (Anna would die if she knew what they were doing to her Louis Quinze) and were stopped in their tracks by Poppy Perry, in a shredded Van Halen T-shirt and micro denim hot pants.

'I don't remember inviting you,' she sneered, giving Leo a death's-head stare.

'What's up with the *bruha*?' Jacqui asked.

Leo looked sheepish. 'She's my ex-girlfriend.'

Poppy's eyes followed them as they moved across the room, where another angry face met them.

'What's the deal?' Luke said, coming up in Leo's face close enough to spitting vicinity. 'Are you here with her?' he demanded, giving his pal a hard shove.

'I'm here with *him*,' Jacqui said, pushing at Luke's chest with a pointy fingernail. 'Do you have a *problema* with that?'

'What's going on, honey?' Karin asked, appearing by Luke's side. 'Oh, hi, Leo. And Jacqui, right?' she said pleasantly.

'Nothing – everything's fine. Get me another beer,' Luke spat.

Karin walked away meekly as the three of them glowered at each other.

Eliza teaches Jeremy
the O.C. drinking game

IN THE PERRYS' PRIVATE SCREENING ROOM THE DIGITAL projection screen blazed a sixteen-foot-tall upset-looking Mischa Barton explaining to Benjamin Mackenzie why she couldn't see him anymore. 'They're breaking up! You need to take a drink!' Eliza cheered.

Eliza had found the only room in the house that wasn't already locked and in use by an amorous couple, or occupied by a group of kids passing a roach around. Not everyone knew about the basement screening room.

On-screen, Ben apologised for being from 'a different county'.

'Chug?' Jeremy asked, holding his shot glass.

'No! Only when he actually says "Chino",' Eliza said, explaining the rules of the game.

'Oh. Sorry. I don't watch this show.'

'If you did, I'd worry. Oh, look, Summer's going shopping. Double chug!'

'I say we do body shots instead,' Jeremy said, pouring another shot of Cuervo and handing her a wedge of lime. 'Hmmm . . . where will I do mine?' he asked, lifting up Eliza's shirt to expose her pierced belly button. She had got it in Greenport one afternoon when he told her he thought they were sexy. He pulled down her skirt a bit to expose her jutting hip bones and bent his head to lick her in the shallow of her stomach.

'That tickles!' Eliza giggled, ruffling his hair and squealing as he began biting her belly.

The door clicked open, and Eliza froze. In the darkness she saw a couple feverishly making out and groping their way to the pool table. A flurry of limbs began throwing items of clothing to the ground. Apparently, she wasn't the only one who knew about the room.

'We're not alone!' she told Jeremy, putting a finger to her lips.

Jeremy smirked when he saw the other couple. 'I guess someone else had the same idea,' he whispered. They giggled quietly.

'Let's go,' she told him, straightening her skirt and collecting the shot glasses and tequila bottle. They inched their way to the doorway, laughing as the couple began making lurid, disgustingly wet sloppy noises along with unintentionally comic expressions of discomfort. 'Ow! Not there! Oops, I think I'm sitting on the remote control! Oh, that's you!' 'Honey, please, stop pinching . . .' 'That's better. Oh, wait, is that your leg or mine?'

The light suddenly switched on, filling the room in a blaze of light.

The two couples blinked. Taylor and Lindsay stood at the front of the room. They were roaming the house, trying to find the source of the music in order to change the CD. The speaker system was wired to the entire house, and you could only take so much vintage Puffy.

'I think they keep the Crestron in here,' Lindsay said, meaning the universal remote that controlled all the electricity in the house, including the lighting, stereo, televisions, burglar alarm, and even the microwave.

'Oh! Sorry!' Taylor said.

Eliza finally got a clear picture of the room's other amorous inhabitants. 'Charlie! Sugar!'

Sugar, splayed out between two Barcaloungers, was topless in a Cosabella thong. She was, indeed, straddling the remote control. Charlie was dressed in his polka-dot boxers and nursing his foot. Talk about compromising positions.

Sugar sat up and shook out her hair, casually sliding her completely see-through cami back on. Eliza willed herself not to look and see if Jeremy was staring.

'Eliza, what are you doing here?' Sugar asked coolly. 'And hey, aren't you our pool boy or something?' she said, noticing Jeremy as she reached for her pack of cigarettes and patted out a stick.

Charlie grabbed at his trousers on the floor and pulled out his lighter. He lit her cigarette and assessed the situation, observing Eliza's crimson face and rumpled clothes and her partner's stony expression and some kind of Pizza Hut uniform.

'Liza,' Charlie drawled, obviously still drunk. 'I didn't know you had it in you to go slumming.'

Eliza recoiled from Jeremy, shaking off his protective hand on her elbow. 'I didn't know you did either, Charlie,' she said, looking pointedly at Sugar. Let her whine to Anna and get her fired. Eliza didn't care.

Jeremy balked. 'When are you going to stop pretending you're still part of this world, Eliza?'

'Excuse me?' Charlie asked, not sure what he just heard. The dude was obviously some blue-collar trash. And Eliza Thompson was Park Avenue born and bred.

Eliza turned to Jeremy, completely horrified that he had just blown her cover. 'You don't even know me,' she spat.

Jeremy's face hardened. He couldn't believe keeping her status with her so-called friends was so important to her. 'You're right, I definitely don't know you at all.' He pushed his way to the door without giving her a second glance.

Lindsay and Taylor were utterly speechless with shock and schadenfreude. Eliza? *Poor?* Could it get *any* better than this?

Sugar, dumb as she was, said matter-of-factly, 'God, you guys didn't know that? Eliza's been working here as an au pair all summer. Her family's totally bankrupt. Hey, don't you have to go burp my brother or something?' she said snidely.

Tears in her eyes, Eliza mumbled something unintelligible and ran out the door as fast as her three-inch-heel Jimmy Choos could carry her.

Luke and Leo are rich white boys who think they're straight outta Compton

'MAN, THAT IS SO LOW,' LUKE SAID, SHAKING HIS HEAD and staring at Leo and Jacqui. 'I can't believe you would tap my bitch like this.'

'Dude, you have a girlfriend,' Leo said in his defense.

Bitch? Jacqui was no one's bitch. What was this, some bad audition tape for a rap video? Who did these guys think they were? Eminem and Dr. Dre? More like Vanilla Ice and MC Hammer.

'You! You *lied* to me!' she said to Luke. 'You had girlfriend the whole time!'

'Listen, *mamasita*. What I do in the States is my business. I showed you a good time, didn't I?' Luke said scornfully. He'd had Jacqui's number since they met. All pretty girls had zero self-esteem. Jacqui was just like every Upper East Side ice princess who pretended to be all that, but melted at a well-phrased compliment.

Jacqui couldn't believe she had ever fallen in love with such a cretin. Or that she had fallen for his whole aw-shucks, nice-guy act.

'Goddamn, Leo, I can't believe you got on my bitch!' Luke said, scowling and folding his arms across his chest, assuming the confrontational pose he had seen Snoop throw down on the BET.

'I didn't. The bitch wasn't taken,' Leo said, stepping back and waving his arms.

'Bitch? What? Listen, you,' Jacqui said, turning to Leo. 'I'm only with you to make him jealous.'

'See. You're being played, man. That is cold. That's cold,' Luke said, smirking.

Leo turned purple and turned to Jacqui. 'What?!'

Jacqui shrugged. Jesus, what did he think he was, some kind of stud? Of course she was only with him to lick her wounds and get even with the so-called love of her life.

It was a whole sloppy-second mess, a complete emotional disaster. But somehow, by the end of the argument, Luke and Leo were slapping each other on the back, calling each other homie and laughing about the whole thing. Dating and dumping the same girl – it was something the two jerks could relate to. It was just like something out of a Bad Boy video, and they thought that was pretty cool. She just provided them with a summer's worth of gross locker room anecdotes, and they couldn't be happier.

But for once it looked like Jacqui was going to have to sleep in the au pairs' cottage. Alone.

Mara can't keep her clothes on

2 A.M.

Almost everyone had left for another party, and the only people left were on the back patio by the pool having another kind of party altogether . . . a more intimate one, shall we say. The table held several empty bottles of liquor, dozens of cocktail glasses, and ashtrays filled to the brim with cigarette butts, and the group exuded a jovial camaraderie as if it were perfectly normal that they were more than half naked. They didn't call it strip poker for nothing.

Mara peeked at her hand. A pair of queens. Not bad. Her dad had taught all three of his kids his favourite game, and Mara always thought of herself as a bit of a pro. No daughter of George 'Texas No Limit Hold 'Em' Waters was going to lose to a bunch of overprivileged softies from East Hampton.

Nonetheless, she was down to her pink Chantelle bra and matching low-rise underwear.

She looked across the table, where Ryan was busy examining his cards, frowning.

The dealer flipped the next card: an ace. 'And that's the river,' he crowed.

'Well, I'm out,' Ryan's friend Corey decided, putting down his cards in disgust.

'Me too,' another friend agreed.

Around the table everyone took a pass, forfeiting an item of clothing in the process.

'I'm in,' Ryan declared.

Mara looked at the ace, looked at her high pair. She scanned the other four community cards – all trash. *There is no way he can beat me. He has nothing! Nothing! He's totally bluffing!* Ryan was the worst player of the night – he was the only one down to his boxer shorts. Well, besides her.

Mara smiled to herself. This was going to be fun.

'I'm in, too,' she said challengingly.

'The Scrabble Master should fold,' he advised.

'No way.'

'Not to be cliché, but read them and weep.' Ryan grinned, putting down a pair of aces. With the dealer's ace, he had three of a kind.

Mara slumped in her seat.

'What have you got?'

She showed him.

'No big deal. You don't have to do it if you don't want to,' Ryan told her, a sympathetic look on his face.

She shrugged. What the hell. It was just like the dressing room at Loehmann's. Except outdoors. In public. In front of Ryan Perry.

'Rules are rules,' she said. All those daiquiris she'd drunk were making her pretty brave.

Taking a deep breath, she unhooked her bra and threw in her underwear as well. Naked as Aphrodite emerging from the sea, she streaked past the rest of the strip poker revellers, through the kitchen, across the porch, through the yard, and dove into the pool.

Far from shy, Ryan took the cue, doffed his boxers, and followed her in. After all, his mother had shipped him to a hippie summer camp in Vermont as a kid. This was all just fun and games.

'WATER FIGHT!' he yelled, splashing up to her.

Mara screamed mid-backstroke and tackled him in the water. She'd never had so much fun in her life. She was liberated, free. The old class secretary Mara would never be caught dead in the wee hours of the morning, completely nude with a guy she wasn't even dating.

Ryan swam up and grabbed her by the waist. 'GOTCHA!'

'Ryan! Let me go!' Mara squealed, loving every minute.

They treaded water for a while, laughing, and Mara suddenly realised she was like, oh, good God, totally naked in front of Ryan! And he was holding her . . . kind of close actually.

She looked into his eyes, which were laughing back at her.

He's going to kiss me, Mara thought. *It's going to happen. Now. Here.* She closed her eyes, but then she suddenly pulled away.

'Ryan, I can't – this doesn't feel right – not that I don't

want to – I really do – but I still have to work things out with Ji – JIM!'

And there, standing by the edge of the pool, was Jim Mizekowski, all two hundred and twenty pounds of him. With a look of absolute disgust on his face.

When arguing naked, be careful how emphatically you talk

MARA STRUGGLED OUT OF THE POOL, RUNNING AFTER JIM. She felt terrible for him – there was so much to explain – if he would just wait.

'Jim, please, listen to me,' she pleaded.

'So THIS is why you couldn't come home this week. You had to 'work'. I get it.' He spat, so angry that a vein throbbed dangerously on his forehead. 'Jesus, I can't even look at you.'

'It's not what you think. Ryan's just a friend. We were just playing a game, that's all,' Mara said, knowing it sounded pretty weak.

'Calm down, buddy,' Ryan said, still laughing, giving Jim his usual disarming smile. 'We're just having fun. You want to join us in a little strip poker?'

Jim ignored him.

'NOTHING HAPPENED, Jim! I SWEAR!' Mara said, energised by the truth. After all, nothing had happened. Yet.

'You know why I came up here?' Jim asked. 'My MOM saw

your picture in the paper. She gets the *Post,* you know. And there was some picture of you from some polo match and some guy you were with – this guy!' he said, motioning to Ryan. 'I didn't even believe it. It's just not like you. Not my Mara. But I saw the picture – you were dressed like a hooker.'

'I'm not a hooker!' Mara cried. Even though she was, technically, still naked. In public. Ahem.

'No, you're worse. You're a slut and a whore. You're nothing better than a two-bit hooker on Worth Avenue.'

Mara gasped. She had never been called such awful names. And from her own boyfriend! She didn't know how to react.

'Hey, dude, that's enough,' Ryan said, coming up to shield Mara from Jim. His voice was quiet, and he was no longer amused. (He had thought the whole thing was kind of funny, really, since he and Mara were still naked, and hey, everything could easily be explained – it's not as if there wasn't a bunch of half-naked people on the porch.) But this guy was acting way out of line.

'I understand you're angry, but you can't talk to her that way,' Ryan said.

Mara couldn't believe what was happening. It was all too much. And she'd had a lot to drink. It was surreal. A total nightmare.

Meanwhile, back on the patio, the music was still blasting and the game continued. Everyone else was totally clueless about the drama going on in the backyard.

'I'll speak to her any way I want,' Jim spat, hulking up. This little fancy pants prep school kid had nothing on him.

'And Mara, you can forget about the discount on that Camry at my uncle's dealership.' With those fighting words, Jim took off through the woods.

It was so absurd Ryan actually began to laugh.

'A Camry?' he asked.

'It's not funny,' Mara said miserably. 'I was counting on that car. It was the only one I could afford to buy and still have money left over for college.'

'God, I'm sorry,' Ryan said, sobering up.

Mara frowned, but after a minute she, too, began to laugh. There they were, standing naked in the Perrys' front yard. 'It *is* kind of funny.'

They walked back towards the house, collecting their clothes along the way.

A few hours later Jacqui walked out of the au pairs' cottage and found the two of them huddled in Ryan's oversized sweatshirts, sharing a cigarette and watching the sun rise.

'I couldn't sleep,' Jacqui explained.

'Glad you made it to the party,' Ryan joked.

'Jacqui – are you okay?' Mara asked.

No, she was really so far from okay, it was laughable. The guy she had loved was a two-timing loser with serious identity issues. And the guy she had replaced him with was an even bigger loser who was more Li'l Romeo than DMX. Jacqui felt empty and used and completely burned out.

'I'll be okay,' she said, hugging herself and shivering.

Mara didn't press for any answers. She knew Jacqui would tell her more when the time was right.

'You want a cig?' Mara asked, offering the only solace she knew Jacqui might accept just then.

'I thought you didn't smoke,' Jacqui said, taking a seat on the grass next to them.

Mara shrugged. 'I thought I didn't do a lot of things.'

Vacation is never long enough, is it?

EARLY THE NEXT MORNING THE PERRY KIDS RAN SCRAMBLING into the au pairs' room. They galloped up the rickety stairs, completely ruining the girls' plans to sleep in. Remnants of the party the night before were in evidence in their little domicile. Jeremy had left his coat under Eliza's bed. Ryan's sweatshirt was draped over the armchair. Several dirty cocktail glasses were breeding fungus in the bathroom.

'We're back! We're back!' Madison yelled, jumping up and down on Eliza's bed. 'Did you guys miss us?'

'Wanna go swimming?' Zoë asked.

Eliza groaned. 'Is it Sunday already?'

Mara couldn't even raise her head from her pillow. 'William, stop pulling my hair, please!'

'Oh my God, I am SO hung over,' Eliza complained.

'Me too,' Mara said, clutching her stomach. She scanned the room. 'Where's Jacqui?'

Eliza gave Mara a blank look. Jacqui? Hello, where had Mara

been all summer? Jacqui was never around. She was their phantom roommate.

'She was here last night,' Mara explained. 'I can't believe she bailed! It's her turn to take the kids somewhere. Ugh.'

'Well, I haven't seen her.' Eliza shrugged, trying to hide underneath the covers.

'Seriously, there is no way I can go to the beach today,' Mara yelled over the clamour as William and Madison fought over who got to sit on the armchair.

'I've got an idea,' Eliza said.

They drove into one of the few movie theatres in town. Unlike the sprawling suburban megaplexes in Sturbridge or the high-tech high-rises in Manhattan, where a movie ticket cost upwards of ten dollars, the East Hampton theatre was a small, brown-shingled building that showed obscure foreign films, art house indies, and, luckily for them, a Disney animated feature that afternoon.

'I wanna see *Alien versus Predator*!' William demanded.

'Sucks to be you; it's not showing.' Eliza yawned.

They ushered the kids into the theatre. Eliza was thankful for the air-conditioning and the darkness. She was planning to catch up on her sleep through the entire thing in an attempt to exorcise the events of the night before from her memory. After she had left the screening room in disgrace, she had tried to look for Jeremy, but all she found were assorted half-naked people passed out on the porch.

He *had* to understand – she'd been put on the spot in front of people she had known her whole life. It wasn't anything to do with him, really. God, it was all such a mess. She gnawed her cuticles anxiously.

Mara walked in with Madison, carrying a huge bucket of popcorn and a Coke.

Eliza stuffed a handful into her mouth and instantly spit it out. 'What? No butter?'

'That motor oil they pass off for butter has more calories than a porterhouse steak!' Mara reminded her, nodding towards Madison.

Eliza knew that. But everyone knew popcorn wasn't really a food. And it tasted like sand without butter. 'I'm getting butter on this and salt,' Eliza said, grabbing the carton.

'Hey, get your own!' Mara said, nodding even less subtly at Madison.

'Why don't we just ask her what she wants?' Eliza said. 'Do you want butter?'

Madison looked at the two au pairs. She really wanted butter, but Mara was giving her such an encouraging look, she didn't know what she wanted. It was Mara who had fixed the hair on her Barbies the other day, combing them until they weren't tangled up anymore. She didn't want to disappoint her.

'No,' she replied, almost like a question.

'Good girl, Mad.' Mara nodded. 'Why don't you buy your own bag?' she asked Eliza in a conciliatory tone.

'Forget it.' Eliza frowned. She had already spent all her money and didn't have a penny to her name till the next pay period.

The lights dimmed, and the strains of the Walt Disney theme built to a crescendo.

While the kids were occupied with the movie, Eliza told Mara what had happened with Jeremy and her friends. 'I swear, I totally didn't mean for that to happen! I was just so shocked, you know?' Eliza said, wanting to be consoled so badly. 'He means more to me than any of them put together.'

Mara nodded. That was a pretty wretched picture Eliza had painted, but Mara could see it was tearing Eliza up. 'I'm sure he'll understand. You're only human.'

In hushed tones she then told Eliza about the scene with Jim and Ryan, complete with a strip poker play-by-play.

'Jeez, what a jerk. I don't even know why you stayed with that white trash Jim for so long,' Eliza said.

Mara was taken aback. That was pretty harsh. Granted, she wanted sympathy, but calling her boyfriend white trash was stepping over the line. Sure, Jim wasn't some heir to a brand-name fortune and he didn't drive a fancy car, and fine, he couldn't pronounce *Quogue* if his life depended on it, but he wasn't that bad. A little dim, maybe, a little overprotective, yes. And very bad tempered when he was provoked. But white trash? Combined with Eliza's callous comments the other night about Jeremy not 'fitting in' with 'this world', Mara felt extremely insulted.

'You really are a piece of work,' Mara said, glaring at Eliza.

'Huh?'

'You know, I felt really bad about what happened with you and Jeremy, but now I think maybe you just got what you deserved.'

'Wait a minute . . .'

'Here's a piece of advice, Eliza: Maybe you should think about what you're saying before you open your mouth,' Mara hissed, grabbing her bags.

'Why? What the hell?' Eliza asked, mystified. It wasn't like she'd had the best night either. C'mon, all her friends thought *she* was white trash now.

'Because you know what's really low class?' Mara asked, her colour high and her voice defiant. 'A total SNOB like you!'

And with that, Mara left all four sugar-crazed kids for Eliza to deal with on her own.

Mara returned to the estate in time to see Jacqui saunter through the front door.

'Where have you been all morning?' Mara demanded.

'I was signing up the kids for the regatta competition down in Shelter Island. I thought they might like it, and it's the last day,' Jacqui explained.

Oh. She was actually doing something nice and responsible for the kids for a change. But instead of putting Mara in a good mood, it just made Mara feel worse about leaving them with Eliza.

'Well, you could have told us,' she snapped.

'What's wrong with you?' Jacqui asked, a little hurt that Mara hadn't even thanked her for the idea.

'Nothing. Nothing. Just – can you just leave me alone?' Mara said.

'Gladly,' Jacqui said.

Everything is getting progressively worse

FOR THE FIRST TIME THE ENTIRE SUMMER, BOTH ANNA and Kevin actually showed up for the weekly progress report in the screening room. Anna was in a good mood. Her co-chairwomanship of Super Saturday was almost locked. She had found a designer with a massive amount of overstock who wanted to sell it all in a prime booth, and it was just a matter of time before the committee anointed her with the title.

Mara and Eliza stumbled in late (projectile poo from the baby getting his diaper changed had delayed their arrival) and were surprised and not too pleased that Jacqui, of all people, was sitting there, conversing pleasantly with their bosses as if it was the most natural thing in the world.

They took their usual seats, perplexed at the turn of events.

'So, anyway, as I was saying, I just want to know how Zoë is keeping up with her reading. Has she moved on to the new Art Spiegelman?'

'Uh, I'm not quite sure, Anna,' Eliza said brightly. 'In fact, you should ask Jacqui since she's been reading to her all summer.'

'Yes, she's completely engrossed in a book, I think it's called *Where in the World Is Carmen Sandiego?*' Mara interrupted.

Jacqui kicked Mara under the table.

Anna beamed. 'And Cody?'

'Oh, we've almost cured him of the whole running-around-naked thing. We're really setting a fine example that clothes are very, very important to one's social development,' Eliza said, glaring at Mara.

Kevin yawned. He was still picturing Jacqui naked below the decks on his Catalina.

'As for Madison, she's learning the value of telling the truth. Especially to her friends,' Mara said, returning Eliza's icy stare.

'And William? Is he taking his meds?'

'Oh, absolutely,' all three au pairs chorused. His doctor had put William on Adderall in addition to the Ritalin and Metadate that he was already taking, so that was true enough. Not that it had done anything to change the kid's personality. He was still a hyperactive little monster.

'Marvellous!' Anna shone. 'Oh, Kevin, aren't these girls perfect? They're nothing like those other ones you hired. I'm so glad.'

The au pairs' ears pricked up. They never did find out what happened to the 'A Team', as they had dubbed the first set of au pairs, and they were slightly worried they would be given the boot as well. Who knew what those girls did wrong? It wasn't as if

Mara, Eliza, and Jacqui were doing anything right. Except Anna and Kevin were so clueless or indifferent, it really didn't matter.

Kevin handed out the fat cash-filled envelopes. 'Thanks, ladies. Keep up the good work.'

He led Anna out of the den.

'Oh, darling, I forgot to tell you,' Anna said as they walked away. 'The landscaper – or the gardener – he quit today. You're going to have to find someone else in town who can take care of the azaleas. Such a shame.'

Mara tried to catch Eliza's eye. But Eliza turned away.

As the girls pocketed their cash, each of them took mental bets on who wasn't going to make it to their final payday.

Mara: 5–1 it's Eliza. The girl was a complete flake. Plus she didn't have anything to stay for now that all her friends had abandoned her.

Eliza: 3–1 on Mara. She liked the odds on the small-town girl feeling homesick and quitting life in the fast lane.

Jacqui: 2–1 on herself. She wasn't sure she could take this any longer. She certainly wasn't having the summer of her life that the job ad had promised. So much for truth in advertising.

That money is burning a hole in Eliza's Stella bag

THE NEXT DAY ELIZA FOUND HERSELF IN FRONT OF THE counter at Cartier. Even after everything that had happened, she felt like herself again inside its gilt doors. Now, this was living. She pondered the classics: interlocking trinity rings, sparkling diamond solitaires with the *C* emblem, the latest from the 'nouvelle vague' collection of sturdy, minimalist gold cube rings that Hamptons housewives were collecting as casually as multistriped sailor shirts from L.L. Bean.

'That one,' she said, pointing to an eighteen-karat-gold Panthère watch set with diamonds.

The salesgirl put the watch on Eliza's tiny wrist. 'It's a beauty.'

Eliza held it up to the light, admiring how it glinted and shone. 'I'll take it,' she said. 'And no need to wrap it up; I'll just wear it out.'

The watch cost significantly more than the amount in the envelope, but Eliza asked the girl to put the rest on her well-worn Visa.

She deserved this watch! After everything she had to put up with. Maybe if she looked at it long enough, she would forget Jeremy's disgusted expression, her friends' scornful laughter, and the fact that she had to return to Buffalo at the end of the summer.

Eliza left the store and spotted Mara across the street, headed to a branch of the North Fork bank. She ducked down before Mara could see her. She didn't feel like showing Mara the watch or facing her just yet.

Someday Mara will have saved enough to buy her own country

MARA LEFT THE TELLER WINDOW. SHE HAD APPROXIMATELY
$6,300 in the bank! She would have had $6,666 if she hadn't
spent so much money on a dress and flip-flops on that fateful
shopping trip. Maybe she could still buy that Camry if Jim found
it in his heart to forgive her. After all, it wasn't as if she and Ryan
had made out or anything, she thought, with more than a little
sense of regret.

She tucked her deposit ticket into her wallet and walked out
the door. She saw Eliza across the street leaving Cartier with a
small red shopping bag. Eliza was pretending not to see her. Just
like on the first day when they had sat on opposite sides of the
bench.

Mara started towards the Pilates studio to pick up the little
girls.

Jacqui just might win her own bet

JACQUI STOOD AT THE TRAVEL AGENCY COUNTER, BITING her lip. She had just enough to take her back to São Paulo. It was so tempting. What was she doing staying in town? She could be back on a real beach in sixteen hours.

She looked across the desk to the flight schedules on the computer screen. See, there was one leaving that evening from JFK.

But maybe running away wasn't the answer? It was such a waste of money. There were only a few weeks left. Her grandmother would be surprised to see her back so early. There would be too much explaining to do, and Jacqui didn't think her *avó* would approve when she confessed that she had spent her summer in the States just to be with a boy. Her grandmother had only allowed her to come to America because Jacqui had told her she had been chosen to participate in an 'educational experience'. How prophetic.

After a month in the Hamptons, Jacqui had learned that thongs were not allowed on the beaches, that her breasts were not considered real, and that the best way to crash a party was to pretend you already belonged.

'Should I make the reservation?' The clerk sat back down at her desk.

'Actually, I think I've changed my mind,' Jacqui said.

Besides, she had promised Zoë she would teach her to read that book she had brought from home, with all the pretty pictures.

So she left the travel agency, her envelope of cash safely tucked inside her purse.

Super Saturday is turning out to be not so super after all

ON THE LAST SATURDAY OF AUGUST, THE ONLY GAME in town was a day-long shopping extravaganza to benefit ovarian cancer. Former luminaries who had cohosted the event included the late Princess Diana (who simply loved the discount de la Rentas), Donna Karan (who turned it into a themed carnival complete with rides), and, of course, the late and great founding chairwoman, *Harper's Bazaar*'s Liz Tilberis. It was a madhouse of billowing white tents, and designers from Calvin Klein, Jill Stuart, Kate Spade, Michael Kors and many more sold samples and overstock and leftovers for a fraction of the original price.

Anna, who had been passed up for hosting duties at the last minute in favour of a more well-financed socialite, nevertheless courageously soldiered on to sponsor the booth for Edgardo DeMenil, an up-and-coming designer who had debuted last fall with a collection of studded leather ponchos. Unfortunately, the world was not ready for studded leather ponchos, and the designer was trying to unload all the merchandise at Super

Saturday. Anna was trying to talk up the 'couture' items with her friends, all of whom were understandably taking a pass.

'Mara, can you take the kids to the pets corner? They're scaring away the clients!' Anna asked in a frantic tone.

'Eliza, will you do it? You forgot to pack Cody's stroller and now I have to hold him all afternoon,' Mara said accusingly, although the truth was that there was something calming about having the baby rest on her hip.

Eliza, whose attention was distracted by all the incredible designer discounts, wandered over at the sound of her name. A pair of Yanuk jeans for $50! A Calvin Klein silk jersey dress for $120! If only she hadn't bought that Cartier watch! She felt poor and irritable and was looking at six straight hours of misery. Nothing's worse than coming to a sale with an empty purse.

'So what? I took him yesterday. He puked all over my Foley and Corrina top,' she said, annoyed. 'Where's Jacqui?'

Nowhere, as usual.

When Jacqui waltzed back, sipping a frosty drink, Mara lost it. 'You're never around when we need you!' she accused in a whispered, hostile tone.

Anna and Kevin were mingling and kiss-kissing friends, randomly introducing a kid when he or she happened to be in the line of vision. Sugar was sitting looking pouty, sexy, and bored, as usual.

'Shhh! They'll hear you!' Eliza warned, hastily wiping Zoë's chocolate-covered mouth.

William decided it was great fun to hang on her hair, and he pulled her backwards just as Taylor and Lindsay walked up, holding several bulging shopping bags.

'William! Please let go! Let go!' Eliza pleaded, trying to wrench the little monkey away from her head.

She looked up and saw Taylor and Lindsay by the Marc Jacobs booth, trying on pinstripe sundresses.

'What do you think?' Taylor asked, smoothing down the front of her peplum skirt. She caught Eliza's eye and turned away in embarrassment.

'Oh, it's Eliza. Hey,' Lindsay said, giving her a weak wave.

The two scooted away as soon as they had swiped their charge cards.

Eliza couldn't decide what was worse – that her friends were ignoring her or that they obviously felt sorry for her.

'Excuse me, miss? Can you get me a drink?' Charlie asked, a twisted smile on his face.

'Can't you see? She's working right now.' Sugar laughed, getting up from her seat. 'Hey, Bill, pull harder,' she told her little brother.

'I got ya!' William crowed.

'Screw you,' Eliza said, looking directly at Charlie.

'Excuse me?' Charlie asked.

'Eliza?' Anna asked primly. 'You know we try to keep that kind of language away from the kids' ears. Spoils their interactive development.'

'Sorry, sorry. I . . .'

'Here,' Anna said, expertly wringing William away and giving Eliza a doubtful look. 'Now go and play with the Kennedy-Cole kids. Over there, over there. Scoot!' she said to her stepson.

'Thanks,' Eliza said weakly, feeling a little humiliated to have been rescued by Anna, of all people.

Mara found a quiet place by the outdoor restaurant to try calling Jim again. He hadn't picked up his phone since Saturday night. She didn't want things between them to end this way, and she wanted to get her story straight with him. It made her furious to think about what kind of lies Jim was probably spreading about her back home. What if everyone thought she was a two-cent hooker when she got back? She was class secretary, after all. She had a rep to protect.

She dialled his number again. Straight to the answering machine.

'Jim, it's me, Mara. I know you don't want to hear it, but you have to. You have to give me a chance to explain. I'm really, really sorry about what happened . . .'

'Hey.'

'Jim, you're there.'

'Yeah.'

'Look –'

'No,' he interrupted. 'I'm sorry I blew up at you on Saturday. It wasn't right and I'm sorry.'

Mara was stunned.

'I don't know what happened between you and that guy, and I don't really want to know.'

'Noth –'

But Jim kept talking. 'The thing is, I kinda knew you wanted the job to get away from here. And I guess I was mad at you for deserting me. But the thing is . . . well . . .' He sounded a little sheepish.

'What?'

'I think I've met someone else,' he admitted.

Mara exhaled. Now that, she hadn't seen coming. She had mixed feelings about his admission. On the one hand, she was in the clear. On the other, what the hell? She'd been so worried about his feelings all summer, but apparently he wasn't really thinking of her at all.

'Who?'

'Stephanie Fortuna.'

The head of the cheerleading squad. Mara had a vague memory of how the little curly-haired minx seemed to jump extra high whenever Jim got a tackle.

'I'm . . . happy for you,' she said, almost actually meaning it.

'Yeah, well. We had some good times, though, didn't we?' Jim asked.

'We did,' Mara said softly. She and Jim had been dating for almost two years. It was the end of an era. It was the most anticlimactic end to an era that she could ever imagine. It was like the last sequel to *The Matrix*.

'Good luck with your job and everything. And I didn't mean what I said . . . about the Camry. It's yours if you still want it,' Jim added.

'Thanks,' Mara said simply. 'You take care.'

'You too.'

'Bye.'

'Bye.'

Mara hung up the phone without saying 'I love you' like they had every time they got off the phone for the last two years. It was weird, especially because she was pretty sure she really didn't love him anymore. She felt unanchored. Free. She wasn't Jim's girlfriend anymore. She was Just Mara, but she wasn't quite sure what Just Mara wanted to do next.

'Hey, Mar, can you lend me a twenty?' Eliza asked, coming over and holding up a cute black sweater. 'Please?'

Mara stared at her blankly. Was she serious? Eliza sure had some nerve. They weren't even officially talking to each other just yet.

'Are you still mad at me?' Eliza bit her lip. She wasn't used to people staying mad at her. Being rude or out of line wasn't new to Eliza, but having to take some responsibility for the things she did, was.

'Listen, I'm . . . I'm sorry about what I said the other day. It's just with everything . . . and I didn't mean to hurt your feelings.' Eliza still wasn't very good at this apology thing.

Mara folded her arms. 'Well, you did.'

'I know. I suck,' Eliza lamented.

'Yeah,' Mara said, noticing that Eliza's eyes were starting to mist a little bit. Now *that* was something she'd never seen before. 'I'm sorry too.'

'For what?'

'Nothing, I just don't want you to cry.'

Eliza giggled, and ran her finger underneath her lower eyelashes to wipe away any make-up. 'So, can I borrow the money? Promise I'll pay you back.'

'Oh, alright. I'm charging interest!' Mara joked.

Eliza hugged Mara impulsively. Eliza bought the sweater and they walked back to Anna's booth, where Jacqui was handing out doughnuts. 'Here you go, Chloë,' she said, giving Zoë a chocolate-sprinkled one.

'Chloë?' Anna asked, looking up sharply from writing up a bill of sale for a particularly ugly poncho.

Eliza elbowed Jacqui. 'Zoë.'

'Zoë . . . Zoë,' Jacqui sang, getting red from her slipup.

'Zoë's been wanting us to call her by different names lately. This week she's Chloë. Last week it was Julie. Right, Zo?' Mara asked.

Zoë nodded, rapturously eating her doughnut. She was only six, but she could be bribed.

When Anna turned her back, Jacqui apologised.

'*Meu deus!* I'm so, so sorry. I totally lost my head. I don't know what I was thinking,' she said, looking completely wretched. 'I don't want to get us in trouble.'

'It's okay. It could have happened to any of us,' Eliza said.

'Yeah, don't worry about it.'

They spent the rest of the afternoon stalking a supermodel whom the three of them were obsessed with. As they piled the kids back in the car, Mara and Eliza were just thinking how the day didn't turn out to be such a washout after all, when Jacqui ran up.

Her eyes were shining and she was obviously very excited about something.

'I'll catch you guys later! I just saw a friend of mine who invited me to this great party at Sting's house!' she said. 'Ciao!'

Mara rolled her eyes. 'What is it with that girl?' she asked Eliza. Mara had had enough of Jacqui. She was getting paid just as much as the rest of them – for doing less than a third of the work. William pulled on a lock of Mara's hair and then ran away. God, another pair of hands sure would be useful to wrestle that little boy sometimes.

Eliza felt extremely annoyed, too, but not about Jacqui ditching them. Hello, a party she didn't know about? The reality of social ostracism was starting to set in.

Jacqui is not a chick gone crazy

RUPERT THORNE SMILED A CATLIKE SMILE AT HIS quarry. He had never forgotten the girl to whom he'd given a ride from the airport that day. Spotting her again at the Super Saturday benefit his wife always dragged him to was indeed a pleasant surprise.

He mentioned Sting was in town – a private concert – and would she care to join him?

They had started the evening by having dinner at The Palm, where Rupert ordered a seven-hundred-dollar bottle of Chateau Latour. 'I'm celebrating something,' he'd explained to Jacqui. Afterwards he had taken her to the bar at the elite Maidstone Club, which was legendary for its stringent exclusionary practices concerning its eighty-acre golf course. Bill Clinton hadn't been deemed worthy enough to tee up during his 1999 visit. Rupert had broken several rules concerning women, foreigners, and Catholics just to impress Jacqui.

The Hummer drove towards an enormous estate overlooking the sea. It was the hundred-thousand-square-foot mansion owned by a former investment banker-cum-techno-DJ (not Sting – Jacqui had misunderstood) who liked to throw wild, twenty-four-hour Vegas-style parties on the grounds, complete with showgirls giving lap dances. The house was frequently rented out for movie shoots, music videos, and twelve-hundred-person bashes like this one.

At the door a woman gave the two of them releases to sign, explaining it was being taped for television. Jacqui signed her name on the sheet without bothering to read it. This wasn't the first time she'd had to sign a release at a party – some cable station or another always seemed to be taping something in the Hamptons. Rupert did the same and gave her his hand as they entered the party.

It was wild. Massive. This was partying on a grand scale. Hundreds of sweaty guests danced under a throbbing laser light show. A two-story-high ice sculpture of a vodka bottle melted in the middle of the fountain. The swimming pool had been turned into a massive grotto. Cocktail waitresses in corsets and tiny boy-shorts handed out free packs of cigarettes.

'Wow,' Jacqui said. 'Where's Sting?'

'Sting?' Rupert laughed. 'I told you D.J. – oh never mind. Let's enjoy ourselves, shall we?'

Roaming camera crews dressed in CHICKS GO CRAZY! hats and logo T-shirts cajoled guests to flash their ta-tas to the cameras. Wait a second. Jacqui had seen these videos advertised on E! once when she was watching that disgusting pig Howard Stone, or whatever his name was.

'What about you?' a bearded, potbellied man asked Jacqui.

'No, no thanks.' She smiled, feeling uncomfortable. It wasn't quite the star-studded event Rupert had led her to believe she was attending. Where were all the big names? Ashton Kutcher and Cameron Diaz? Sarah Jessica Parker and Kim Catrall? Or at the very least, Tara Reid and Paris Hilton? It wasn't an elegant A-list bash. In fact, most of the guests were cheesy guys in shiny shirts and polyester trousers, and most of the women were overly tanned, silicone enhanced, and wearing cheap spandex dresses.

'Uh, I think I'll just get a drink,' she said.

'Good idea,' Rupert agreed, licking his lips.

Rupert kept refilling her glass even when it wasn't empty, so she wasn't even sure how many drinks she had. In her growing anxiety Jacqui drank a lot more than she had intended. The piercing light of a filming camera suddenly flashed onto Jacqui. She squinted to see several hefty bodyguards and camera crews standing at the doorway.

The twenty-eight-year-old topless-video entrepreneur who was throwing the party took a bullhorn. 'It's that time of the night, ladies and gentlemen. Any woman who isn't naked in five minutes better leave now.'

'What?' Jacqui said.

Rupert grinned. 'Oh c'mon. It's no big deal. Everyone knows these parties always end this way.'

'I didn't!'

'Hey, you signed the waiver at the door. C'mon, let's have a little

257

fun,' Rupert said, reaching over to pull down the straps of her shirt.

'Wait! Wait!' Jacqui said, pushing his hand away.

Rupert scowled. 'What's the matter?' he asked. 'I show you a good time, I take you to dinner and the Maidstone, and this is how you thank me? C'mon, I just want to have a little fun,' he said, keeping his hand on her breast with a little too much force.

'Of course we're going to have fun,' Jacqui said, her mind racing. 'I just need to go to the bathroom and take care of a few things.' She winked, her heart pounding.

All around them women were stripping down and shaking their breast for the cameras. It wasn't a fun, careless goof like Mara and Ryan skinny-dipping in the pool. This was business. This was frightening. This was not what she bargained for when she said she'd like to see Sting play a private concert.

'I'll wait right here,' Rupert drawled.

Jacqui stood unsteadily on her feet. 'I'll be right back,' she promised.

It was four in the morning and she was in the middle of nowhere. She didn't have money for a cab, and she didn't even know where she would call for one. No one at the party would take her home.

She found a phone in the hallway and dialled the first number that came to mind.

'Luca! It's me – I really need your help!'

'Who is this?' a sleepy female voice demanded. 'Who's calling?'

'It's Jacqui. Can I talk to Luca?'

'He's sleeping right now. What's this about?' the suspicious voice asked.

No use. Jacqui dialled another number.

'Leo! It's me, Jacqui. I really need your help.'

'Jacqui?' Leo asked. He was still awake, having played fifty-four straight games of John Madden Football on his PlayStation. 'The girl who said I was just a mercy screw?'

'Leo – please.'

But he had already hung up.

Jacqui was in tears. In a few minutes Rupert would storm out looking for her and God knows what she would do then. She dialled the last number she could remember.

The phone rang and rang, and Jacqui had almost resigned herself to walking down the four miles of the Montauk Highway when Mara's voice answered.

'Hello?'

'Mara. It's Jacqui. I really need your help. Can you guys come and pick me up?'

Mara sat up in bed and looked at the clock. 'What the hell? Just because you blow everything off, doesn't mean we can just up and get – '

'Mara, please,' Jacqui said, starting to cry.

'What's going on?' Mara asked, suddenly realising something was wrong here.

'I'm at this party – Sting isn't here – it's just – I need to get away.'

'Where are you?'

Jacqui told her. 'I'm really scared, Mara.'

'We'll be there in a few minutes. I have to get Eliza up, I don't know how to get there, but I'm sure she will. Hang in there.'

Jacqui put down the phone and tiptoed out the front gate. It was getting cold outside from the ocean breeze, but she would rather freeze than walk into that house again.

Sometimes people actually forget that the Hamptons is Long Island

A FLASH OF HEADLIGHTS AND A FAMILIAR CLUNKY RED
Volvo pulled up to the front door. Mara threw open the car door.
'Jacqui?'

Eliza lit herself another cigarette. God, talk about drama.

Mara had hastily explained why they had to get up and go get
their lost roommate, but Eliza still wasn't sure exactly why she
had to leave her comfortable bed at four-thirty in the morning.

They found Jacqui huddled by the steps. When she spotted
them, she burst into tears.

'Oh my God! What happened!' Mara said, fearing the worst.

'Nothing – nothing. I just didn't know if you were actually
going to show up,' Jacqui whimpered.

She was shaking and so upset, a totally different person than
the confident, glacial, sophisticated South American who was so
jaded about everything. In the moonlight she looked all of her
sixteen years.

'I was stupid,' she said. 'I should have known something like this would happen.' She told them all about Rupert, the bait and switch, the sketchy party, the leering guys, the video cameras.

'You're under the age of consent,' Eliza said. 'We could put them in jail.'

'I signed the release form,' Jacqui admitted.

'Who cares? That doesn't matter. That's never going to hold up in court.'

'C'mon, let's get out of this place before they try to get new recruits,' Mara suggested.

Jacqui sniffed and wiped her nose with the palm of her hand. She looked at the car. 'You guys took the Volvo?'

They drove west – all the way west – to the part of Long Island where it was more strip mall than stripper party. After all, it's not *all* about the Hamptons. By now they were a little sick of the place, to be honest. All that posing, primping, and posturing. The constant need to match one's bikini, sarong, handbag, and flip-flops. It took hours just to get dressed to go nowhere.

'Look, there's a Denny's,' Mara said. 'I haven't been to one in so long.'

'Anyone up for breakfast?' Eliza asked.

'Sounds perfect,' Jacqui agreed.

They found a corner booth by the window and opened menus.

'What can I get ya?' a waitress in a checkered uniform with a beehive asked them. She was so far from the sylphs who doled out minuscule plates of tofu at Babbette's that the girls couldn't help but grin at each other. This was exactly what they needed. A dose of reality.

'I have lumberjack special,' Jacqui decided.

'Three eggs, two pancakes, bacon, sausage, *and* ham?' Eliza asked in horror. There was absolutely nothing on the menu that was under her four-hundred-calorie-per-minimeal ratio.

'Sounds great. I'll have the same,' Mara decided, snapping her menu closed.

'Two 'jacks. What about you, hon?'

Eliza contemplated. The bacon alone was three hundred calories. But she was really, really hungry. 'Make it three.'

They wolfed down their greasy breakfasts and filled each other in on the latest news.

'And you haven't even spoken to Jeremy since?' Mara asked after Eliza updated Jacqui on what happened.

'No.'

'You've got to find him and tell him how you feel,' Mara stressed. 'It's important. You guys can't just leave things like this!'

'I know, I know.' Eliza sighed, spearing a fat brown sausage with her fork and popping it in her mouth.

'Jeremy – the guy who cuts the lawn?' Jacqui asked. 'He's really nice. I saw him looking for you the other day. Sorry. I forgot to tell you.'

'He was?' Eliza asked. 'Oh my God.'

'See – I'm sure he feels the same way. But you've got to go to him first.' Mara had a major romantic streak.

'Okay. But only if you break up with Jim. You deserve so much better than that bonehead,' Eliza said. 'And he is a bonehead.'

'We broke up already,' Mara said. 'Yesterday, actually.'

'And you haven't told Ryan?'

'No, why should I?' Mara said obstinately.

Jacqui and Eliza exchanged a look. 'Only because he is so into you,' Eliza said.

'Is love,' Jacqui announced. 'I know when men love. He is sick with passion. He can't get enough of you. He's so in love,' she said dramatically.

'No, he isn't,' Mara said. 'He has a girlfriend.'

'That Camille girl? She's history,' Eliza said. 'He told me the other day, he just wasn't feeling it. He broke it off that week the kids were away.'

'So what? It's not like he would ever be interested in someone like me,' Mara said quietly. She knew how guys like Ryan felt about her – she knew it the first time she saw him – guys like that were so out of her league.

'What on EARTH are you talking about?' Eliza yelled, so loudly that the truckers having breakfast at the counter turned around. 'You are a bombshell! Have you looked in the mirror lately?' Eliza asked, pulling Mara to look at her reflection in the glass.

Jacqui nodded vigorously. 'In São Paulo we call girls like you, how do you say . . . hot.'

'You guys are really sweet, but you're just blowing smoke up my butt,' Mara said as she turned. There was Eliza, the spitting image of Cameron Diaz, who, even totally hung over, still radiated that *InStyle* cover girl glow. There was Jacqui, the sultry, Latin sexpot. Then there was her. The plain one. But for once Mara took a good look at the reflection. The haircut Pierre had given her brought out the angles of her cheekbones, and the new blue shirt Eliza had helped her pick out made her eyes look bluer than they ever did. While running after the kids half the summer, she had even lost a few pounds. Were they right? Had she transformed into a hottie overnight?

'See,' Eliza said smugly. 'Told you.'

'Now, you go get that boy,' Jacqui said. She was so happy to be just where she was at that moment. As she looked around at Mara, who was brushing her bangs away from her face with a wistful smile, and Eliza, who was motioning for a round of milk shakes (Hey, what else goes well with a lumberjack special?), Jacqui realised that after everything that had happened this summer, they really were friends.

Eliza, Mara, and Jacqui find the best part of the Hamptons

THE SUN WAS RISING WHEN THEY DROVE BACK UP Route 27 towards East Hampton. Roadside farm stands were opening up for business, and Eliza convinced them that they couldn't pass up this chance to buy the freshest fruit and vegetables for the house.

'Anna always goes to the one in Amagansett, but it's always so picked over. This one is so much better.' Eliza sniffed as they walked around, looking at all the stalls.

The corn was piled high in the palest emerald green stalks, and inside, they were ivory white or as yellow as daffodils. Grapefruits the size of basketballs, oranges that glowed with an almost fluorescent light. Carrots as long and thick as your arm. Radicchio, endive, arugula, and every other fancy lettuce for less than a dollar a bunch.

Eliza showed them the bakery table, set up with loaves of gluten- and wheat-free pumpernickel, sourdough, and challah bread.

They spotted Cindy Crawford behind a baseball cap, sniffing persimmons.

'Hey, look, there's a homemade peach-and-blueberry pie,' Mara said, walking over to the delicious smell. 'Let's get one for the kids.'

'Madison will love it,' Eliza agreed.

'Peaches! Zoë's favourite.' Jacqui nodded.

'William would like throwing it against the wall.' Mara laughed.

They bought Cody a SpongeBob-shaped balloon and filled up the trunk with baskets of citrus, loaves of freshly baked bread, fat red-orange tomatoes on the vine, cauliflower and broccoli blossoms, and enough grapes to make their own barrel of wine.

Eliza dropped them back off at the house.

'Where are you going?' Mara asked.

'Jeremy always gets up early to go running in Montauk. I'm going to try to find him.'

'Good,' Mara said, squeezing Eliza's arm. 'I'm going to go and find Ryan.'

'Go get him, sista.' Eliza smiled.

Jacqui impulsively put her arm around both of them, which was actually rather hard to do, considering Eliza was still in the car. 'You guys are the best.'

Eliza drove off and Jacqui and Mara walked to the back of the house to the stone pathway.

'I'm going to go get some sleep,' Jacqui said to no one in particular as she climbed the rickety attic stairs.

But only after a long, hot shower so she could start with a fresh, clean slate.

Mara finally
makes her move

THE MAIN HOUSE WAS EMPTY WHEN MARA SNUCK inside; not even the kitchen staff was awake yet. She walked up the back stairs to Ryan's room and opened the door.

'Ryan?' she whispered. 'Are you up?'

Now that she had decided she knew exactly what she wanted – *him* – she couldn't wait to break the news. And if he didn't want her, she could live with that – what she wouldn't be able to live with was if she never told him.

She creaked open the door and walked inside his room. On his desk rested the pack of playing cards from the other night, a few twigs they'd picked up from the beach as potential marshmallow sticks, and the book she'd lent him to read – *Zen and the Art of Motorcycle Maintenance*. He'd said he'd never read it and she had chastised him for his lack of literary education.

His surfboards and skateboards were lined up against the wall.

But his bed was still made. The blue comforter was turned down perfectly.

Her heart sank. He probably never even came home last night. If it wasn't Camille, it was someone else. It wasn't as if he was going to wait around for her the whole summer, was he? Mara remembered all the girls at the many parties they attended this summer who had made their interest clear.

She closed the door behind her. By this time he'd probably found someone to keep him company, maybe one of those Bush nieces or Hearst heiresses who hung on his every word. Or maybe even one of the cute Irish girls who worked at every café, bar, and kayak rental shop in the Hamptons.

'Good morning, miss,' Stevens, the butler, greeted as he passed her on his way to opening the curtains in the master den.

She nodded to him shyly.

The pool sparkled in the morning light and she told herself she was still really, really happy she'd spent the summer in the middle of such gorgeous beauty. The knife edge of the pool blended with the blue horizon of the ocean. It was a sight Mara would never get tired of.

She absentmindedly picked up strewn children's toys as she walked back to the au pairs' cottage. Zoë's Disco Elmo, William's missing Gameboy, Cody's blankie, Madison's duelling Britney and Christina dolls.

As she turned the corner, she caught her breath.

There, in the hammock behind the au pairs' cottage, was Ryan, asleep.

She kissed him softly on the lips to wake him up. Her sleeping prince. His nostrils flared slightly with every breath. She felt a wave of tenderness and affection.

His eyelids fluttered, and when he saw her, he smiled. 'What was that for?'

'I just felt like it.' She smiled back.

'I was looking for you all night. Where'd you go?' he asked.

'Nowhere. I was looking for you, too.'

'Fancy that.'

She leaned down to the hammock, and he pulled her down to cuddle with him. It swung underneath their combined weight and threw them closer together.

'What about Jim?' he asked, gently grazing her bare arm with the back of his hand.

'We broke up,' she said.

'And you're okay with that?'

'I should have done it a long, long time ago.'

'Good,' he said sleepily, and closed his eyes.

Mara nestled into the crook of his armpit, savouring his strong arms around her. She never wanted to let go.

The hammock swayed in the breeze, and they fell asleep to the sound of crashing waves on the shore.

Eliza goes to Montauk
for the first time
all summer

PLEASE, PLEASE, LET HIM BE THERE, ELIZA PRAYED. *Please, please, please.*

She parked the car in the lot and walked down to the beach. A few brave swimmers were doing laps in the early tide, but otherwise the beach was empty. Then she saw him. He was wearing a dirty anorak and his running shorts.

'Jeremy! Jeremy!' she called.

He turned back, saw her, and kept running. Faster.

Eliza tossed away her high-heeled platforms and ran to keep up with him.

'Jeremy, please!' she begged. 'Please wait.'

But he kept running.

'I LOVE YOU!' she cried.

Finally, halfway down the beach, he stopped and took off his earphones. 'What did you say?'

She ran down, not caring if little broken pieces of seashells were piercing the soft soles of her feet. She stopped right in front of him. His face was shiny with sweat, and his hair had kinked in the humidity. But she thought he was even more handsome than she remembered.

'I'm so sorry about that night. I don't know what I was doing – no, I did know, and I'm so embarrassed. I love you. I've never felt this way before, and you have to know that.' Eliza looked for a trace of feeling on Jeremy's face. Nothing. 'Why did you quit the Perrys'?'

'You think I could work there – seeing you – knowing what you really think of me?' he asked.

Eliza could see how much she'd hurt him. 'Please forgive me. Can we start over again? Please?' She held her breath.

He had to say yes, he just had to. She told him she loved him. She'd never said those words aloud to anyone – ever.

'I don't know,' he said, looking at the sand. 'I think we're too different.' He shook his head. 'It's not that easy.'

'Can't we just try?' She tried grabbing for his hand, but he pulled away.

This wasn't how it was supposed to happen. He was supposed to kiss her right now and say everything was forgiven and forgotten. But his face was grim.

'It's not a faucet I can just turn on and off,' he said. 'I'm . . . I'm going to have to think about it. You have to give me some time.'

He put his earphones back on and began to jog away.

Eliza watched him, not sure how to react. It was the most

vulnerable she'd ever been with another person, and she had been rejected.

He'd asked for time. But it was almost Labor Day. She didn't have any more time. She was going back to Buffalo in a week.

Mara finds happiness
in a hammock

'MARA AND RYAN SITTING IN A TREE! K-I-S-S-I . . . ,' Madison and Zoë chorused, waking up their big brother and the au pair in his arms.

'MARA AND RYAN ARE IN LOVE!' William sniggered and made loud sloppy kissing noises.

'Shush,' Ryan said, batting at his smaller siblings.

'Wake up! Wake up, sleepyheads! We wanna go swimming!'

Mara blinked and smiled. 'You guys go and get changed and we'll meet you in the pool.'

Instead the girls climbed into the hammock with them, so that William, who never liked being left out, scrambled in, too. 'Oof! You're heavy!' Ryan said, hugging his younger brother.

Mara laughed as the kids began wildly swinging the hammock. 'We're all going to fall off! Okay, if no one's going to get out, I will!' she threatened, trying to grab hold of one side of the hammock so she could climb off safely.

'No, you don't, you're staying right here,' Ryan said, reaching over to pull her back against him.

The two little girls whispered to each other on the far end of the hammock, cupping their mouths with tiny hands.

'Zoë and I decided,' Madison said, in a very serious tone, 'that you are a LOT prettier than Ryan's old girlfriend.'

'Oh, thanks.' Mara winked at Ryan. 'So I'm prettier than Camille, am I?'

Madison and Zoë looked confused. 'Camille?'

'Um, Ryan's old girlfriend?' Mara asked.

'You mean Sophie?' Madison asked.

'Or Annette?' Zoë chimed in.

'There's more than one?' Mara asked.

'Maddy! Zo! Don't answer that!' Ryan said in a half-jestful manner.

'There are *tons,*' Madison assured Mara.

'Lots.' Zoë nodded.

Mara raised an eyebrow at Ryan. 'Lots, eh? How many were there?'

'Do we have to get into this now?' Ryan laughed. 'It doesn't really matter, does it? I mean, we're together now.' He noticed Mara looking downcast. 'My sisters don't know what they're talking about.'

He cupped Mara's chin and kissed her again. 'You're the *only* one I want. Okay?'

'Okay.' As long as they were clear on that.

The little girls sighed happily. It was just so romantic.

*   *   *

A few minutes later Jacqui appeared, wearing sunglasses and shorts and carrying a croissant and a coffee cup from the Hampton Coffee Company. She held several newspapers and magazines underneath her free arm.

'Who are you?' William asked on his way to the pool.

'I'm Jacqui – I've been taking care of you all summer!' Jacqui joked.

He looked puzzled.

She smiled when she saw Mara and Ryan together.

'Look what I found,' Jacqui said, holding aloft copies of *New York* magazine, *Hamptons* magazine, the *New York Post*, the *New York Daily News*, and the *New York Times*. There were photos of Mara everywhere, with photo credits from her friend Lucky Yap.

'The summer's latest IT girl – and she didn't have to run over the back wall of a club or tape a sex video to do it!' blared the always-restrained Page Six.

'Hey, you're more famous than me,' Ryan said, noticing that the latest round didn't even mention the 'Perry heir'.

Mara paged through the magazines and newspapers with a thoughtful smile on her face. She felt confident and blissfully happy – not because she'd achieved in one season what most Hamptonites crave their whole lifetimes, but because she was with the guy she loved.

Jacqui is a miracle worker

JACQUI ROUNDED UP THE KIDS AND TOOK THEM TO the pool. She pumped up Cody's water wings and tugged them on his chubby arms.

'Let's go!' She whooped, jumping into the deep end.

Amazingly, he followed her in, splashing and kicking like a duck.

'Good boy! Good boy!' Jacqui said, laughing.

She didn't even realise how miraculous this was – Mara and Eliza had been trying to get him in the water all summer, but as far as ever-absent Jacqui knew, Cody was a born swimmer. William jumped in the pool too, almost knocking out his brother.

'Be careful!' Jacqui chided.

The little boy stuck his tongue out. 'DUNK!' he said, and pushed Cody's head under water.

'WILLIAM!' Really, that one was such a monster.

Chortling, William let his brother go and swam to the other end of the pool.

Cody kicked and splashed happily.

'Not bad,' Kevin Perry said, kneeling down. 'Hey, Jacqui, right? You want to hit the steam bath later? We just put in a new showerhead. It's amazing.'

Jacqui swam to the edge of the pool. She was sick of being watched, being slobbered over, and after the night at the party she'd had it with older men.

'I don't think your wife would appreciate you talking to me that way,' she said evenly.

He looked confused. A lot more confused than he should have. 'Sure. I'll, uh, see you around,' Kevin said.

Jacqui nodded. She felt relieved. After years of kowtowing and bowing and scraping and flirting with men for a tip or a ride or another drink or an invitation to a party, she had finally stood up for herself.

It felt fantastic.

The second-best thing
Anna ever said

ONCE AGAIN ANNA WAS SITTING AT THE HEAD OF THE TABLE when the au pairs trooped in for the weekly progress report. Did miracles never cease?

The three au pairs took their seats across the table.

'Where's Kevin?' Eliza whispered.

Jacqui shrugged.

Now that Jacqui had made it clear she wasn't going to tolerate his advances, Kevin had found better things to do with his time.

The girls were all a little tense. They were supposed to get their final payment at the meeting – that is, if they didn't get fired first. They still had no idea why the first batch of au pairs was let go – and Super Saturday was not their best moment.

But Anna was positively glowing at them.

'Well, I hope you had a wonderful summer,' she said. 'I certainly did.' She had been asked to donate her tennis court for the annual Cartier tournament, putting her right up there with the Swids,

Kravises, and Davises of the town. It sort of made up for the Super Saturday debacle. Sort of.

The girls nodded.

'I just can't be more pleased with your obvious devotion to the kids,' Anna said. 'In particular, Cody swimming this morning was amazing!' Anna held a hand to her chest. 'To see him conquer his greatest fear – a mother couldn't be more proud!'

Mara and Eliza nodded, trying to figure how the hell Jacqui had done it.

'And that Portuguese book you're teaching Zoë, Jacqui! We were just hoping we could get her to read in English, but to have her bilingual to boot, it's spectacular. Her admissions counsellor thinks this will put her over the hump for next year. She said Zoë is Dalton material for sure.'

Again Eliza and Mara exchanged confused glances. When exactly did this happen?

'Better yet, Madison's lost ten pounds!' Anna cheered.

The kid had been eating them out of house and home all summer, and the weight loss was just from shedding baby fat, but none of the girls would tell Anna that.

'Of course, William's still a bit twitchy. But nothing's perfect. At least he's stopped biting people,' Anna continued. 'It's just so easy to get off track in the Hamptons. The social life here is just frenetic, what with the parties and nightclubs and all.'

The girls looked a little guilty at that.

'I never told you guys this, but we had to let our first au pairs go for that very reason! They were out every night!'

The girls all exchanged sidelong glances.

'So we just want to congratulate you on a job well done. Here's the last of your payment, with a little bonus inside.' Anna winked.

Eliza sighed with relief. Those Visa bills had been piling up. She was going to make a dent on them this time instead of adding to the total. Seriously. As soon as she got her hands on the gorgeous tweed coat she saw at Scoop the other day. Hey, it was almost fall, and a girl needed back-to-school clothes.

Mara hugged herself. She had made more than ten thousand dollars this summer. Woo-hoo! College and a ten-year-old Camry. Life didn't get better than this! Sure, she'd got a bit more fabulous this summer, but underneath it all, she was the same small-town girl she'd always been.

Jacqui put her envelope away. When she got home, she was going to buy her grandmother the biggest statue of the Virgin Mary the old lady had ever seen — it was the one gift that would tell her how much Jacqui loved her, and that's exactly what she wanted to say.

But Anna wasn't done.

'By the way, we'd love to have you girls with us this Christmas. We always do two weeks in Palm Beach, and our regular nanny goes to England at that time, so we're strapped. Do you think you'd be interested? We'll pay five thousand dollars. We can all meet in New York and we'll go in our private jet.'

Palm Beach? Christmas? Five grand? A jet? Where did they sign?

P. Diddy knows how to throw a party

IT WAS TIME FOR P. DIDDY'S ANNUAL LABOR DAY WHITE Party, the last big bash before the summer was over. Eliza had worked the phones for three days straight, trying to make sure they all got invitations. Kit had come through again, and Lucky Yap had sent over a couple, so they were all covered.

Mara hung out in Ryan's room, watching him change into a white linen suit. He buttoned up his shirt in the mirror and caught her eye.

'What are you looking at?'

'My gorgeous boyfrie – ' she answered, then caught herself. Did she just say THAT WORD? How could she do that? She didn't even know what he thought they were doing. Maybe they were just fooling around. Certainly she didn't want to label their relationship so early.

Seeing the distress on her face and knowing what put it there, Ryan turned and climbed up on the bed, then crawled up to kiss her on the cheek.

'I'd rather look at my gorgeous girlfriend,' he whispered.

Mara leaned back, pulling him closer, tugging on the rawhide necklace he always wore around his neck. The pillows were still warm from their earlier activities.

Ryan kissed her closed eyelids, her nose, her cheeks. 'Maybe we shouldn't get dressed yet,' he murmured.

'Maybe not,' she agreed.

Eliza looked at her closet askance. How could this be? Everything white that she owned was dirty, or yellowed, or stained. She had absolutely nothing to wear to the biggest party of the season.

Or did she . . .

She walked furtively to the main house. The diaphanous white Versace dress Sugar had asked her to send to the cleaners earlier that week was still hanging in her walk-in closet, waiting to be worn. But Sugar wasn't going to get back from her bikini wax for a while yet.

Sugar would just look washed out in it, Eliza thought. *Really, I'm doing her a favour.*

Eliza grabbed the dress. It was her last night in town. And didn't she deserve to wear it? She was the one who had taken such good care of it all summer.

Jacqui yawned as she put on her white shirt and a calf-length skirt. The most conservative outfit she owned. For once she didn't feel like attracting any attention to herself. Guys were just too much trouble these days. She was enjoying being single.

The group met at the driveway. Mara and Ryan walked out of the main house, holding hands, apple cheeked and glowing in their matching white pantsuits.

Eliza met them at the door in the borrowed (fine, stolen) Versace.

'Isn't that . . . ,' Ryan asked, thinking the dress looked familiar.

'It's mine,' Eliza declared. At least for the night. If she couldn't have Jeremy, she could at least have a Versace dress.

Jacqui walked up from the garden pathway, looking devastating in her "conservative" outfit. 'Everybody ready?' she asked.

Mara and Ryan took the Aston Martin, and Eliza and Jacqui thought it would fun to ride in on the Vespas. It beat having to worry about parking.

They drove to an imposing modern mansion on Settlers Landing with P. Diddy's initials carved into the wrought iron gates. Several billowing white tents were set up near the entrance to facilitate the guest check-in.

Eliza told them that she'd heard the entire city of East Hampton had to be insured for up to five million dollars against any incident related to the party and that Puffy had paid for an eleven-thousand-square-foot tent with a ten-inch plastic foam wall on one side to keep the dulcet tones of Funkmaster Flex from reaching a nearby neighbour.

'I heard he even had a whole orchard planted the week before to make it look more countrylike!' Eliza said.

At the receiving line they spotted Leonardo di Caprio getting patted down by several hulking bodyguards. Leo was a vision in white, from his cream-coloured baseball cap to his snow white shoes. There was Topher Grace hanging out with Ali Hilfiger, Gavin Rossdale walking in with Gwen Stefani, and Eve, Li'l Kim, and Busta Rhymes mingling with Zac Posen, Paz de la Huerta, and Claire Danes.

The three girls held their collective breath as one of the huge bouncers waved their invitations underneath a laser. It seemed an eternity before it pinged as authentic.

'Go right in.' The doorman in the pristine three-piece suit waved them inside.

A cocktail waitress in a white lace dress brought over a tray of champagne flutes. 'Cristal?'

They each took a glass and toasted each other.

'To all of us,' Mara said. Sure, it was a little cheesy, but she was allowed – she was a Hamptons It girl.

It pays to tip the valet well

THEY FOUND AN UNOCCUPIED TABLE NOT FAR FROM where Amanda Hearst sat in deep conversation with Andre 3000. Puffy's annual barbecue was the perfect mix of old money and mo' money. Waspy blue bloods traded tall tales with gold-toothed gangbangers. New York's fanciest socialites boogied down with Hollywood hotshots and hip-hop stars. A white Moroccan-style tent was set up on the grounds, and belly dancers in ivory-and-pearl-embossed ensembles were clacking their finger cymbals as they gyrated through the crowd.

'Check it out! His logo is, like, everywhere!' Mara said. Their host's monogram was engraved into the bottom of the pool, on the napkins, even on the towels that hung in the bathrooms. In fact, on every beach, bath, and dish towel on the premises.

'Yeah.' Eliza sighed. Somehow the fact that she had scored a legitimate invitation to the best party of the season didn't do anything to improve her mood.

'Don't be so down,' Mara said. 'It's our last night together!'

Eliza managed a weak smile. 'I know. I'll try.'

Jeremy had never bothered to call. He said he needed time to think about it, but for Eliza time had run out. Kit, the only friend who still talked to her after she was 'outed' as poor, had offered to drive her back to the city next day, and she had a ticket on the Greyhound back to Buffalo.

'Who knows, he might surprise you,' Mara said.

'I know. I feel like it might still work out,' she said a little hopelessly. 'I gave him my number at home. Who knows, maybe he'll still call me.'

'If he doesn't, there are a million other guys who would die to go out with you,' Mara said loyally. She would never have thought she could be best friends with someone like Eliza – but there you had it.

'Maybe,' Eliza said. The summer had been spectacular – but humbling as hell. Before this summer the thought that she would lose her heart to the gardener was laughable, even ludicrous. She was Eliza Thompson; she could have anyone she wanted.

But Eliza Thompson didn't get everything she ever wanted anymore. She was starting to learn that.

Lindsay and Taylor walked by. They did a double take when they saw Eliza. What was *she* doing here? Nevertheless, they decided to stop by Eliza's table and show her how bighearted and generous they could be. Besides, it wasn't like they were going to have to hang out with her in the city anyway. They knew all about Buffalo.

But when they walked up to the table, Eliza looked the other way. Eliza knew it wasn't their fault they were the way they were, but that didn't mean she had to pretend to like them anymore. The truth was that she had never really liked them. Not really. Not in the way she liked Mara and Jacqui.

'Um, hi?' Lindsay said.

Taylor cleared her throat.

Eliza pretended to be extremely fascinated by the contents of her cocktail glass as she purposefully ignored them.

The two girls stood there as Ryan, Mara, and Jacqui smirked without saying anything.

And with that, they flipped their perfectly Sahag-layered hair and walked away in their four-hundred-dollar shoes, and for the first time Eliza was really, truly happy to see them go. She went back to staring at the bubbles in her glass, thinking about how none of this really mattered to her anymore. How much money she could have saved on bags alone if she'd realised that a few years ago. How she'd give up her Marc Jacobs Stella bag, her orange Tod's purse, her black Prada bag that was the same as Gwyneth's just to have another shot with Jeremy.

And then, as if she'd finally thought the magic words, Jeremy appeared.

'Hey, Eliza,' Jeremy said. He was wearing a white valet uniform. He had his hands in his pockets and he looked utterly miserable.

'Jeremy! What are you doing here?'

'I got a job parking cars,' he said.

'Why?'

'I knew you would be here. I wanted to see you,' he told her.

'You did?' She seemed so small and vulnerable just then, and for once she wasn't trying to be like anything but who she was.

The rest of the table took that as their cue to make a graceful exit.

Eliza stood up. She looked into his eyes and saw how much she'd hurt him.

'I didn't want you to leave thinking that I didn't care,' he said.

Her eyes misted with tears. Real tears this time. She wanted to jump into his arms, wipe that awful, wretched look off his face, and tell him that nothing mattered – it didn't matter that they had been apart for so long – what was important was that he was here now.

So that's exactly what she did.

Eliza leapt from her seat and threw herself in his arms, in front of Puffy, Demi, Leo, and her two ex-friends.

Caught off guard, Jeremy fell backwards, and the two of them tumbled on the grass, hugging and kissing and smiling at each other. Screw the Versace dress – she was with Jeremy.

'Oh my God . . . what the hell! Is that Eliza kissing the *valet*?' Lindsay asked, an eyebrow raised.

'You know what, he is kind of cute,' Taylor allowed.

And finally they started to see: Eliza knew something they didn't.

It's called
Karma

JACQUI SMILED AT ELIZA AND JEREMY. MARA AND RYAN
were cuddling by the pool, and Jacqui thought she would just slip
away. All her friends looked pretty busy. She was thrilled for them
but a little sad for herself, too. She certainly hadn't bargained for
the kind of summer she had ended up having.

She shook her head at the passing tray of canapés.

But she did help herself to a goody bag at the exit. A crisp
white shopping bag emblazoned with the ubiquitous logo contained a white terry cloth robe, terry cloth slippers, and a bottle
of Absolut (the party's corporate sponsor that year).

'Leaving so soon?' A very handsome and very familiar-looking
guy stopped her on the way to the gates.

'You look even more beautiful when you aren't crying.' He
smiled. 'So I guess your summer ended up getting a lot better?'

It was Nacho Figueroa – the hot Argentinean polo player
from the big match!

'Hey! Jacqui, right?' She turned, and standing by the Mister

Softee truck parked in the driveway (you never know what the guests will want if they get the munchies) was Eliza's friend Kit – the nice guy who had given them their party invitations.

'Hi, Kit,' she said, kissing him hello.

Kit beamed. Nacho took a step back, a quizzical look on his face.

She smiled at both of them, but just then her mobile phone rang. *'Espere um momento,'* she told Nacho. 'Excuse me,' she told Kit.

'Pronto?'

'Jacqui, it's Luke. Your Luca.' He was obviously drunk, but Jacqui wanted to know what this was all about.

'Sim?'

'Someone called my house at three in the morning and my girlfriend – I mean, my ex-girlfriend – she flipped. We broke up, and, well, I miss you, Jac, I really do.'

'Oh, *coitado,'* Jacqui said scathingly.

'And she's with Leo now, can you believe it?' He was slurring a little. 'What is it about that guy? One eye isn't even quite straight.'

'So what do you say? Me and you? I know you don't like to be alone,' Luke breathed. 'And I'm so lonely.'

Jacqui laughed to herself. So there was justice in this world after all. 'That's a shame, Luca. But *não. Thcau.'*

She turned the phone off and turned back to Kit and Nacho. Hmm . . . the rakish polo player or Eliza's childhood friend?

Jacqui paused for a moment. *Isn't 'polo player' just a long way of saying 'player'?* Nacho seemed nice, but Jacqui was tired of men who played games.

'Drive me home?' she asked, linking an arm in Kit's. '*Tchau tchau*, Nacho.'

Kit grinned. Maybe they were wrong. Maybe nice guys did finish first.

It's the last night of summer, but it's the first night for other things

A FEW MINUTES AFTER MIDNIGHT MARA CREPT UP THE stairs to their attic bedroom. She found Jacqui asleep in the top bunk.

'Jac? Are you awake?' she asked.

Jacqui raised her head. 'Now I am.'

Mara sat on the bed and took off her shoes. When she looked up, Eliza was walking through the door. 'Hey.'

She was glad all three of them were together on their last night.

Eliza sparkled in her white dress when she kicked off her shoes. 'Help me with this, Mar,' she said as she began pushing her single bed up against Mara's bottom bunk. 'Get down here, Jac,' she whispered.

The three of them snuggled on the one makeshift king-size bed, feeling comfort in the warmth of each other's bodies.

Eliza told them about how she and Jeremy got back together. 'I just love him so much,' she said, burying her face in the pillow at her own cheesiness. 'But Buffalo is so far.'

'I'm sure you'll see each other,' Mara said. She could have slept in Ryan's bed, but she didn't want to for some reason. Their last week in the Hamptons had been something out of the middle part of *Titanic* – before the ship sank, while everything was perfect and hot and steamy. But on the last night here, she wanted to be in the au pairs' room. It was the only thing that felt right.

Jacqui told them how Kit had offered all three of them a ride back to the city in his car. That was good. At least they wouldn't have to take the Jitney. So why were they all so bummed?

'We'll see each other at Christmas,' Eliza said, voicing the emotion they were all feeling. They were going to miss each other. They had gone through a lot this summer. 'We'll need winter bikinis!' Eliza added.

'In Palm Beach,' Mara said dreamily. Another chance to get out of Sturbridge.

'What's it like?' Jacqui asked.

'Awesome,' Eliza yawned. 'Parties and galas and we'll all need new clothes!' Her eyelids dropped. Mara was falling asleep, too. Jacqui turned on her side, grabbing for the covers.

Their summer was over. They had done everything they wanted to do and some things they shouldn't have. Tomorrow they would drive out on the Montauk Highway for the last time. They would return home older, wiser, and certainly more glamorous.

In the end, it *had* been the best summer of their lives. Maybe there was truth in advertising after all.

Acknowledgements

Many heartfelt thanks to the wonderful folks at 17th Street – my absolutely fabulous editor, Sara Shandler, the inspiring Josh Bank, and the encouraging Ben Shrank. Thanks to Les Morgenstein for invaluable insight. Immense gratitude to Emily Thomas for all her brilliant ideas. Thanks to Claudia Gabel and Jennifer Unter for thinking of me for this project. As always, I'm very grateful to Deborah 'superagent' Schneider, a guardian angel in high-heeled shoes.

Thanks to Jason Oliver Nixon, Andrew Stone, Paige Herman, and Juliet McCall Dyall at *Hamptons* magazine for giving me a reason to write off my summer rental. Thanks to Karen Robinovitz, my partner in crime, an invaluable resource and a true friend.

Thanks to the de la Cruz and Johnston families for all their support. Thanks to my dad for letting me hog his computer to write this book when mine broke. Thanks to my mom for asking if the naughty parts would be 'normal or perverted' (I've never laughed so hard, Mom!) Thanks to 'Hotel Chit' in New York. Thanks to Aina and Steve for sharing their stories about the Hamptons. Thanks to Kim, David, and Diva for a fantastic summer. Thanks to Jennie for coming out to visit. Thanks to Tristan, Gabriel, Tyler, Peter, Andy, and the rest of The Gang for being The Gang.

Thanks to my husband, Mike, for getting out of the city every Friday night, no matter how late it got.

About the author

MELISSA DE LA CRUZ is the author of the novel *Cat's Meow* (Scribner 2001), which was published as *The Girl Can't Help It!* in the United Kingdom, where it was a Top 10 best seller. She is the coauthor of the tongue-in-cheek guidebook *How to Become Famous in Two Weeks or Less,* which was optioned by Walt Disney Studios for development as a major motion picture and by Reveille Productions/Universal Studios for development as a reality television program. Her work has been translated into several languages. She writes regularly for *Marie Claire, Gotham, Hampton,* and *Lifetime* magazines and has contributed to the *New York Times, Glamour, Allure,* and *McSweeney's.* She recently moved from New York City and now lives in Los Angeles with her husband. She has never *dared* to use her mobile phone on the Hampton Jitney.